SLEEPWALKER

M. A. HUNTER

Boldwood

First published in Great Britain in 2024 by Boldwood Books Ltd.

Copyright © M. A. Hunter, 2024

Cover Design by 12 Orchards Ltd

Cover Photography: Shutterstock

Every effort has been made to obtain the necessary permissions with reference to copyright material, both illustrative and quoted. We apologise for any omissions in this respect and will be pleased to make the appropriate acknowledgements in any future edition.

A CIP catalogue record for this book is available from the British Library.

Paperback ISBN 978-1-80549-561-1

Large Print ISBN 978-1-80549-562-8

Hardback ISBN 978-1-80549-560-4

Ebook ISBN 978-1-80549-563-5

Kindle ISBN 978-1-80549-564-2

Audio CD ISBN 978-1-80549-555-0

MP3 CD ISBN 978-1-80549-556-7

Digital audio download ISBN 978-1-80549-557-4

Boldwood Books Ltd
23 Bowerdean Street
London SW6 3TN
www.boldwoodbooks.com

For all the dreamers.

1

NOW

How has it come to this?

The boat continues to bob in time with the sound of waves crashing against the bow. Ahead of us is nothing but a wall of white; the fog fully encompassing the whole vessel now. I don't envy the captain of the MS *Oldenburg* having to navigate through this. I can only hope there is state-of-the-art navigational equipment in use, but looking at the rusted bench frames and chipped paint of the well-trodden walkways, it's hard to imagine anything modern exists onboard.

Affectionately referred to as 'the old and buggered', the MS *Oldenburg* is a ship that was built in the 1950s and, according to the pamphlet I'm clasping, crosses from Bideford and Ilfracombe to Lundy Island three times a week. The twelve-mile trip should take us just short of two hours and as far as any of the other passengers are concerned, Detective Fahey, Max and I are just three acquaintances making the trip from Ilfracombe. I'm grateful Fahey didn't cuff me before we boarded.

It doesn't feel real; none of it does. Less than a month ago, Lucy and I were talking about booking a holiday abroad. Somewhere warm with a pool and food that our five-year-old daughter Sienna wouldn't fuss about. Lundy Island couldn't be further from that dream. And none of us would ever have imagined I'd be standing trial for murder.

I look over at my brother Max. Over six feet tall, he inherited male pattern baldness from Dad's side of the family in his early twenties, and now keeps the top of his head fully shaved; a means of exercising what little control over it he has left. I want to ask him for the umpteenth time if this is all just a nightmare from which I seem unable to wake; a bad practical joke that has been taken too far. As angry as I would be to find myself the butt of the joke, I would give absolutely anything for Lucy to still be alive.

Whilst this feels like a waste of everyone's time, Max assures me it buys him extra time to find Lucy's real killer.

So much blood... like something out of a horror movie.

Those were the words of the Crime Scene Investigator I over-heard from the back of the ambulance while I struggled to make sense of why someone had erected a large white canopy outside my front door. I refused to accept that Lucy was dead until Max entered my room at the hospital and confirmed the devastating news.

But even now, I've not come to terms with it.

And the worst part is how they could believe that I am responsible. They claim to have found my bloody prints on the handle of the knife that inflicted the fatal wound, and her blood soaked into my pyjamas. But what they seem unable to accept is that I could never hurt Lucy. I loved – *love* – her with all my heart, and wouldn't have been able to do any of the things they are accusing me of.

I thought a person was innocent until *proven* guilty, but Detective Fahey and his team appear to have attended a different school of thought.

And I genuinely can't tell whether Max is just using the suggestion that I was sleepwalking when the crime occurred to buy more time to find the real killer, or whether there's a part of him that actually believes it.

In the UK, a person who commits any offence whilst sleepwalking can be considered not guilty, or 'legally insane' if it can be proved the offence occurred while they were asleep. This is how Max explained it to me when he first proposed it as a defence at the plea hearing. I've asked him what he believes and he always gives me the same answer: 'It doesn't matter what I believe, little brother, only what I can prove.'

Hardly the ringing endorsement I was hoping for, but then Max and I have never been that close. It was a relief when he volunteered to represent me when Fahey arrested me for Lucy's murder within days of me being released from the hospital. They don't seem to care that I suffered a blow to the back of the head the same night that Lucy and I were discovered in the kitchen, and that I have no recollection of what really happened.

What's more logical: that I was sleepwalking, stabbed my wife to death, and somehow managed to knock myself unconscious; or that someone broke into our home, knocked me unconscious, and murdered my wife?

We're sitting against a railing that would do very little to stop anyone falling overboard. I'm not the strongest of swimmers, so any attempt to escape into the choppy, icy waters would fail before it began. And with the fog as thick as it is, it would be so easy to become lost anyway.

Fahey doesn't speak, his cheeks an unnatural shade of green, but I've never been a fan of small talk anyway. What would we talk about? He's already warned me that he won't answer any questions about the investigation. And as far as he is concerned, he's caught his suspect. What troubles me most is the prospect that they're no longer looking for alternative suspects.

Max returns, pocketing his phone and pulling his coat around him. I'd give anything for a hot drink to fight off the chill, but the *Oldenburg* doesn't have any refreshment facilities. I should get up and move about, but I don't want to give Fahey the wrong idea. Max has already told me not to do anything that might cast further suspicion, but it's almost as if he's also forgotten I'm an innocent party in all of this. I'm not sure either appreciate just how much I've lost.

No, correction: just how much has been taken away from me. Lucy's body has yet to be released by the coroner, which means we've not been allowed to lay her to rest. How am I supposed to process my grief when I haven't had the chance to say goodbye? Although I was discovered beside her, my last memory of Lucy is of her laughing, so none of this feels real. And I would give anything to suddenly wake and for the nightmare to be over.

'Shouldn't be too much longer,' Max says, blowing warm air into his hands. 'We should be able to see the island soon enough.'

Three miles long and half a mile wide, Lundy Island lies off the coast of North Devon where the Atlantic Ocean meets the Bristol Channel, and is a National Trust property. There are no hotels or lodgings available, according to the pamphlet, and the only method of transportation is the *Oldenburg*'s twice-daily visit. Anyone who misses the crossing back will have to battle the elements, and at this time of year, it isn't something I'd want to face.

The island is also the base for the Lundy Clinic for the Study of Sleep Disorders. Max has promised that they will be able to fully assess my mental state and predisposition to sleepwalking in less than a week. Again, this is going to be a waste of time, because they will conclude that I don't sleepwalk, which only serves to support my assertion that someone else killed Lucy. So what is Max really hoping is going to happen while I'm locked inside the clinic? All I can pray is that he has some masterplan up his sleeve, and this week will buy him the time to implement it.

The only way he could convince the judge was telling stories of when I sleepwalked as a child; stories I have no recollection of either. And I'm certain that if it is something that continues to affect me, then Lucy would have mentioned it. And I'm also sure that members of my various forces' teams wouldn't have kept it a secret.

Fahey stands suddenly, clutching his mouth, and tells us not to go anywhere, before hurrying towards the toilet sign. The fog is so thick here that Fahey disappears from sight before he's even made it to the door into the hull. The irony that a similar impenetrable fog surrounds my own memory isn't lost on me.

Why can't I remember what happened that night? The swelling to my head is gone, and I'm no longer suffering with the agonising headaches, and yet the glaring hole remains. I overheard Max on the phone yesterday asking one of the medical specialists whether the lack of memory could be as a result of disassociation; that I could have killed Lucy and been so shocked by my actions that my own psyche has wiped it from my mind like someone deleting a file on a computer. When he caught me eavesdropping, he was quick to reassure me that he's simply playing devil's advocate and trying to pre-empt what the prosecutors will ask, but the look on his face told me he's not totally convinced by my protestations. What chance have I got if I can't even convince my solicitor – my only brother – that I didn't do it?

The boat rises and drops, and my stomach turns. Looking over the side, I can't even see the water through the white shroud, but spray bounces up and catches my chin. The smell of salt and sewage is so pungent that I have to look away.

'Planning your escape?' Max murmurs beside me.

I don't answer, shaking my head instead.

'Nobody would blame you,' he continues quietly. 'Given everything you're facing, and what's happened...'

'I have no reason to run,' I say firmly. 'I didn't kill Lucy and I'm going to prove it one way or another.'

He lights a cigarette and inhales deeply, before offering me the packet. I shake my head, though I could do with something to take the edge off. I cough as his exhaled smoke blows into my face. He apologises, and stands, moving across to the other side of the ship, and leans over the railing. I'm so cold that I also stand, and move about to try to get the blood pumping. I move to the front railing and try to peer through the fog in search of the island, but it's no good. There could be land a stone's throw ahead of us and we wouldn't see it until too late.

And then suddenly, there's a break in the dense swirl, and a dark shadow appears on the horizon. The boat begins to slow, and as the mist continues to disperse, the shadow begins to take shape. Spiky shards pierce the thick blanket of cloud, and as we near, the shadows take on hues of dark green and brown as the scale of the large hilly mass becomes apparent. It's as if someone took a giant moss-covered rock and dropped it into the water. It's like something out of a horror movie, the kind of place that is probably very pleasant in the right conditions, but just looks sinister in low light. I can't escape the feeling that nothing good will come of this.

2

We head towards a long wooden pontoon cut into the water, and the boat begins to slow as we near. Fahey appears beside me, and he takes my wrist in his hand as if to remind me that I'm not a free man. He continues to hold on to my arm as the boat docks and the other passengers head along the drawbridge to dry land. It is only when everyone else is off that we venture forwards. It feels like I am being led somewhere from which there is no return.

Whilst the rest of the passengers have headed towards the left of the pontoon, where a sign confirms the start of the marked trail around the island, we venture to the right, where a track leads up and around the hill directly in front of us. A man with a prematurely grey beard, dressed in a navy-blue overcoat, is standing beside a large map stencilled into a placard of wood. He approaches Max and extends a hand.

'You must be Max Meredith, right?'

There's a Belfast twang to the bearded man's accent, and he gives me a serious frown as Max shakes his hand and introduces me and Fahey. He makes no effort to shake my hand, but there's no look of fear or concern behind his grey eyes.

'My name is Stuart Coyle and I'm the facility director and clinical lead. I thought it only right to come down and meet you all personally. How was your crossing?'

'Choppy,' Max replies. 'Is the clinic far?'

'Only a five-minute walk. I hope that's okay? There are no motor vehicles allowed on the island, so we either have to walk or run. The choice is yours.'

What kind of place prohibits motor vehicles? I can't escape the feeling that my living nightmare has taken a darker turn, and I'm being imprisoned here against my will.

Coyle leads the way, Max beside him, and Fahey with an ever-watchful eye next to me. A more natural colour has returned to his cheeks now that we're on dry land, and I'm the one feeling sick to the gills. Is this what it feels like being marched to the gallows?

'Have any of you been to Lundy Island before?' Coyle asks.

'No, never,' Max answers for all of us.

'Well, I'd offer to give you a whistlestop tour, but there isn't much here really. There's a small street of houses on the south side of the island for the twenty-eight of us who call the island home. The majority of those work at our facility, whilst a handful of others run the bar and café for the visiting tourists.'

I catch sight of a monument as we pass. A bronze statue of a bearded figure in a cloak and hood, a cross in one hand, with the other pointing back out to sea. There is text etched on a tablet near the statue's feet, but when I try to read it, I realise it is written in Latin.

'For the souls of all who are lost,' Coyle translates when he sees me reading it. 'This is St Brendan the Navigator, Lundy's shrine to all those who've died traversing these rough waters, whether through sinking or misadventure.'

He looks at me directly as he says this, and the hairs on the back of my neck stand. I stare back out to sea, the mainland cut off by the thick wall of fog. I've never felt so isolated, and all I want to do is get back home where Sienna is waiting for me. It's been too long since I spoke to her, and I promise myself that as soon as I'm settled, I'll find a phone and call her.

I can't even begin to imagine what she's going through, with her mum gone and now her dad ripped from her life. I know Lucy's sister Geraldine will do a great job of taking care of her, but she shouldn't have to. It should be me helping Sienna to process her grief, and her helping me.

Maybe I should have instructed Max not to pursue this course of action. Maybe I should have just pleaded not guilty and allowed the judicial system to run its course. On the stand, I know I could convince a jury of how much I love Lucy, and if they could see how much pain I'm in, they'd see through Fahey's mistake. They'd see that I couldn't possibly have killed Lucy. At least then I'd be at home and better able to support Sienna.

Is it too late to tell all this to Max now? Surely he could reach the judge and advise that me being at this clinic is just a waste of everyone's time. The judge could then tear up the order that I be detained here for the next week and we can get back to finding Lucy's real killer. Ultimately, that's what we're going to have to do when Coyle and his team conclude that I am not someone who sleepwalks. But I can't get to Max. He's several metres in front, in deep conversation with Coyle, and with Fahey and I struggling to keep pace with them, a greater gap is growing.

'Hold on there,' Fahey says with more than just a hint of warning in his voice. 'You might have convinced everyone else that you didn't stab your wife, but the evidence tells me a very different story. You can continue to lie to yourself, tell yourself that you didn't commit this heinous crime, but at some point you're going to have to come to terms with what you did. And for the sake of your daughter, I hope that you realise the truth sooner rather than later. She deserves to know why her mum died, and she deserves a father who doesn't lie.'

I know now that there is nothing I'm going to be able to say or do to convince him of my innocence. As far as he is concerned, he's solved the case, and that means he won't even contemplate the possibility that someone else could have killed Lucy. If Max can't find the person responsible and somehow obtain their confession, I have no way of proving my innocence.

Coyle continues to lead the way up and around the hill until we reach what looks like an abandoned hotel. It stands out against the blanket of thick cloud blocking out the sky. The paintwork is grey and weathered, and the windows on the front side are covered in grime. It looks like the sort of building they use in horror movies; devoid of any kind of life. If it wasn't for Coyle leading us here, I never would have guessed this is supposed to be a state-of-the-art facility.

'Welcome to the Lundy Clinic,' Coyle says, with a smile on his face that could belong to the devil himself.

3

It's only when we've entered through the automated doors that I finally accept we're in the right place. The reception area is the total opposite to the decrepit exterior. The carpet is a deep maroon colour and must be relatively new as I can feel the bounce of the tread as I walk across it. The walls are clinically white, and there is a gentle hum of air conditioning. The place is so tall and airy, like we've walked into an airport lounge. I can almost picture suited pilots wheeling their cases along with a smile on their faces and a twinkle in their eyes.

The other thing that makes me think of an airport is the presence of four men in dark green shirts and trousers, carefully stationed at each corner of the room. The radios clipped to their belts and their athletic physiques mark them out as security, but it isn't yet clear to me whether they're a permanent fixture or have been drafted in because of me. The fact that there are no other patients or guests in the square room is also a red flag, though it wouldn't surprise me if everyone is on high alert as a suspected murderer arrives. Although Max hasn't said it in so many words, I know it was he who arranged this stay, and had to get the judge to agree to the assessment being carried out here. Just how much Stuart Coyle and the rest of the clinic team knows of this isn't yet clear, but given they'll be supplying their report to the judge, they must have some detail of what's happened.

Coyle escorts us to an elongated counter that looks more like something I'd expect to see in a hotel, and even the woman behind the desk looks as though she's stepped off a plane. Coyle speaks on our behalf and asks the receptionist to let Dr Carpenter know that we've arrived. A moment later, a door to the right of the reception desk opens and a blonde woman in a pencil skirt and knitted jumper steps through. She can't be much older than twenty-five. She straightens her white coat, and walks towards us purposefully, her expression firm but welcoming.

'May I introduce Dr Carpenter,' Coyle says, stepping back and placing a protective arm behind her back. 'She will be overseeing Jake's care while he's here with us.'

There are no nerves as she shakes hands with Fahey and Max. Then she looks straight at me, smiling amiably.

'It's a pleasure to meet you, Jake.'

Her handshake is as sincere as the warmth emanating from her. Maybe I was wrong to assume they know the trouble I'm facing.

'You will need to surrender any communication devices you're carrying on your person,' Carpenter says calmly, accepting a plastic box from the receptionist.

My mouth drops open. How will I phone Sienna without a phone?

'My brother isn't in police custody at this time,' Max interjects.

'It's a requirement of the clinic that no recording devices are permitted through to the inner sanctum. It is for our patients' safety as much as our own. As a private medical facility, our clients' privacy and wellbeing is at the forefront at all times. Any personal items are stored in a secured room here at the entrance. And when his stay with us is complete, he'll be able to collect anything he's secured.'

'I need my phone,' I say firmly. 'I have a daughter I need to be able to speak to.'

'I understand,' she says, offering a sincere nod, 'but we can't allow you to bring the phone in with you. There is a telephone inside the facility which patients can access to let loved ones know they are okay.'

'But she won't have that number. What if she needs to phone me? She has this number only.'

'Once you're settled in, you can call her and share the number of the facility. That way, if she needs to speak to you, she can phone here and we can pass on the message.'

She's not listening to me. I only agreed to come here knowing I'd be able to phone and message Sienna. I can't be cut off from her altogether.

'Then I'm not staying,' I say, taking a step back before feeling the weight of Fahey's hand against the small of my back.

'Jake, you have to stay,' Max says firmly but quietly. 'You need to be assessed.'

I grab his arm and pull him away from the others, and he extends a hand to keep Fahey away from us.

'Why are we doing this, Max?' I whisper. 'We both know I didn't kill Lucy, and all you need to do is show the jury that someone else did.'

'We discussed this a long time ago, Jake. You're here so they can assess whether you sleepwalk.'

'But I know that I don't. In fact, you're the only person in the entire world who believes I ever have.'

'I promise you there was a time when you used to sleepwalk on a regular basis. It used to freak out Mum.'

'But I spoke to Mum and she has no memory of it.'

'I know,' he exhales. 'I spoke to her too, but you have to remember her memory isn't what it once was. She still occasionally forgets that Dad is dead.'

It breaks my heart whenever I speak to her and she tells me what Dad and her have been up to. Most of the time I don't correct her as it upsets her to be reminded.

I let out a deep sigh.

'I did not kill Lucy while sleepwalking,' I say through gritted teeth.

'Then stay here and be assessed to prove that.'

'I shouldn't need to prove it, Max.'

But as soon as I say the words, something clicks in my head. I'm not just here to buy Max time, he actually thinks I may have killed Lucy in my sleep.

'Your being here gives me another week to dig into yours and Lucy's lives before we return to court. That time could be invaluable if I'm able to find something – *anything* – that substantiates what you're saying. The police say nobody broke into the house because there was no forced entry, but have they considered someone else might have got hold of your keys? Or that maybe the front door wasn't locked? I need you here, Jake, so I can do what is needed to find the truth about what happened that night.'

'But I can't cope without being able to speak to Sienna. And how am I going to be able to check in with you and find out what you've discovered?'

'Listen to me, I will speak to Sienna and let her know why you don't have your phone, and I will phone you here every day to provide updates on the case. Okay?'

'And you'll give Geraldine the number for the facility so Sienna can phone me?'

'Absolutely.'

I remove the phone from my pocket as we walk back over to the reception desk, and I turn it over in my hands several times, before passing it to Dr Carpenter.

'I promise you it's the same rule for all our visitors. And considering we're looking to assess your sleeping patterns, the removal of distractions like social media and messenger apps will only benefit our assessment and potential treatments. After a few days, our other guests usually report they find it easier getting to sleep because they're not tied to their phones.'

'Other guests?' Fahey says, spittle forming on his lips. 'But Meredith will be isolated, right?'

Her lips curl slightly to one side. 'This isn't a prison, Detective Fahey. I am fully aware of Jake's circumstances, and if you're worried about the prospect of him trying to escape, I can assure you that we have an increased security presence, as per your stipulations. In addition, every inch of the clinic is covered by video cameras.'

I'm half-expecting Fahey to object and insist that he stay in the room with me, but before he has a chance, Coyle whisks him away towards one of the security guards, presumably to continue the conversation.

'If you want to follow me,' Dr Carpenter says, moving back towards the door, 'I'll show you to your room, and fill you in on what you can expect while you're here with us.'

I look to Max to see whether he's planning to take off or tag along, and am relieved when he nods and ushers me to follow Dr Carpenter.

She scans the pass hanging from her neck, and the door beside the reception desk slides open with a whoosh. We find ourselves in a narrow, dimly lit corridor, the ceiling so low that Max almost needs to duck as we progress along it. Above our heads there is no ceiling, just a glass roof, some four storeys high.

There are eight closed doors, including the one we've just entered from, spread evenly around the walls. I imagine it would be easy to become disoriented. I can't escape the feeling we've stepped into some kind of labyrinth.

Dr Carpenter moves towards a door off to our right and again scans her pass against a panel. As before, the door slides open with a whoosh and we follow her through to another narrow corridor and into a much smaller enclosure. It's only when we're inside that I realise this is in fact a lift. We begin to ascend, though when the door slides open and we step out, there are no panels or numbers to indicate how high we have climbed.

The walls here are as white as those in the reception area and the air smells of sweet flowers. I feel some of the tension ease from my shoulders for the first time all day. I'm not sure what I was expecting the clinic to be like inside – maybe some kind of insane asylum – but there are no bars on any of the large frosted windows that look into the rooms to the left and right of us. At the far end of this long corridor is a large red door, but rather than going through it, we stop halfway along, and Dr Carpenter opens a door to one of the rooms. There is a bed covered with neatly pressed white linen against one of the walls, with an array of equipment either side of it. There are two soft leather chairs below a window that looks out over the island. I can see the sea, though the crashing waves are muted.

'This will be your room while you stay with us, Jake. This is the dorm floor, as we call it. You'll have seen the red door at the end of the corridor? The brown door beside it leads through to The Butterfly Room, which is the main communal area where guests can interact if they so choose. There are some board games, a radio, and a number of fiction books to read. The Butterfly Room is also where meals are served, though there's plenty of space, so don't feel that you *need* to speak with other guests. Some suffer from lack of sleep and so may be irritable, and others suffer from other psychological comorbidities, so it's understood that you don't have to engage.'

I wasn't sure what to expect of this place, but this isn't it. I feel as though I've been checked in to rehab against my will.

'You'll soon get the hang of things,' she adds with a disarming smile before turning to Max. 'Remember: the purpose of Jake's stay with us is to determine if he suffers from somnambulism.'

I frown.

'Better known as sleepwalking,' she clarifies.

She begins to explain the many different types of sleep disorder they study and treat, but I can't keep up with all the terminology.

'Please don't underestimate what we're capable of here. I can't go into too much detail, but some of the things we're currently studying would literally blow your mind.' She smiles at her own joke. 'One of our most experienced nurses, Brenda, will be along with your hospital attire in due course.'

Max and I both raise our eyebrows at this.

She laughs. 'Don't worry, there are no bottom-revealing hospital gowns here. We have special pyjamas that contain sensors which allow us to monitor blood pressure, heart rate, and the like, so we can see how different stimuli affect you both during the day and when you're asleep.'

'And at the end of the week you'll be able to reach a conclusive decision about whether he sleepwalks or not?' Max asks.

She nods.

'And can your equipment fail?' He looks at me as he says this. 'Your findings could come under significant scrutiny and challenge in court.'

'The equipment we use to assess patients is top of the line. Your brother isn't the first person we've assessed facing charges for this condition. We are very good at what we do here, Mr Meredith.'

Something crashes into the open door of my room, and we all start. A woman in a white uniform and chequered tabard wheels what looks like an old tea trolley into the room. She has the look of someone who's seen and heard it all, and can no longer be surprised by anything. She is hunched over the trolley, her back and shoulders now rounded by time and service.

'Ah, and here is Brenda now. Brenda, may I introduce our latest guest. This is Jake Meredith, and his brother Max. And that is my cue to leave so you can get changed and settled. Brenda will be your first point of call from here on in.'

'Oh, I thought Mr Coyle said you would be overseeing me,' I say, confused by this change.

'Dr Carpenter deals with all the head stuff, but I'll look after your day-to-day needs,' Brenda interjects.

Her Welsh accent is strong, but I sense she's toned it down so it's easier to understand. She puffs out her cheeks and wipes her forehead with the back of her wrist. Her hair is thick with greying curls, and the large glasses cover most of her cheeks and temple. She reminds me of a childminder Max and I had when we were kids who we referred to as 'Auntie Roz', even though she wasn't family.

Brenda puts an affectionate arm around Dr Carpenter. 'She's brilliant at her job, but lousy at making beds and cleaning bathrooms.'

They laugh, before Dr Carpenter takes her leave. Brenda moves to a door at the far side of the room that I hadn't noticed before, opens it and reveals a toilet, basin, and walk-in shower. Again, it's all in brilliant white, which is beginning to make my eyes ache.

'There are towels hanging behind the door, but just shout if you need any more,' she adds, returning to the trolley, and lifting out a transparent plastic pouch. 'If you can get changed into these, I'll give you a tour of the rest of the clinic.'

She shows Max out of the room and closes the door. I was told not to bring anything with me and that all my needs would be dealt with, but I pull out one thing I snuck in from my pocket. It's a photo of Sienna and Lucy laughing while on a spinning teacup ride from a funfair. I remember the day so well. We ate chips out of paper bags while huddled together on the end of Teignmouth pier.

One way or another, I won't stop until I've proved my innocence and get back to my little girl. Losing one parent at such a young age isn't fair, and I won't let her lose another.

4

FOUR WEEKS BEFORE THE MURDER

Jake starts awake, the drumming in his ears unbearably loud. He blinks several times, trying to place the noise and khaki-coloured wall of a jet plane. He turns to look out of the tiny porthole-sized window behind his head, and sees the grey of runway behind him, but for a moment can't tell if they're about to take off or are landing. The inside of the cabin rattles as the plane continues to roll, and he sees they are no longer taxiing towards the runways but away from them. And then the realisation that he's home – returning from serving for the final time – hits him, and he can't keep the smile from breaking across his face. Any minute now, he'll be off the plane and back in Lucy and Sienna's arms. His heart throbs with excitement.

He looks around the cabin and spots the faces of another six men chattering excitedly. He recognises one of them, but none are from his platoon.

'We're home!' one of them yells at the top of his voice, and everyone else on board cheers and whoops.

Jake has always told Sienna that being away from home and family while on deployment is the toughest part of his job, but returning always makes it feel worthwhile. Jake cannot wait to kiss Lucy and tell her how much he's missed her, but he's also terrified that he'll barely recognise Sienna because kids grow so quickly and change so much at that age. Lucy has been sending him photos of the two of them, but it isn't the same.

He reaches down to the sports bag between his feet and pulls out the stuffed camel toy he brought back for Sienna, and smooths out its fur where it's become crumpled in the bag. He then reaches below that and pulls out the long, thin jewellery box, snapping open the lid and adjusting the chain of the silver necklace and pendant. He's put pictures of himself and Sienna inside so that Lucy will always have them close to her heart.

He's hoping it serves as a distraction when he breaks the news that he's resigned his commission, and is officially unemployed. He knows she won't be happy to assume the role of sole breadwinner, but he doesn't intend to remain unemployed for long. He's worked out that they'll survive financially for at least two months, but wants to find something sooner rather than later. A smarter move would have been to delay handing in his resignation, but after what happened – not what everyone thinks happened, but what *really* happened – he doesn't want to risk staying any longer.

Disembarking, he can feel the adrenaline pumping around his body as the cool wind blows against his face. It's good to be home after three months in the heat of the desert. Even the splashes of rain against his cheeks are welcome. He passes through security and immediately spots the huge cardboard sign being held lopsided by Sienna:

WELCOME HOME, DADDY

He runs and scoops her into his arms, the sign quickly discarded to the floor as Sienna throws her tiny arms around his neck. She smells of vanilla and strawberries, but he buries his face in the crook between her neck and shoulder.

'I've missed you so much, pumpkin.'

He can feel the warmth of her tears as they trickle onto his cheek. 'I love you, Daddy.'

'I love you too, sweetheart.'

He pulls her back so he can look into her beautiful, innocent eyes. He dries her tears with his thumb, and smiles warmly at her. 'Thank you for my sign. Did you make it yourself?'

'Mummy helped spell the words.'

He looks to Lucy, and takes Sienna's hand into his, so he can use his left to pull Lucy towards him. The kiss is hard and passionate, because he wants her to know how much he's missed her too. She reciprocates and it pushes any lingering memory of what happened in the desert out of his mind.

Sienna groans in morbid horror as they continue to kiss, and squirms until they break apart.

Home is a three-hour drive from Wattisham Airfield, during which Sienna tells him all about school and how she's really enjoying it. He doesn't interrupt, cherishing every moment. And it isn't until he recognises the road they're driving along that he realises something isn't right.

'What are we doing here?' he asks, still feeling pretty drained and desperate to have a shower and change out of his army fatigues.

Lucy looks over at him, and makes an apologetic face. 'Sorry, I just need to pick up a few papers from Geraldine's. I'm in court in the morning and I asked her to take a look at my documents. Four eyes are better than two and all that.'

She parks on the side of the road.

'Don't be too long,' he says, flashing her the grin he knows she can't resist. 'I thought we could get home, put Sienna to bed and then maybe you and I could... you know, have an early night as well.'

He lifts her hand to his lips and kisses the back of it.

She flashes that smile of hers, and he's putty in her hands.

'I won't be long. Why don't you come in too? I'm sure Ray would love to see you.'

Jake wrinkles his nose in revulsion at mention of his golf-loving brother-in-law.

'I don't want to see Ray. He'll start talking golf at me, which you know I can't stand, and then he'll try and pressure me into going to the driving range with him.'

She chuckles, not realising he's being serious.

'He's not that bad. Just come in with me. I'm sure a beer will make things easier.'

Jake shakes his head. 'I've been travelling for eight hours, I'm in dirty clothes, and I just don't have it in me to be sociable with anyone right now. I'll wait in the car.'

'Please? I might be twenty minutes or so going over any revisions with Geraldine. Please?'

'Yeah, come on, Daddy. I can introduce you to Auntie Geraldine's cat.'

They've ambushed him, and a flash of memory of the platoon being attacked pricks his mind's eye. On that day he swore he would do anything to be back with them and his resistance weakens.

'Okay, but one beer and then we're on our way. Agreed?'

Lucy smiles again and climbs out. Jake pushes open his door and follows suit, hanging back to help Sienna out before following them up to the front door. As he's standing on the doorstep, he happens to glance over his shoulder, suddenly conscious of just how many cars appear to be parked along the street. His brain connects the dots just as the door opens and he sees familiar faces gathered just inside. He inwardly groans when he sees the 'Welcome Home, Hero' banner hanging between lampshades in the expansive hallway, before a chorus of 'Surprise' rises from those gathered inside.

He wants to grab Lucy and Sienna's hands and drag them back to the car, but it's already too late. He's grateful that so many people have decided to come out, but desperately wishes they hadn't bothered. Given everything that's happened in the last few weeks, a party isn't appropriate. If they had any idea of what he did over there...

He chases the thought away, plasters on a smile he's in no way feeling and follows Lucy inside. There are pats on the back, warm hugs, and messages of congratulations. It's overwhelming. It looks as though Lucy and Geraldine have been busy planning this for weeks. The dining table is filled with finger foods, and the sideboard is stacked with bottles of wine and spirits. He can't believe so much effort has been made for him.

His stomach grumbles as he smells the steaming pizza that's just been carried to the table by Ray. He waves as their eyes meet, reaching into his back pocket and passing Jake a bottle of beer, quickly apologising because he forgot to bring a bottle opener, and disappearing back out to the kitchen.

'A hero's welcome,' Max's deep brogue mutters, right before he slaps a hand on the back of Jake's shoulder. 'Welcome home, little brother.'

Jake turns, surprised Lucy managed to get him to come along. The last time they spoke, bitter words were exchanged, and although their mum has been on at them to clear the air, between Max's busy lifestyle and Jake's deployments, they've left things to fester.

'Hey, how's tricks?' Jake asks, uncertain what else to say.

'Couldn't be better, but my exploits in the criminal justice system pale against your heroism overseas. Mum hasn't stopped telling everyone she knows how her baby is being awarded the Victoria Cross for gallantry in the face of the enemy.' He raises his glass of wine in a toast. 'Congratulations.'

Jake clinks the unopened beer bottle against the tip of the glass. 'Thanks, but I only did what anyone would in my position.'

'Mum said she wasn't certain why it is being awarded. Are you able to enlighten us?'

He now spots his sister-in-law, Catarina, standing just behind his brother.

'It's highly confidential. I could tell you, but then I'd have to kill you,' he jokes.

It isn't true, but he isn't prepared to tell anyone what really happened out in that desert. Being awarded the VC has blown everything out of the water, and as grateful as he is to be recognised, being allowed to return early from deployment is the only reward he wanted.

'What if I promise not to tell anyone?' Max presses. 'I'm good at keeping secrets.'

Isn't that the truth, Jake thinks but doesn't say. He's relieved when Ray returns, now wielding a bottle opener, reaching for the neck of the bottle and popping off the small metal cap.

'Would you mind if I borrowed the hero of the hour?' Ray asks, placing a hand on Jake's shoulder and leading him away. 'There's something I want to show you,' he whispers as they cross through the room and towards the kitchen.

But they don't stop there, continuing through the internal door and out to his garage. He flicks on the light and both cough as the dust is disturbed.

'What do you think?' he asks, his eyes wide with excitement.

Jake looks around the garage, littered with offcuts of wood, but all he can see is Ray's bag of golf clubs beneath the light. Jake winces when he sees the large red bow wrapped around the top of it.

'I decided to treat myself to some new clubs, and I was going to sell my old ones on, but then when Lucy said you were coming back and were due some leave, I thought...' His cheeks bristle excitedly. 'I know you two don't have a heap of disposable cash, so I'd be honoured if you would accept them as a gift from Geraldine and me.'

'I – I don't know what to say, Ray,' he answers honestly.

Ray slaps him hard on the back. 'I knew you'd be speechless. I thought it might be an idea for us to take them to the driving range later in the week so you can get a feel for them, and then we can start with a nine-hole, and slowly build up to an eighteen.'

Jake hands him the bottle of beer, excusing himself as he races out of the garage and towards the downstairs toilet, closing and locking it behind him. Whilst he appreciates the effort Lucy has gone to, she knows how much he hates surprises and being the centre of attention. If she'd let on sooner, he would have told her how physically exhausted he feels.

He desperately twists the taps, willing the water to run, staring back at his pallid reflection in the mirror above the sink. His heart is racing so fast that he thinks he may pass out at any moment. He doesn't know what's happening to him, but is terrified he's having a heart attack.

5

I stand, feeling the thin cotton pyjama top and bottoms tight against my skin. The label on the packet they came in claims there are tiny sensors secreted within the material able to measure heart rate, pulse and blood pressure, and it makes me wonder just how much my stay here is costing, and who's footing the bill. Max and I haven't discussed his fee for helping me, but I know my brother well enough to realise he isn't acting pro bono. There will be a cost at some point, and frankly if he keeps me out of jail, I'll pay whatever it is.

Fresh flowers stand in a shapely glass vase on the windowsill, reminding me of the days when Mum would do the laundry when we were growing up. She was always testing new detergent scents; whenever there'd be a television commercial for a new brand or fragrance of washing liquid or tablet, she'd be out buying it the next day. Our home always smelled of fresh flowers and the great outdoors. I wish she was here right now, to hold me close and tell me everything is going to be okay.

I bury the negativity of my thoughts with a firm shake of my head. I know I am innocent, and the British justice system is designed to try and punish the guilty. I have to keep believing that an innocent man won't go to prison. That said, the thick wire mesh covering the outside of the windows gives this whole room a prison feel. Dr Carpenter told Fahey that they'd adopted additional security measures for my stay, so maybe that must mean even the doctors think I'm guilty.

I look down at the photograph of Lucy and Sienna in the spinning teacup again, and can't escape how different they look from each other. Sienna has Lucy's hazel eyes, but her hair is much darker. Still blonde, but more straw-coloured than platinum. And she definitely inherited that withdrawn look from my side of the family. Poor kid. At least she seems to have received her mum's brains, because Sienna is bright as a cookie, excelling in maths as well as creative writing. She can be anything she wants to be when she's older. University educated like Lucy hopefully, and then a choice of careers: law, accounting, or maybe medicine. When I try to picture her as an adult, I can't, because the possibilities for her are endless.

My eyes prick with tears at the thought of not being able to see her grow up, and so I stand and move to the small bathroom. I don't want her to have to come and visit me every weekend in prison. She deserves so much better, and I'm suddenly overwhelmed by all the weeks of her life I've already missed from serving overseas. I don't want her to grow up resenting me for not being there when she took her first steps, spoke her first words, and mastered using the toilet. Lucy used to send me photo messages with each achievement, and each time my heart would break a little more. That's one of the reasons I resigned my commission, although not the only reason. The day I handed my resignation over to my Commanding Officer, I never expected I'd spend more than a day or so away from my family ever again. And now look at me; accused of my wife's murder and voluntarily confined to this place when I should be at home with Sienna.

I run the tap until the water warms and then splash handfuls of it onto my face. My hands brush the stubble on my chin, and the reflection staring back at me looks exhausted. I seem to have aged so dramatically in the days since I woke in the back of that ambulance. Where once I used to get asked for identification by nightclub bouncers well into my twenties, the figure staring back at me looks twice the age. I guess that's the unwritten consequence of grief.

A knock at the door is followed by Max poking his head through to check that I've finished changing.

'I was asked to drop your clothes at reception on my way down,' he tells me, entering and folding my combats and long-sleeve vest top. 'They said you can keep your coat, as you'll be allowed out into the grounds for fresh air and exercise.'

I exit the bathroom and close the bedroom door, taking the pile of clothes from Max's grasp. I place them on the end of the bed.

'Tell me this is the only way,' I say to him, hoping to break through that thick wall of disengaged armour he permanently wears.

He slumps down on the bed.

'I wouldn't have brought you here if I thought there was any other way.'

'Are things really that bad? I thought the onus was on the prosecution to prove my guilt, rather than me proving my innocence.'

He can't seem to bring himself to make eye contact, his brow furrowed.

'It is, but from what I've heard they feel confident in their case, and from the evidence I've seen, they have good reason. They can place you at the scene, and they have your prints on the murder weapon, which is all compelling.'

'But hardly a stretch given I live in the house and must have used that knife a hundred times to chop onions.'

'But your prints were made in her blood, which means you held it after she'd been stabbed.'

He holds his hands aloft, as if surrendering before I unload both barrels at him.

'But the real killer could have placed the weapon in my hand whilst I was unconscious beside her.'

He nods in agreement.

'Absolutely, and that's the sort of thing I now need to prove. Our best means of keeping you out of prison is by casting doubt on the prosecution's case against you.'

'They also need to prove I had motive for wanting Lucy dead,' I say, the words bitter in my mouth.

He slowly exhales, before finally meeting my gaze.

'They think they can prove that as well.'

'What?' I snap, angered at the suggestion that anyone could think I would want Lucy dead. 'How?'

His face is stoic, showing no emotion.

'They have witness accounts of shouting and arguments. Apparently, the police were called around one evening a few days before she died?'

I can't tell if he's asking this as a question, or he already knows the answer.

'That was nothing,' I say dismissively. 'Lucy had had a bad day at work, and she came home, angry that I hadn't prepared anything for dinner. Her shouting was just a means of releasing some of her frustration. It was her who threw the plate at the wall, not me. So, if anything, the police being called around has nothing to do with me having the propensity to lash out.'

He nods sympathetically.

'I get it, and it isn't me you need to convince, but – and I'm purely playing devil's advocate here – how do you think the jury will react to the news that the police were called around because of a violent altercation between the two of you? Even if we argue you were the victim in that situation, it still plays into the prosecution's hands, because they can argue you acted out of fear of how she might escalate next time. Even in self-defence arguments, there's still an admission that in that moment – however brief – the killer wanted that person dead.' He sighs heavily. 'I'm not trying to make you feel worse about things, Jake, but I think you need to face up to the reality of your situation: you're on trial for murder, and the evidence supports the prosecution's charge against you.'

I slump down on the bed beside Max, the wind firmly knocked from my sails. Placing my reliance on the British justice system is somewhat naïve when there are too many miscarriages of justice to ignore.

'How do we find the person or persons who killed Lucy?' I ask.

'First of all, I will draw up a list of people who could have wanted to harm either you or Lucy.'

'That'll be a short list. Don't you remember that Fahey asked me for the names of people who could have wanted Lucy dead and I couldn't give him a single name? Everyone loved Lucy.'

'Yes, they did. But don't forget, just because she's the one who died, it doesn't mean their intention wasn't to also kill you. Or their objective could have been to kill her and leave you to take the blame. Lucy and Geraldine ran a practice specialising in family law, and they will have acted on behalf of divorcees and on a number of family custody hearings. So, I will speak to Geraldine and find out a list of all of their recent cases so I can identify those who may have had an axe to grind.'

I can't get past the words *leave you to take the blame*. I can't think of anyone I could have pissed off enough to have planned such a cruel retaliation. But what if there is someone out there pulling the strings to see me hung out to dry for something I didn't do? Just because I can't think of a name doesn't mean it isn't a prospect. I would have hoped that Fahey and his team would have explored this possibility during their investigation, but it would have been difficult to ignore all the evidence pointing at me.

'And I'll be speaking to all of your neighbours to see which of them have security cameras at their properties or switched on in their cars. This is something the police should have already done, but there's no harm in repeating the process. All we need is evidence of someone acting strangely near the property, and it opens the possibility that an intruder was lurking nearby. I promise you, little brother, your being here now isn't a waste of time. I have so much work I need to do, and little time to complete it. So, do me a favour, play along with everything they ask of you here, and allow me to do what I do best: find the dirt that nobody else wants to acknowledge.'

I pull him into a hug, and feel my warm tears blotting against his suit jacket.

'And if all of that fails,' he continues, 'and the experts here at the Lundy Clinic *can* prove you're susceptible to sleepwalking, it gives us a contingency plan.'

His words are like a punch to the gut. For all his claims to the contrary, there's clearly a part of him that genuinely believes I sleepwalk, and he isn't totally convinced by my proclamation of innocence. And as much as I hate to admit it, if the shoe was on the other foot and I was presented with overwhelming evidence that he'd done something wrong, I too would question whether he was capable.

I move away, and look out of the window, down at the large expanse of water, the fog having now cleared. What would stop me attempting to swim back to the mainland? If I made it, I could grab Sienna and we could leave the country and start over. I know that would make me look guilty but coming here in the first place also suggests culpability.

I think back to the night when Lucy and I first met. I remember still feeling angry with the manner in which Max had used our dad's failing memory to force him into early retirement, thus handing over the business to Max. Meredith and Sons had been handed down from father to son for four generations, and I didn't begrudge Max taking the reins, just the way in which he had manipulated things to fulfil his destiny. Dad could have been allowed to take a back seat, but still maintain control for a few more years to ensure a tidy pension, but Max had ensured that wouldn't be the case.

I can't deny that it's exactly that level of ruthlessness I now need fighting my corner.

He stands and refolds the pile of clothes.

'Is there anything new you can tell me about that day?' he asks casually. 'Has any of your memory started to return?'

'Nothing,' I admit, unable to explain just how frustrated I am with the black hole blocking everything out from that day.

'What did you have for dinner that night? It was a Thursday, did you have plans to go out anywhere?'

I shake my head.

'I don't think so.'

'What about Sienna? Did she have any afterschool clubs you had to take her to?'

I shake my head again.

'No, Lucy used to say she couldn't cope with Sienna doing stuff during the week as she never knew when she'd have to work late from home. Don't forget, a lot of the time, it was just the two of them, because I was serving overseas.'

'And how were things between you and Lucy? I know Fahey was asking questions about your relationship, but it's just the two of us here now. What was really going on between the two of you?'

'We were fine,' I say through gritted teeth, angry that he would be suggesting otherwise.

He raises a sceptical eyebrow.

'Come on, Jake, I've been married for over twenty years, and I know how tough things can be without even throwing in the pressure of managing a long-distance relationship.'

'Me and Lucy are – *were* – fine. I loved her.'

'Lucy wasn't happy you'd resigned your commission, though, was she?'

'No, that's not true. She was supportive of my decision.'

'Okay, so let me rephrase: she wasn't happy you'd failed to find a new job.'

I can't deny that, but I don't think either of them appreciates how hard it is to find a new job in the current climate, especially with no qualifications to bulk out my CV.

'How do you know about that?'

He shrugs. 'She was my sister-in-law, Jake. I kept an eye out for her and Sienna when you weren't about. Would you expect anything less?'

I don't want to tell him that Lucy used to tell me how much he made her skin crawl, and hated the way he dominated conversations at family gatherings.

'What else did she tell you?'

I narrow my eyes. I find it hard to believe that Lucy would ever share such intimate details with Max of all people. I wonder whether his comments now are the result of second-hand information. Lucy and Catarina were quite friendly and it feels more likely that Lucy might have confided something to her rather than Max directly.

He doesn't answer the question, but slaps both hands against his legs and stands.

'I'd better get going or I'll miss the ferry back to the mainland.'

I don't press him, because he's right when he says he's the only person on my side. I embrace him again, and he pats my back a couple of times before breaking free of my grasp.

'Call me as soon as you find out something new,' I say to him. 'No matter how small, I need every glimmer of hope you can throw my way. Please?'

'I will do my best. Don't give the doctors and nurses any trouble here. At the end of the week, Dr Carpenter will be writing a report on you for the judge's attention. It can't paint you in a bad light.'

He leaves the room on that bombshell, and I want to chase after him, but I hear Dr Carpenter's voice in the corridor as she escorts him back towards the lift, and I don't want to give her the wrong impression. I'm going to have to be on my best behaviour while I'm stuck in here. What she writes in her report at the end of the week could have a far greater bearing on my future than anything Max can find out.

6

Cool, damp air crashes into my cheeks. I'm standing in a doorway, looking out at a sea of green, engulfed by a medieval-like tall, grey wall, weathered and overgrown in moss.

'Are you going out or not?' I hear Brenda's Welsh voice behind me. 'I haven't got all day.'

The overhead light glimmers off the glossy white plastic sleeve over my arm. I don't remember putting on a cagoule, nor how Brenda and I have made it from my room to the ground-floor entrance to the clinic's grounds, but the freshness of the breeze is intoxicating. I step outside.

'You shouldn't get too wet if you stick to the stone path,' Brenda says, 'but there are umbrellas just inside the door here if the rain gets heavier. They've been predicting a storm all week, but the meteorologists on the mainland get the forecast wrong as many times as they're right, so better to be safe than sorry.'

She speaks so quickly that it's hard to get a word in edgeways, so I simply nod my understanding, and watch as she closes the patio door, and raises the handle, before heading back along the corridor to complete her tasks.

The walled gardens must be half the size of a football pitch, and the stone path Brenda alluded to is a series of interconnected grey slabs that form an unconventional circle around the dew-covered, ankle-length grass. There are a couple of others dressed in thin white cagoules across the other side of the grass, but I'm in no mood to be sociable, so I make no effort to catch up with them. The canvas shoes I'm in pinch my skin with every step, but the sole feels firm, so I commence a circuit of the track. The cloud overhead is a thick blanket of white and light grey, like candy floss devoid of colour. The air is salty and if it wasn't for the thick insurmountable prison-like walls, I could almost allow myself to believe I've chosen to come here for rest and recuperation.

I've certainly been in worse places than this. If the rest of my unit could see me now, I don't think they'd be quick to play their violins for me. But I bet if they were around and could see what I'm facing, there isn't a single one of them who wouldn't step forward and take my place. But they'll never get the chance.

I don't want to think about what happened to them in the desert. I was labelled a hero for my actions, but a real hero wouldn't have allowed us to wind up in that mess in the first place. I physically shake my head, desperate to force the memory back in the box I've been struggling to keep it in. That is all done; behind me now. I walked away so nothing like that could happen again. Besides, I have far more important things to worry about.

Max says he needs to focus on finding someone else with a motive for wanting to hurt me or Lucy, and I should be focusing on the same thing. But it angered me when he dared to suggest that there were difficulties in our marriage. We were happy. Of that I am certain. Lucy wouldn't have organised that awful homecoming party at her sister's house if she didn't love me. As much as I hated being dragged around from one group to another, as well as the anxiety attack that gripped me in the bathroom, I know her heart was in the right place. Her heart was always in the right place.

I remember when we returned home after the party, she told me she immediately needed to return to Geraldine's to review some notes ahead of their next court date. I asked her what the case was about, but like always she quoted client confidentiality. It was our way: me feigning interest in her work, and her protecting me from a subject she knew I had little interest in. We both knew it and had come to terms with it.

But should I have shown greater interest in her current case? Could it have something to do with what happened? As a solicitor specialising in family law, most of her cases focused on divorce and custody battles over children; she didn't mix with the criminal element in the same way that Max does, so out of the two of them, I'd have thought he'd be at greater risk of reprisals. But maybe he's right and it was one of her clients who broke into our home and attacked us. What that theory doesn't explain is why they didn't kill me as well; unless of course they thought I was dead.

He said he is going to ask Geraldine about their recent clientele, but maybe that's something I can do. She's looking after Sienna for me, and I'm sure she'll want to see me cleared and back to take care of Sienna sooner rather than later. Maybe I should ask Dr Carpenter if I can use the telephone she said I can access in order to phone Geraldine and ask that question.

I complete a first lap of the garden, but my head feels cloudier than when I began. I feel like I'm missing something so obvious, right under my nose and yet out of reach.

Lucy was smart, funny, beautiful, and loving. Why anyone would want to hurt her is genuinely beyond me, and yet someone, somewhere decided that she deserved to die, and unless I can figure out who that is, there's a strong possibility that her killer will go free, with me taking the fall instead.

I don't know enough people outside of the army to even begin drawing up a list of prospective suspects. The only people I have socialised with in recent weeks are Ray and Max, and neither of them had motive to want Lucy dead. The only member of my platoon who returned from our last tour was Tariq, and with him in the state he is, there's no way he could have broken in and attacked us; not that he'd want to anyway. He's the reason I was awarded that stupid medal, so he means me no ill.

That doesn't leave anyone else who would want to see me suffer in this way. The only other conversations I've had in recent weeks have been with recruitment agents and neighbours, but conversation with them hasn't veered much beyond which bin to put out.

Of course, the one thing Max and I didn't discuss is the possibility that the intruder was someone that neither Lucy nor I knew. What if he was just an opportunist burglar who we caught, and he went to extreme lengths to escape? I don't know if Fahey considered that. He certainly didn't ask me whether anything had been taken, and I certainly didn't check. The fact that I haven't been allowed back inside my house since that night means I've no way of knowing if anything has been stolen. It's definitely something I will raise with Max when I speak to him later. He promised he'd call once he made it back home, though it will be late by then, so I may not hear from him until the morning.

I should definitely try to phone Sienna. Dr Carpenter promised me I could use the telephone once I was settled, and I definitely am, so that needs to be my next priority. I'm all Sienna has left, and she needs stability in her life. I need to give that to her, but I've never had to cope without Lucy and I don't know if I'm capable. I mean, I'm going to have to be, but I can't say it doesn't fill me with trepidation. Lucy was exceptional at managing the home, and Sienna and her job, and I just plugged gaps when I was back. Now, I have to take on all of that, and I'm terrified I won't be good enough.

I don't know how much she's been told about everything that's going on. She's only five, so I don't know if she knows what it means when a person is arrested and charged by the police. Will she understand that people can be accused of things they didn't do? I'm sure Geraldine will have told her something about why I'm not there right now, but I should check exactly what yarn has been spun so I don't say the wrong thing when I next speak to Sienna. God knows, I don't want to confuse matters any more than they already are. I don't want to think about the possibility that I'm found guilty and she spends the rest of her life hating me for taking away her mum, even though I didn't.

I need to call her and explain that there's been a huge mistake, but that her Uncle Max is working hard to fix it and get me back to her. If I could manifest such an outcome, I would spend all my energy trying to do so. My daughter deserves so much better than this.

I flinch as the door to the hospital slams open and a man who looks frailer than the force of his door shove steps out, pulling his cagoule tight around his body. He freezes when he sees me looking over, and I immediately avert my gaze. If I had to guess, I'd say he's in his late fifties, judging by the large, round face, with a nest of greying hair, and a smooth crown. He is huddled over, and I can still feel his stare, so I turn back to face him, only to realise he's already swallowed the distance between us and is standing beside me.

'You got the time?' he asks, his voice deeper and fiercer than I'm expecting, with a noticeable East Coast American accent. I pull up my sleeve, forgetting I left my watch at reception.

'Sorry, no.'

He's a good foot or so shorter than me, and the extra-large pyjamas he's wearing hug his figure tight. He holds out a cigarette packet, but I shake my head, and begin to walk on.

'You must be new here,' he says, matching me stride for stride.

'What gave me away?' I say, trying to ease the tension.

'Hope. It's in your eyes. They haven't beaten it out of you yet.'

My brow furrows at the statement. He's speaking as though he's a convict in a prison movie doing hard time.

'What do you mean?'

'You got a name?' he says, deflecting my question.

'Jake.'

'Well, Jake, you'll probably figure it out for yourself at some point, but spoiler alert: you can't trust no one here.'

He lights the cigarette, and inhales deeply, before blowing a cloud of smoke in my direction, which I swat away. I can't say why, but there is something off about this guy, and I want to put as much space between us as possible.

'I don't mean to be rude,' I say as casually as I can manage, 'but I need to go in and make a phone call.'

'Ha! Good luck with that.'

Every instinct is telling me to stay quiet and head back inside, but I relent.

'What do you mean?'

He leans in closer, the smell of the tar on his breath filling my lungs. 'There's only one way to make contact with the outside world.'

I wait for him to expand, but hear someone calling my name, and when I turn, I see Brenda standing at the door to the hospital. She is waving and there is a sense of urgency to her movements.

7

THREE WEEKS BEFORE THE MURDER

Jake closes the front door behind him, and takes a deep breath, slowly exhaling while trying to focus on the list of tasks ahead of him. With Sienna due to stay at a friend's place, he has the house to himself, but only a couple of hours until Lucy will return.

He carries the overflowing shopping bag into the kitchen, and drops it on the counter, before emptying it and putting away each item. The risotto will take twenty or so minutes to cook, according to the recipe, and then he'll stuff the peppers with it, and they'll take a further thirty minutes in the oven. So, that gives him an hour to get the rest of the house tidied and hoovered. With the shopping away, and a mug of tea on standby, he starts with the upstairs bathroom, brushing inside the toilet, cleaning every surface, and washing the glass shower door. He doesn't enter Sienna's room, knowing how she'll react to his presence in there, so closes the door instead, figuring out of sight is out of mind. He makes the bed in their room, and whips the hoover around the spots he can reach, before hoovering the landing and staircase.

He's sweating by the time he makes it back downstairs, but doesn't stop, continuing to work from room to room, ending in

Lucy's office. When they moved in, they agreed that the converted garage really wasn't big enough to be used as a guestroom, and Lucy staked her claim. With him often away from the house for long periods, his argument to turn it into a mancave quickly failed.

She used to spend a day or so a week working from home, but she hasn't used it at all in the week since he's been back. He dusts the desktop, careful not to dislodge any of her papers, and vacuums the carpet. Despite his best efforts, he accidentally knocks a pile of receipts to the floor, and stoops to pick them up, skim reading them in the process. They are mostly receipts for cafés and restaurants, and she is organised in keeping them all together so she can complete her annual tax return. He spies one for a hotel that surprises him, given the locality of the address, but dismisses it just as quickly, and places the stack back on the desk. He will try to remember to let her know they may no longer be in order.

Satisfied that the house looks cleaner than when Lucy left this morning, he heads into the kitchen and begins to prepare dinner. His exhaustion makes him question whether all of this is still such a good idea, but he reminds himself why he is going to this effort. He knows how hard Lucy has been working since he got back, and he wants to show her how much he appreciates her. Dinner is one of her favourites, and he has also bought a bottle of her favourite wine. When she arrives home, he will have a glass poured and ready, lead her into the living room while dinner cooks, and then massage her feet until it's time to eat. And if all goes to plan, they'll head to bed, and he'll show her how much he's missed her.

They haven't been intimate since he returned from Basra, as after the surprise party she had to return to Geraldine's to discuss their case and he was already asleep when she got back. He doesn't want to think badly of her, but there have been a lot of late nights since he got back. He doesn't blame her for taking advantage of him being here to watch Sienna. He knows he owes them both a huge debt and won't complain. And given she's the current breadwinner, he can't ask her to work less. If he wants her to find a better work-life balance, he needs to find a new job so that she doesn't feel so compelled to work all this extra time.

He has an interview at the end of the week. It's working as a delivery driver for a supermarket, but it's the only application he's made that hasn't been rejected within a day of applying. He just wants to find a job to help tide them over until he can figure out what he wants to do with the rest of his life. Serving in the military is the only thing he's ever been good at, but he won't go back.

The nightmares he's having most evenings are leaving him exhausted every morning. Lucy has mentioned them once or twice, but she doesn't press when he tells her it's all under control. She has mooted the idea of him seeking a referral for counselling, but he can't risk opening up on what happened over there. That's all in the past, and that's where he intends to leave it.

Just before six, he opens the wine and pours two glasses, placing them on the table he's set, and lights the two tall red candles. The stereo is primed with the CD of her favourite songs he created first thing this morning, and he will set it to play as soon as she opens the door. He steps back and surveys the room, a sense of satisfaction that he hasn't felt in an age slowly seeping through his body. Everything looks perfect, and he can't wait to see the look of surprise on her face when she gets home.

At half past six, he extinguishes the candles, removing the mound of wax that has congregated in the bottom of the candle holder. He will relight them as soon as he hears her car on the driveway. He has already drained his glass of wine, and is worried that Lucy's is no longer sufficiently chilled, so he pours a fresh glass from the bottle, and begins to drink the warmer version. He switches off the oven and removes the peppers as the cheese on the top is starting to brown. She must be running late with a client, though she hasn't messaged to say that's the case.

At seven, he is staring through the curtains at the dark night sky, his excitement building with each set of headlights that approach, but none stop and pull onto the drive. He has messaged to ask for an ETA, but she hasn't responded yet. He tries to ignore his growing frustration. In her defence, Lucy had no idea what he was planning, and although she said she should be finished by six, he didn't tell her he had planned anything. He knows she struggles to keep regular hours, often working late into the evening once Sienna has been collected from school. His daughter has told him as much.

By seven thirty he is starting to panic slightly. She hasn't replied to any of his messages, and when he tried calling her, the phone was off. He is assuming the battery has died and that is why she hasn't seen any of his messages. But it annoys him that she could have phoned from the office to give him an update on what time she will be back.

By eight o'clock he has phoned and left a message on the answerphone, and he has called Geraldine, but she didn't answer his call. The dinner is now cold, the bottle of wine all but empty, and his frustration has been replaced by major anxiety. He can't stop thinking that something bad has happened. There's no logical reason he can think of for her radio silence. If she'd broken down, he's sure she would find a phone or a means of contacting him to let him know. The only thing that would stop her phoning is if she'd been in an accident and had no means of letting him know. But if she'd been taken to the hospital, he's sure the staff would have called him as her next of kin.

At quarter past eight, he can't sit on the sofa any longer and reaches for his jacket ready to go and search for her, when he hears keys in the front door, and a tired-looking Lucy walks in a moment later.

'Sorry I'm late,' she calls out to nobody in particular.

He is so relieved that he can barely contain himself, hurrying over to her and hugging her.

'Something smells nice,' she comments as the whiff of the ruined dinner floats out from the kitchen.

'I made your favourite,' he tells her, but a heavy frown falls across her face.

'Oh, did you? I wish you'd said. I've already eaten. Geraldine and I grabbed a pizza at work. Sorry. Do you think it will keep until tomorrow?'

His heart sinks, and it's late enough that he's lost his appetite as well. Not wanting to ruin the evening, he leads her through to the living room, and plonks her on the sofa, before attempting to remove her shoes, but she pulls her feet away as he starts to massage one of them.

'I'm sorry, but I have a ton of work still to do tonight. Do you mind?'

He gently lowers her foot, and tells her he understands, and watches as she stands and heads off to the little office, closing the door behind her.

8

'No joy?'

My eyes widen as I find myself inside a small office, tall filing cabinets covering every wall, and only stopping where the wooden door stands open with Brenda leaning against the doorframe.

How did I get here? I was outside in the gardens with the smoking man.

'Maybe try again later, love. What do you say?'

I meet Brenda's stare, but don't understand what she's saying, until she steps forward and extracts something hard and plastic from the fingers of my right hand.

A phone? Who was I calling? Why can't I remember how I got in here?

'I need to call my daughter,' I blurt out, remembering the last thing I was discussing with that man.

It's Brenda's turn to look confused, as the crow's feet beside her eyes bunch together.

'But you just did try and ring her; nobody was home.'

I pull up the sleeve of my pyjama top, only now realising I'm no longer wearing the cagoule, but am equally frustrated to recall I don't have my watch.

'What time is it?'

Brenda looks up at the wall behind me. 'Nearly five o'clock, love. Maybe they've gone out for dinner.'

Turning, I see the clock on the wall over my shoulder. How can it be so late? I'm sure we left Ilfracombe at ten and it should only have taken two hours to cross, so we must have arrived at the clinic a little after twelve. Have I really been here for almost five hours?

'Can I try again, please?' I ask Brenda, holding out my hand for the phone.

She spends what feels like an age considering my request, before handing the phone back. I take it in my hands, my mind temporarily blanking. It's been so long since I had to remember a number, as usually I just locate the name in my mobile. Sienna will be at Geraldine's, so if I've just phoned there, I must know what the number is.

'Can I have some privacy?' I ask, trying to buy some time for my memory to kick in, and Brenda reluctantly leaves the room, leaving the door ajar as she stands guard outside.

I try to visualise my mobile's phone screen, Geraldine's name and the numbers that usually appear beneath it. Keeping my eyes closed, I try to picture the digits in my mind's eye, until they look right, and then punch them into the phone.

It begins to ring, so whatever number I have dialled at least exists, whether it's Geraldine's or not. I listen to the rings counting down to the moment when I'll be able to hear Sienna's sweet, angelic voice, but I have no idea what I'm going to say. Hopefully, Geraldine will be the one to answer the phone and she can let me know what story has been told to Sienna, so I don't end up saying the wrong thing. I imagine Geraldine will hover nearby to monitor what I say anyway.

I will just tell Sienna what she needs to hear: that I love her and that I'll be home soon. But to be honest, I don't know which of us needs to hear that most.

The phone continues to ring, but then the answer machine cuts in and the robotic-sounding voice announces that nobody is home. I could leave a message for Sienna, but part of the reason for phoning was so I could hear her voice and answer any questions she might have. Leaving a message feels like cheating. I end the call before the machine beeps and return the phone to the charging port.

'Still not home,' I tell Brenda as I pull the door open, and she offers a sympathetic frown.

'As I said, you can try again later. They could be out to dinner now. You'll have better luck next time.'

She begins to move away, encouraging me to follow her.

'Can I go back outside for some fresh air?' I ask, the corridor feeling stale and lifeless.

She leans in conspiratorially. 'Probably best to avoid the garden for now to be honest, love.'

'How come?'

'Well, with Sully doing his rounds... trust me, better to stay away from that one.'

She must be referring to the guy with the nest of grey hair, talking like he's doing hard time in a prison movie.

'Is that the man who was speaking to me?'

Brenda nods. 'Far be it for me to speak ill of any of our guests, but there's more going on there than just sleeping issues. If he gets his claws in, he'll tell you all sorts of conspiracy theories; many of them sound so plausible until you understand his background and mental health concerns.' She pulls a face of admonishment.

'I've already said too much. Just steer clear if you can.' She glances at her watch again. 'It's nearly supper time, though, so it would be better if you head to The Butterfly Room now and get some food.'

For her to speak so candidly of someone who can only have been here a couple of days feels wrong, but before I can challenge her, she's off again, quick marching along the corridor. She leads me through the brown door, to a further corridor, past a room marked for staff only, and then to a large room adorned with paper butterflies. Each one has been haphazardly cut out and coloured with felt tip pens, like you'd expect to see in a primary school classroom. The room is huge, the hardwood laminate floor stretching to large, covered windows, filling the space with natural light. There are square tables to my right, each with four aluminium chairs stationed beneath, and against the wall is a large table, covered with lidded hot plates. The air is as stale as the corridor, so I don't think they've brought out the food yet.

To the left there are three easels, large drawer units, and three faux leather sofas in a U-shape around a television screen. There are two men in white pyjamas sitting on one of the sofas playing cards, but neither look up as we approach.

'Make yourself comfortable, and supper will be out soon. I think Dr Carpenter will come and collect you after you've eaten.'

She doesn't say goodbye as she turns on her heel and exits the room, leaving the door open. I nod in the direction of the two men playing cards, but neither acknowledges me and they continue with their game. Beyond them is an old wooden bookcase, and I cross to it to scrutinise the covers. There's a range of genres in no discernible order. Not alphabetised by title, cover or set out in genres, and not by any authors I'm particularly familiar with; not that I'd call myself a voracious reader. Lucy was the bookworm out of the two of us, but she tended to read on her Kindle, so we didn't keep books on shelves, other than those picture books that Sienna still loves to read.

She must be finding it so odd to be staying at Geraldine and Ray's house. They don't have children of their own, so she'll be bored out of her mind unless the police have allowed them to collect more of Sienna's toys and books from home. The only blessing in all of this is that at least she's being looked after by family. Geraldine spoils her rotten most of the time, and Ray buys her sweets whenever they're out together. It could be worse for her.

'Jake?'

I turn and see Dr Carpenter smiling back at me.

'Have you come to collect me already? Brenda said you'd stop by after—'

She shakes her head to interrupt. 'No, I will be by later. I just wanted to introduce you to someone.'

She half-turns and I see a woman with hair as dark as night sitting at one of the square tables. She must be about my age, pretty, but nervous. I follow Dr Carpenter over to the table and sit when instructed to do so.

'Jake, this is Katy, another of our new guests. I thought, given your backgrounds, and unfamiliar surroundings, you might be able to support one another.'

We nod at each other, but I don't know what to say. Small talk has never been a strength, and this feels painfully awkward, like when my parents would introduce me to children of their friends and just expect an instant connection.

'Jake is also a soldier in the forces,' Dr Carpenter continues.

This seems to pique the woman's interest.

'RAF?' she asks.

I think back to what Max told me earlier. He wants me to play along with everything the doctors and nurses ask of me. I need to convince them that I truly believe I suffer with sleepwalking and am genuinely interested in their assessment, even if this only serves to buy Max more time to find the real culprit.

I shake my head. 'British Army.'

'I'm sure you will have much in common, but remember you only have to share what you're comfortable with. You're not obliged to disclose any personal information.'

She offers the obligatory smile, and pats Katy's shoulder, before departing.

'Where are you stationed?' I ask, uncertain where else to begin.

'Northolt. You?'

'Camberley.'

'Are you an insomniac as well?'

I shake my head, hesitant to reveal the real reason I'm here. 'Sleepwalking.'

She raises her eyebrows at this. 'I had an ex who used to sleepwalk.'

'Oh, yeah?'

'Yeah, but he grew out of it when he was like fifteen, I think. He left home – where his father was abusing him – and it just stopped when the trauma did.'

So much for the clinic's policy for not oversharing.

'What do they think is causing yours?' she continues.

I shrug. 'That's what I'm here to find out, I guess.'

She bites at her lip as she considers this. 'I suppose it would make sense. I'm assuming you've seen action?'

I nod again cautiously, not ready to be as open as she clearly is.

'PTSD could be a trigger,' she concludes, as if it's that easy. 'At least it was the cause for my ex.' She pauses. 'How long have you been here?'

'Arrived at lunchtime.'

'No way. Were you on the 10 a.m. boat as well?'

'Yeah.'

'You got kids?'

The switch in topic is so quick that it leaves my head spinning. I focus on the reason I'm here: to buy more time.

'A daughter,' I confirm.

The smell of fried onions and garlic fills the room. Staff in blue aprons are now carrying food to the hot plates and beginning to lay out the options. My stomach growls involuntarily. I can't remember the last time I ate.

'What's your daughter's name?'

'Sienna.'

'And how old is she?'

'Five.'

A frown crosses her face but disappears almost as quickly.

'Is there a problem?'

She shakes her head. 'No. No problem. I assumed she'd be older.' She pauses and forces a wide smile. 'I can see from the way you're smiling that she's the apple of your eye.'

I nod.

'Must be hard for her when you're overseas.'

For the briefest of moments, it's like I've been transported back to the police station with Fahey and his partner firing questions at me, making assumptions about my family situation and twisting my words to make me appear guilty of their charge. Katy probably isn't trying to be so intrusive, but I'm not enjoying this interrogation. Dr Carpenter clearly introduced us for a reason, and I don't want to just storm away, but something feels off.

'I've no doubt, but she doesn't complain. Her mum...' My words trail off as I catch myself. 'She's a great girl, and I'm looking forward to getting out of here and back to her.'

Katy leans closer, grinning. 'Where's the strangest place you've ever woken up?' she whispers.

It's an impossible question to answer, because as far as I'm concerned, I've never sleepwalked. 'I'd rather not say,' I say, but she raises her eyebrows and must conclude that the answer is something far more scandalous.

'At least you're getting rest while you're asleep. You've no idea how exhausting insomnia is. I spend all day concentrating while on duty, and then I get home feeling shattered, but the moment I lie down it's like someone lights a fire in my brain. I do usually manage to drop off, but never for more than an hour or so before I'm wide awake again. I can't remember the last time I got more than three hours' kip. My CO told me to get it sorted once and for all. Hence why I'm here.'

We both look up as a figure approaches our table, and I immediately recognise the face of Sully, the man I encountered outside.

'You newbies shouldn't be sitting here,' he says without making eye contact.

There are a dozen other vacant tables.

'Didn't see your name here when I sat down,' Katy fires back, sitting back and making herself more comfortable.

'I don't give a shit. This is my table. You two fuck off and find somewhere else to sit.'

I stand and move to the next table over, wary of what Brenda said about avoiding Sully, but Katy remains where she is. I nudge my head in her direction, trying to pass her a silent warning, but she is staring Sully down.

'Get outta my fucking seat,' he shouts, before slamming his hands down on the metal tabletop.

Katy's eyes meet mine, and this time I do see something close to fear, but she doesn't retreat.

'There's room for both of us,' she tells him firmly.

He moves so quickly, flipping the table up and away from her, before grabbing the back of her chair and tipping it forwards, trying to use gravity to help in his quest. Katy falls to the floor, and I immediately stand to go to her aid, but an alarm sounds overhead and a moment later three orderlies in white uniforms run in and drag Sully away. He wails out in defeat as they carry him out, leaving the rest of us watching on in disbelief.

9

'Welcome.'

I'm no longer in The Butterfly Room, instead standing in a darkened corridor, an open door ahead of me and Dr Carpenter peering out from behind it.

'Won't you come in?'

Dr Carpenter steps back and opens the door wider, allowing me to enter what looks more like it should be a broom cupboard than an office. The only natural light comes from a window high up in the ceiling, but the sky overhead is darkening, and so we're bathed in the artificial glow of halogen. There is a small antique desk against one of the walls, holding a closed laptop, a tall stack of folders and papers, and an empty mug stained with tea and lipstick on the rim. For a place that's felt so clean and modern inside, I would have thought they'd afford their lead clinician a more spacious office.

There is a chaise longue across from the desk and an armchair perpendicular to it, which Dr Carpenter heads for.

'Should I sit or lie down?' I ask, indicating the vacant stretch of green leather.

'Up to you,' she says, sitting in the armchair and crossing her legs. 'Whatever you feel most comfortable doing.'

I choose to perch on the chaise longue, not entirely sure whether we're meeting for some kind of counselling session or something else.

'Comfortable?'

It's not the word I'd use, but nod, nonetheless.

'Good. And how are you settling in so far?'

She says it like I'm not being held here against my will. I can't say I feel particularly relaxed, and there's definitely something odd happening with my ability to recall transitioning from one area to another. I can't be blacking out or someone would have said something. I have twice come to in the presence of Brenda and she didn't question whether I was okay or feeling off. And now Dr Carpenter seems oblivious to the fact I have no idea how I got from The Butterfly Room to her office. Brenda had said Dr Carpenter would stop by to collect me after dinner, but does that mean I've eaten? Why can't I remember that? The last thing I saw was Sully causing a commotion and being dragged away by three men. Did something happen after that? Did they clear the room because of the disturbance and Dr Carpenter chose to collect me before food?

I run my tongue around my mouth, searching for unfamiliar flavours. I no longer feel hungry, so does that mean I have eaten? If so, what?

Why can't I fucking remember?

'Jake? Are you still with me?'

I blink several times and force myself to look at Dr Carpenter.

'That's better. That was so odd... it was like you were here physically, but your mind was elsewhere. Can you tell me where you went?'

I don't know how to begin answering that question. It feels like someone is physically removing chunks of my short-term memory, and that may explain why I can't remember what happened the day that Lucy was murdered. I assumed the amnesia was related to the blow to the back of my head, but what if there's some kind of injury to my brain that's causing these troubles? They scanned me at the hospital – or at least that's what I was told – but what if they missed something? A tumour? A hematoma?

I should speak to Max and tell him about it first. I don't want to tell Dr Carpenter anything that will reflect badly in the report she prepares for the judge. I should definitely check with Max whether I should mention it. A brain injury might explain so much and put a dent in Fahey's case against me.

'I was right here,' I tell her reluctantly.

She narrows her eyes slightly but doesn't challenge me.

'Are you happy with your room?'

Maybe all this is her way of checking I'm okay, and that if I answer her questions, she'll let me return to my room, or more importantly try to phone Sienna again.

'Room seems fine,' I tell her. 'I've slept in worse places.'

'Like where?'

Given she knows I've served overseas, I thought she'd pick up on the inference.

'I'm afraid I can't tell you that; I'm not allowed to discuss my military service with a civilian.'

'Is that your rule or theirs?'

She's firing these questions so quickly that again it feels like some kind of interrogation. I'm being paranoid. Of course Dr Carpenter has questions. Before we boarded the boat, Max did warn me that they would be looking to explore my history in order to try to identify potential causes of sleepwalking. I just need to treat this as any regular medical examination the army doctor would give.

'All I can tell you is that I have fought in wars in countries that I can't disclose for reasons of national security.'

'In case it wasn't obvious, anything the two of us discuss is protected by patient–doctor confidentiality.'

'So, should I think of you like a member of the clergy hearing my confession?'

She scoffs. 'It's interesting you chose to put it that way. What is it you feel you need to confess?'

For the briefest moment, I'm back in the heat of the desert, the wind whipping grains of sand into my face. And the fear creeps across my shoulders.

I chase the memory away, and realise my palms are clammy. I wipe them on my pyjama bottoms.

She uncrosses her legs and reaches for a notebook from the desk, slipping a pen out of the spine and then pushing a pair of black-rimmed reading glasses onto her nose. She's in her mid-twenties at best guess, so how can someone so young have any idea what I've experienced fighting for my country? I doubt she's experienced love and loss in the same way as I am right now, so what gives her the right to try to empathise with my situation?

But maybe that's the point of all this. The judge was very quick to agree to Max's petition to have me assessed here, but was that because he hoped it would prove my guilt sooner? Maybe placing me under the care of a doctor this young and pretty is supposed to trick me into lowering my guard and saying things that will reflect me in a bad light. And if I'm supposed to be this dangerous murderer, why would they allow me to speak with Dr Carpenter without the presence of at least some form of security? For all they know, I could lash out and kill her with that ballpoint pen.

Plunged into her neck, I could catch the carotid artery before she even has a chance to scream.

Not that I would, because *I* know I'm not a murderer, but even as I think these words, the heat of the desert is trying to call me back to that day. I can't let her know what happened over there; it certainly wouldn't look good in the court report.

'I'd like to talk to you about your life, Jake, to help me better understand if there is anything that could be triggering the disturbances in your sleep. Is that okay? Anything you don't feel like answering, you only have to say, but I hope you will indulge me, as the more I know, the easier it will be for me to make a thorough assessment. And as I've already said, anything you do tell me will be treated with the utmost confidence. I'm not your enemy.'

I shouldn't be surprised that she'd say this, but it's clear I'm going to have to keep my wits about me. One wrong word, and I'll have no means of recovering.

'What do you want to know?'

'Well, your brother informed me that you used to sleepwalk as a child, so why don't we start there. Do you know how old you were when the sleepwalking began?'

She should really be asking Max this question, as he's the only person with any memory of these episodes. Maybe I should have quizzed him more about them; asked him some detail so I'd be able to lie convincingly to Dr Carpenter. I try to recall what he told me in the police station when he first mentioned my history of sleepwalking.

'Honestly, I don't really remember ever sleepwalking, but my brother told me I was about five or six.'

'He told me you used to suffer with horrendous night terrors, do you remember that?'

I have a flash of memory: sitting bolt upright in bed and screaming for my mum and dad. It was always Mum who came to my rescue and would hug me until my breathing settled. And then she'd lie me down and stroke my hair until I drifted back off to sleep. I haven't thought about that in forever, but I can now recall Mum being worried about all my nightmares. She kept phoning the school, demanding to know what was happening to cause such terrifying dreams.

'Yeah, I used to have nightmares at times, but most kids do, right?'

She nibbles on the end of her pen. 'Do you recall waking up in any strange places with no recollection of how you got there?'

Max mentioned me coming into his room when he was fifteen, which would have made me six or seven. He said I turned on his main light, which woke him, but I didn't respond when he asked me what I was doing. Then, I proceeded to open the built-in wardrobe, before heading out of the room, returning a moment later with the wastepaper basket which I placed inside the wardrobe, before pulling down my pyjama bottoms. He called for Mum when he thought I was about to urinate into the basket, but she reassured him that I hadn't and led me back to bed.

But those are Max's words, not mine. He sounded genuine when he told me the story, so I've no reason not to believe him, but I'm worried that if Dr Carpenter does conclude that I am prone to sleepwalking, the court will automatically conclude that I killed Lucy in my sleep, and the real culprit will evade capture.

'Nothing that I can remember, but it was a long time ago.'

'Your brother told me your mum took you to the GP to be reviewed. That doesn't ring any bells?'

I have vague memories of Mum taking me to see the GP and him asking all sorts of questions about my dreams, but I can't really remember what I told him.

'None, I'm sorry. I'm not trying to be difficult, but I really don't remember ever sleepwalking.'

'Your brother Max told me you used to appear in your parents' bedroom, standing over your mum fast asleep. He even told me she once found you walking about outside, which meant you'd managed to unlock the front door, but you have no recollection of that?'

'I'm sorry, but no.'

'That's okay, Jake, it's often the case that the individual doesn't remember it happening, and in many cases if the sleepwalker manages to return to bed without being woken, there's no reason they'd have any clue that they'd done it.'

'Can I ask you a question?'

'Of course.'

'How many people have you treated for sleepwalking?'

'A fair few, but we do treat all manner of different conditions here.'

'But those who have sleepwalked, are they... I don't know how to ask this... are they like me? Do I have the air of someone who sleepwalks?'

She narrows her eyes and removes her glasses, scrutinising me.

'There isn't anything that distinguishes someone with the condition from someone without it. Once the lights are out, your behaviour will reveal whether it is a condition you suffer with.'

'And what if because I'm here in unfamiliar surroundings, I don't sleepwalk? Does that mean I never have or never will?'

'Not necessarily, but it isn't just whether you get out of bed that we'll be monitoring. That's the point of the sensors in the pyjamas you're wearing. We know what happens to breathing capacity, blood pressure and heart rates during the various cycles of sleep. Whilst there are differences from person to person, we will monitor your results to help determine any abnormalities. I don't want to bore you with the science behind it all, but I can provide some reading materials if that would help?'

I hate reading books with jargon that I don't understand, so I politely decline.

'Getting back to that period in your childhood, what can you tell me about your experiences?'

'What do you want to know?'

'I don't know, um, how about where you went to school.'

'What does that have to do with anything?'

'Well, was it a state school? Private? Grammar?'

'State school.'

'And how did you perform at school? Were there any subjects you excelled in, or were you a jack of all trades? Did you do much by way of sports? What was your circle of friends like? Were you ever bullied? Did you regularly get into trouble? Did you have any learning difficulties?'

My head is spinning with all the questions. And I can't understand what any of this has to do with whether I sleepwalk or not.

'I don't know. I had a normal upbringing, I guess. I worked hard at school, but I wasn't top of the class in any particular subject. I enjoyed design and technology because I liked working with my hands, and I struggled with maths and science. I enjoyed playing football, and I would occasionally play the fool in class, but was never suspended. And I had a close group of five or six friends who were like brothers.'

'Do you remember anything traumatic happening during that time?'

'Like what?'

She shrugs. 'You tell me.'

Nothing immediately springs to mind. My childhood was no worse than anybody else's as far as I'm aware. In fact, probably better than some, given my parents didn't separate like those of some of my friends. As a lawyer, Dad worked long hours, so Mum was the primary caregiver, but I wouldn't say that caused any undue stress. It's like she's searching for answers where none exist.

'How about any childhood illnesses? Is there anything from your medical history that might have been particularly traumatic?'

I stare back at her blankly. 'Just the regular colds and flu like anyone else.'

She scribbles a note in her book.

'The common causes of childhood sleepwalking include lack of sleep, irregular sleep schedules, illness or fever, and stress. Although less common in adults, sleepwalking is often caused by stress, migraine, fever, medicinal side-effects, or certain neurological disorders including but not limited to Parkinson's disease.'

She pauses, and the prospect that my recent bouts of amnesia could have an underlying medical reason hangs heavy on my mind.

'I will have you reviewed by a neurologist to rule out PD, but I'm more inclined to believe that stress – specifically PTSD – may in fact be the root of your condition. However, we won't rule out anything until we're certain.'

She closes her notebook.

'We will continue to talk in the morning, and I hope you will feel able to open up more about matters in your life to help me better understand potential causes.'

She stands and crosses to the door, opening it and inviting me to follow her back to my room.

I want to trust Dr Carpenter. I want to believe she has my best interests at heart. But I also have to consider whether she's been planted by the court to trick me into saying something that might implicate me in Lucy's murder.

10

I am still wide awake in my room, and I recall everything from the moment I came to outside Dr Carpenter's small office. Definitely no mini blackouts or waking in unfamiliar surroundings. But also, no sleep, and it must be at least three or four hours since I came back up here. The Butterfly Room is out of bounds from ten o'clock, so it's not like I can even go and find myself a book to read. So that leaves me with only the voice in my head for company.

My throat is unusually dry – maybe the constant air conditioning is to blame – and I finally decide to do something about it, grabbing the empty beaker from the windowsill and heading through to the bathroom. I run the tap for several seconds, splashing it against my fingers until it cools, and then fill the cup to the brim. I take a long sip, swallowing most of the water, but it tastes stale, and I fear I should have run the tap for longer to clear the pipes.

I flick off the bathroom light and walk slowly back towards the bed. Sleeping on a strange mattress is always difficult, but I'm sure part of the issue I've had with dropping off to sleep is these pyjamas. Even in winter, I never sleep with a top on as I tend to overheat. The room itself is warm, which also doesn't help, but I try to push such thoughts from my mind.

I roll onto my right side and tuck an arm under the pillow, keeping my eyes closed, and focus solely on Lucy's face. I lie like this for what feels like an age, but I'm still awake, so I roll on to my left side, tucking the opposite hand beneath the pillow. I kick off the thin sheet, before regretting it, and place it just over my feet. I still can't get comfortable, and the longer I lie still, willing sleep, the more frustrated I grow.

I know the reason I can't sleep isn't just the unfamiliar feel of the bed. I mean, it's not my bed and these are not the pillows I'm used to, but it's more than that. I've slept in all manner of strange places in my time, including a puddle in a trench at one point. No, the reason I can't get to sleep is my brain won't still for long enough for my subconscious to take control. Every time I close my eyes, I picture Lucy's face and it feels like I'm living in a nightmare. She can't be dead. She was too young; too sweet; too innocent. I just can't get my head around the fact that she's gone, and that someone took her from us.

And then my mind wanders back to the fact that I am the one wrongly accused of her murder and am facing trial and imprisonment. It isn't fair and I'm not used to being so out of control. The army has taught me to fight for what is right and to find ways to exercise the utmost control in any given situation, but I feel as though I'm falling into a black hole and there is nothing there to grab onto, or anyone to pull me back from the precipice.

I hear Fahey's words from the interview: *Lucy was feeling the strain of you being away from home so much.*

He didn't say it in so many words, but could he have been intimating that she was having an affair?

I quickly dismiss the thought. Not my Lucy. She was growing increasingly frustrated about my overseas deployments, and that was one of the reasons I'd stepped away from the service, but she loved me, and wouldn't betray our vows.

I roll back onto my right side, trying to push all thoughts from my head, but it's no use. The pyjama top snags as I wriggle and I momentarily fear that I've ripped it, but there's no obvious damage save for a tearing sound.

I wish I'd managed to get through to Geraldine and Sienna earlier. By the time Dr Carpenter had finished with me in her tiny office, it was well after seven, so Sienna would undoubtedly have been in bed. I will try again in the morning. I miss the sweet sound of her voice, and I need to reassure her that everything is going to be okay. If I can make her believe me then maybe it will be enough to convince myself too.

But I also want to speak to Geraldine and make sure she believes me too. She didn't say in so many words, but when Fahey arrested and led me away, I saw the look she gave. She must know I'd never do anything to hurt Lucy, though. I am not a violent man. I need her to tell me she believes I didn't kill Lucy. And I need her help to figure out who did. She and Lucy were more like best friends than sisters, and as business partners she would know what cases Lucy was working on and whether any threats existed. Divorce hearings and custody battles were her bread and butter. How many disgruntled spouses and bereft parents did she leave in her wake? Who's to say that a bitter ex-husband didn't come seeking revenge because Lucy helped her client win a huge settlement? Surely that's just as – if not more – likely than Max's suggestion that I could have done it in my sleep.

Max should be back here by lunch tomorrow and hopefully he'll have spoken to Geraldine and will have a full list of Lucy's recent cases. I'd like to think Lucy would have told me if she thought she was in danger, but maybe she didn't want me to worry, or maybe she underestimated the risk. Either way, that's an avenue that Max needs to explore.

I roll onto my back again, and stare up at the white ceiling, which has taken on a grey hue. I don't feel at all sleepy, but I don't want Dr Carpenter to think I'm deliberately staying awake to prevent her from assessing me. Max told me to do everything they asked of me, and as much as I don't want them to conclude I'm prone to sleepwalking, I need to show I'm open to the process. I decide to go in search of Brenda, or whoever is her nightshift equivalent, to ask for something to help me drift off.

I open the door and peer out into the corridor, half-expecting to see some kind of nurse or orderly struggling to stay awake while on duty, but there is nobody out here. I'm surprised by just how bright the corridor is. From inside my room, I would have said the lights were off, but I see now that the frosted window is shaded to prevent too much light penetrating through.

I stand in the corridor for a few minutes, waiting to see whether my presence is being monitored via the cameras in the ceiling, but nobody appears, and so I venture further out, this time waving my arms, but there is still no sound or apparent movement.

The large red door looms but before I reach it, I arrive at a room where the door is ajar. A loud humming noise is coming from within. Curiosity gets the better of me, and I push it wider, spotting the mound of a figure beneath the bedsheet. The whirring sound is louder inside the room, and I step inside, trying to make sense of what I can see. The layout is identical to mine, even down to the purple hue lighting the edges of the walls, but beside the bed there is a large cube-shaped machine that resembles an electricity generator. This machine is the cause of the vibrating sound.

I move closer, conscious that I don't want to wake whoever is sleeping. Being inside another patient's room is forbidden, particularly at this time of night, but I can't resist moving closer still, now seeing that there is a tube connected to the machine and running to a large mask over the face of the person in the bed. I'm assuming the person is male based on the shape of the body beneath the sheet, but it's impossible to see features beneath the large mask.

The person stirs, and I freeze, waiting for a panicked scream, but it doesn't come; instead, a low baritone gurgle erupts beneath the mask. This is the moment I realise this patient must suffer from some kind of sleep apnoea and that the machine they're attached to is a CPAP machine. I read about it in one of the clinic's pamphlets that Max showed me.

I tiptoe back towards the bedroom door, when I hear voices in the corridor, so I quickly duck out of sight. If Brenda and whoever she's speaking to come in here now, I'm going to be in big trouble.

The voices pass the open bedroom door but don't stop, much to my relief, but I hear the urgency in Brenda's tone when she speaks next.

'That's what I'm telling you: I don't know how he got hold of a knife, but I've managed to sedate him and have removed the weapon from the ward.'

'There's a reason we don't allow patients like that to have access to sharp implements,' Coyle responds, his Northern Irish accent even harsher now.

'I know, I know. I'm so sorry. I will instigate a thorough review of all staff to see who brought it into the clinic.'

I don't hear what else is said as their voices are now too far away. I poke my head out into the corridor just as Brenda's frame disappears behind the large red door. I hurry to it, but by the time I get to it it's already closed. I push against it, but it holds firm; secured in some way. There's no obvious sign of a scanner, but there's no way I'll be able to follow Brenda through.

Frustrated, I return to my own room and lie back down. What lies beyond the big red door?

11

TWO WEEKS BEFORE THE MURDER

Jake crashes into the plate glass wall, and loses his footing, crashing to the hardwood floor of the court. Max takes a breath to compose himself, before striding over and offering a sodden hand. Jake hasn't felt this breathless since running laps at the camp in Basra, and accepts the hand, allowing Max to pull him back to his feet. Both their T-shirts are soaked through with sweat, and although Max's cheeks are looking red, Jake is the one who looks as though he's just completed a marathon.

'You'd never guess I'm the older brother,' Max says, bouncing the ball several times, ready to serve again.

'Can we... just take... a minute,' Jake stammers, struggling to get his breath back.

'We only have the court for another ten minutes,' Max replies, ignoring the request.

'Yeah, but you're already three games up... so it's not like there's any doubt... about who the winner is.'

Jake rests his hands on his hips, trying to inhale deeply, the racquetball racket hanging precariously from his fingers.

Max continues to bounce the ball, until Jake moves away and

collects the water bottle from his bag. Jake takes a long drink, just grateful not to be charging around the court for a few minutes. Part of the reason he suggested they meet up was to ask his older brother for advice. In the week since he pulled out all the stops to surprise Lucy, she's been late home every night, and spent most of the weekend away at the office. Jake has made the most of his time with Sienna and has loved getting to see how much she's learning at school, watching old movies together and hanging out. He knows it won't be long until she no longer thinks it's cool hanging out with her old man.

He's tried raising the subject with Lucy, but it feels like she's been trying to avoid speaking to him. She sets her alarm for 5.30 every morning to get up and go for a run. She returns and hits the shower at 6.30, and by the time she's dried and dressed, Sienna is up and asking her mum to do her hair. And then Lucy is gone before 8 a.m., leaving Jake to walk Sienna to school.

He tried to speak to her about his concerns as soon as she got home last night, but she told him she was exhausted and wanted a bath before she could handle anything remotely close to conversation. Jake prepared their dinner and when he went upstairs to tell her it was ready, he found her fast asleep in bed. He doesn't want to add to her heavy workload and stress, but he misses the intimacy and is desperate to get back to how things used to be. It's not just about sex. He wants her to share her work troubles and worries. He wants to be more than just a househusband.

But as soon as he arrived at the sports complex and saw how pumped Max was about the racquetball match, he chickened out of saying anything. They've been playing for half an hour and Jake can't do any more. It's not like any of the games have even been that close in terms of the score.

'Come on, we can squeeze in one more match before our time's up,' Max says. 'If it helps, I'll even play lefthanded.'

Jake narrows his eyes, well aware Max is taunting him to get a reaction, but Jake can't resist the challenge.

'Your right hand getting too tired, is it?' Jake fires back, wiping his hairline with a towel and joining his brother at the service line. 'I'd have thought that would be the strongest part of you with all the action it's probably seen down the years.'

Max smiles thinly but doesn't react, bouncing the ball and smacking it with his racket. Jake charges after the ball, returning it with a deft flick, and fist pumping the air when Max fails to return the shot.

'You only won the serve. It's still love all,' Max says, flinging the ball towards him.

Jake doesn't care; he has to take the small victories when he can get them.

'It's Mum's birthday next week,' Max says, when the match is over and they're in the changing room cooling down after showering. 'I think we should do something nice for her and Dad. What do you think?'

Jake doesn't want to admit he'd forgotten her birthday was so soon, though vaguely remembers seeing it written on the calendar at home.

'Sure, what did you have in mind?'

'I was thinking something like a city break to London, including dinner and a show. Should only be a couple of hundred each.'

Jake looks away, not wanting Max to see the shame on his face. He has less than a hundred pounds in his account, and with no job offers forthcoming, he can't afford it. He attended the interview for the role of delivery driver at the supermarket, but later learned he'd been unsuccessful, though he isn't entirely sure where it went wrong. He doesn't want to have to ask Lucy for the money.

'I was thinking we could do something nice for her instead of buying a gift,' he tries.

Max dries his face with the end of his towel and sits down beside him.

'What did you have in mind?'

'I don't know. A party maybe?'

Max wrinkles his nose in disgust.

'She hates being the centre of attention.'

'Yeah, but it wouldn't have to be a party with music and dancing. I was thinking of something more intimate. A nice meal that you and I could cook for them, us and a small selection of their closest friends.'

Max shakes his head.

'They have dinners with their friends all the time, so it won't be very special. She's always wanted to go and watch opera live, so she'd be blown away by the city break idea.'

Jake takes a deep breath.

'The thing is, Max, I can't afford it. I'm sorry, but things are tight since I got back. I've been unable to find a job anywhere, and we're going to have to tighten our purse strings if I don't find anything soon. In fact, you're not aware of any jobs going anywhere, are you? You're not looking for help at the firm?'

He raises a sceptical eyebrow in Jake's direction.

'And what exactly do you think you could do at the firm? Unless you have a law degree tucked away that you never told me about?'

'I don't know. I'd do anything. I could man the phones. Or I could make cups of tea for your clients.'

Max shakes his head.

'Delia handles all communications and makes drinks for the clients already. You're not asking me to sack Delia, are you? She's been with the company since Dad took it over from our grandfather.'

'No, I don't want you to sack Delia. But you must have friends who own their own businesses. Are none of them hiring?'

'I can ask around for you. What skills can you offer?'

Jake doesn't know where to begin.

'I have people leadership experience, I have a full driving licence, um, I can defuse improvised explosive devices.'

'Not much call for that here in Camberley, I'm afraid. But hey, listen, I will ask around and let you know what they say. Have you visited the job centre yet?'

Jake nods, remembering the embarrassment that he couldn't find a single role he was qualified to undertake.

'How's Lucy finding having you back?'

It's the 'in' Jake has been waiting for, but as he opens his mouth to speak, and explain the growing gap between them, he can't bring himself to say. He doesn't want to show his more successful brother just how much he's struggling.

'Things are great. She was so thrilled when I told her I'd resigned my commission. And once I find a new job and am back on my feet, we've even talked about trying for another baby.'

Max can't hide his surprise as he chokes on his own spittle.

'A second child? I thought you'd decided not to after the complications Lucy had with Sienna's birth.'

'That was then, but I think it will bring us closer together.'

In truth, when he raised the subject, albeit briefly, the day after he returned, she laughed, thinking he was joking. But the more he's thought about it, the more he's sure another baby could be the missing piece of the jigsaw, and exactly what they need to rekindle their romance.

12

The pressure of someone shaking my shoulders stirs me, but when I open my eyes, I'm not expecting the sight of a dozen or so butterflies flapping only inches from my face. My arms flail as I swat them away in blind panic, feeling their paper-thin wings flutter against my fingertips. I dare to part my eyelids, squinting at the swarm, only to realise they're not nearly as close as I thought, and are in fact paper shapes, no bigger than a fifty pence piece, cut to resemble butterflies.

'Careful. The staff won't be happy if you vandalise anything in here.'

Turning my head, I gasp at the large, round face staring back at me.

'Morning,' Sully says, his American accent seeming somehow stronger today.

Lifting my head, I see I am stretched out on one of the sofas in what appears to be The Butterfly Room, my paper antagonists hanging from a ring as part of the room's ornate décor.

What am I doing in here?

My last memory is hurrying back to my room after Brenda

almost caught me snooping about in that other patient's room. I remember getting back into bed and pulling the sheet up to my face, convinced someone would have seen where I'd been and would come to confront me about it. There are so many security cameras in the ceiling that must have captured my late-night stroll along the corridor, and entering another patient's room is strictly forbidden, so I can only assume my reprimand is coming, or nobody happened to be watching the feed at the time.

It still doesn't explain why I now find myself sprawled out in The Butterfly Room. When Dr Carpenter told me the room was out of bounds after 10 p.m., I'd assumed the brown door that leads to the room would be locked, but it can't have been if I made it through.

Sully is kneeling beside the sofa, still watching me intently. I suppose I should be glad that it was he who found me in here and not one of the staff; that doesn't mean he won't report finding me here, though something tells me that Sully is the last person who will go telling tales.

I stick out a hand, and he grabs it, helping me to sit up properly. My back aches from the firm cushions, and there's a dull throb between my shoulders that I can only put down to my head being propped against one of the wooden armrests. I must assume I've been lying here for some time given the pain I'm feeling in virtually every muscle group.

Standing, I stretch out the last of the twinges, and run a hand over my shaved head, surprised at how much the hair appears to have grown in such a short period since I last had it clipped. Regardless of how much sleep I've had, I feel exhausted, and should probably try to return to my room before anyone notices I'm not there. Sniffing the unwelcome pong emanating from the pits of my pyjamas, I realise I should probably shower as well.

With no memory of how I got here, the only conclusion I can

reach is that I sleepwalked here during the night, and the realisation that Max could be right hits me like a steam train. I don't
want to consider the possibility that the reason my bloody prints
were found on the knife is because I am the one who stabbed
Lucy. Until now, I've been adamant that isn't what happened, but I
have no other means of explaining how I've woken up with no
recollection of how I got here.

Presumably the security cameras will have captured my movements and I'm keen to view the footage just to check that my
being here definitely is a result of sleepwalking and not someone
playing tricks on me. Who's to say that I wasn't in such a deep
slumber that someone was able to lift and carry me from my room
and place me here? Sully is too short to have managed it single-
handedly, but he could have been helped.

I almost erupt with laughter at the thought. So desperate am I
to believe that I don't sleepwalk that my imagination is conjuring
absurdly alternative theories. Why would anyone want to make
me think I sleepwalked if I didn't? The only person with anything
to gain from Dr Carpenter diagnosing somnambulism is techni-
cally me, as it gives Max the defence he's seeking on my behalf.
The staff have no reason to make me think I'm a sleepwalker.

'You feel better now, Bambino?' Sully asks, plonking himself
down beside me.

'That depends; are you still mad at me for sitting at the wrong
table last night?'

He waves his hand dismissively. 'I should probably apologise
for my outburst. My meds were messed up and I may have overre-
acted to the situation.'

I assume that's his attempt at an apology.

'I can't place your accent,' I say instead. 'Where are you from?'

'Queens.'

It fits his accent, but I can't figure out how someone from New

York City could end up in a sleep clinic in the middle of the Bristol Channel.

'I'm confused. How did you wind up on Lundy Island?'

'You know, you ask a lot of questions.'

'I'm sorry,' I say, remembering what Dr Carpenter said about patients not having to engage.

I turn and look at the hot plates. Two orderlies are carrying in large metal dishes and placing them beneath the lids. The air fills with smells of cooked meat and eggs, and my stomach grumbles. It takes all my willpower not to race over and steal a rasher of bacon.

'You managed to make that phone call to your kid yet?'

I frown at his question, then remember we'd discussed it when we'd met in the garden yesterday afternoon.

'Yes, they were more than happy for me to use the phone.'

'Yeah? And how'd that work out for you?'

'Nobody was home.'

He scoffs and raises his eyebrows sardonically.

'What? It's not like they stopped me making the call.'

'You dialled the number?'

My brow furrows further. 'Yes.'

Although now that I think about it, when I came to in the administrator's office, it was Brenda who told me the call had gone unanswered. But it was definitely me who tried to call Sienna at Geraldine's afterwards.

'They weren't home, that's all.'

'Convenient.'

'What is that supposed to mean?'

'They let you try again yet?'

'No, but it's still early so I'm sure they will later on today.'

Sully puffs out his cheeks sceptically.

'Sure they will.'

'Is there something you want to say, Sully?'

He holds his hands up, his palms facing out in a pacifying manner. 'Hey, if you want to believe that they're going to let you make as many phone calls as you like, then who am I to dampen that hope?'

I remember what Brenda said about there being something not quite right about Sully and how he would reel off conspiracy theories to anyone willing to listen.

He leans in closer, his cheek touching my shoulder.

'When you decide that all is not as it seems here, you come and find me. If you want to make a real phone call and speak to your kid, I may have access to a phone that isn't controlled by this lot.'

He instantly stops talking as one of the orderlies enters the room and looks over to us. Sully immediately shuffles away from me, as if he's expecting to once again be dragged from the room. He's so tense that I feel my own shoulders tightening as the orderly stares us down.

'No trouble here, boss,' Sully calls over to him. 'Just showing the new guy the ropes.'

The orderly holds his stare for several seconds, before turning and leaving the room.

Sully shrugs. 'Sometimes the appearance of obedience is enough, but don't ever let yourself believe they're not in control. You and me? We're here because they let us be.'

I think back to Brenda's warning. I should try and put some distance between Sully and me. I stand and slap my belly.

'I'm hungry.'

I cross the room towards the steaming hot plates, but feel Sully close behind like a shadow.

'An all-you-can-eat breakfast buffet, or so they call it,' Sully says, as he hands me a warm plate from the stack on the end, 'but that isn't quite true, because they only have a limited supply of each item. And believe me when I tell you once it's gone, it's gone. It's a good thing we got here early, as we get to choose what we want. I pity the suckers who rock up near the end and are lucky if they even manage to get a slice of toast.'

I take Sully's advice with a pinch of salt but make a mental note to arrive in The Butterfly Room promptly for breakfast each day, just in case. I collect the tongs from the side and load my plate with fried bread, scrambled eggs, bacon, and sausage. It's a feast but feels like the first sight of food I've had in days. Sully sits down at the table he overturned last night and leaves me no choice but to join him.

'So, what you in for?' Sully asks, dipping the end of a sausage into ketchup. He funnels it into his mouth with his fingers.

'Sleepwalking. You?'

His eyes narrow as if confused. 'That it?'

I'm not ready to tell any of the other patients about the Damocles' sword hanging over me, and nod instead.

I lift the slice of toast from my plate and use my knife to scrape off the burned crumbs from the edge, before taking a bite. It still tastes bitter, but I make do.

'You like burnt toast, huh?'

'Not particularly,' I say between mouthfuls.

'Nor me. That's why I'm a firm believer in the burnt toast theory.'

He says it with a knowing nod like I should automatically understand.

'Okay, Sully, you've got me: what is the burnt toast theory?'

He begins to strip the fat from the rasher of bacon between his fingers before pushing the greasy trimmings between his lips.

'You really don't know?'

I shake my head.

He licks his sausage-shaped fingers before wiping them on his pyjama top, leaving a transparent stain.

'So, let's say hypothetically you wake up and get dressed and then fix yourself some toast before you set off for some busy day. Right? You could be going to work, or meeting some friends socially, or have an appointment, or whatever. Doesn't matter. When the toaster ejects your cooked bread, it turns out it's burnt. And I'm not talking like the shit on your plate right now, but I mean like practically charcoal. Right?'

I nod along, wishing I'd been brave enough to end the conversation and sat at a different table.

'You're not going to eat this fucked-up toast, so you chuck it in the garbage, but you're still hungry and decide to drop another slice in the toaster, being sure to turn it down this time. You wait patiently, and then it pops out and you eat it. But now you're running late for whatever it is you're doing with your day. How late do you reckon you are at this point?'

I sigh. 'Three or four minutes maybe?'

'Exactly! But what if that delay then prevents something bad happening to you? Let's say you're now in your car driving to wherever, and you see a major pile-up that you would have been part of had you left on time. Or you're late arriving for your appointment, but that then means you wind up meeting your soulmate whose path you wouldn't have crossed had you been three or four minutes earlier?'

He pauses and takes a bite of his own toast.

I wipe my face on a paper napkin. 'Okay, so what you're saying is...?'

'Sometimes the universe burns your toast because it's trying to reset your course,' he says, smiling. 'You ever experienced something like that? Something bad happening that then leads to something far better you couldn't have imagined. Ever been turned down for a job interview, only to be offered a better opportunity a month down the line? It's the burnt toast theory.'

It isn't a concept I'm familiar with, but I can see the positivity of the idea.

'So, you're saying I'm now destined to be doomed because I didn't ask for a fresh slice of toast?'

'No, I'm saying that the reason you find yourself here right now is because the universe is trying to reset your path, Jake.'

My mouth drops open. I'm about to ask how he knows my name, but three orderlies rush in and apprehend Sully, dragging him away.

'Where are you taking him?' I ask.

'Patients who can't behave have to go to the secure unit,' one of the orderlies retorts before turning back to Sully. 'And don't try to escape this time? Mr Coyle warned you what will happen if you do it again.'

13

I'm suddenly in a corridor and the weight of someone's hand is dragging down my arm. I stumble as I suddenly realise we're walking at a brisk pace, and am only just able to stop myself from tumbling. I look to the figure holding my arm and see now it is one of the orderlies. I've not managed to catch any of their names yet but this one looks like all the rest: dark hair, cropped at the back and sides, with dark eyes that don't seem to trust me.

I try to shrug off his hand, but he only grips my arm tighter. I'm about to ask where he's taking me, when we arrive at a set of lift doors. He scans his pass, and the doors part immediately, and he pushes me inside, never releasing his grip on my arm.

Have I done something wrong?

The way he is manhandling me reminds me of when Fahey was arresting me in front of Sienna. It's like this guy is afraid that I might... I don't know... escape? Attack him in some way? I want to offer him reassurance, but when I open my mouth to speak, he grizzles and shakes his head.

I guess they must have figured out I didn't wake in my room this morning. Maybe the sensors in these pyjamas revealed that I took a late-night jaunt to The Butterfly Room. Or maybe they watched it all courtesy of the security cameras. But just because I did sleepwalk on this occasion doesn't mean that's what happened that night.

And even if I was sleepwalking that night, I know in my heart there is no way I could have killed Lucy. It's just a coincidence that Max was right, and I can – on occasion – sleepwalk. It will prove to the judge that he didn't just admit me here to buy more time for my case. The reaction of this orderly feels a bit extreme, though, unless Coyle and Carpenter now see me as more of a threat because they've witnessed the sleepwalking.

We travel in an upwards direction until the doors separate again and suddenly it's like we're in a different building. I no longer feel as though I'm in a hospital. It is so bright up here, and the air smells cleaner somehow. Floor-to-ceiling windows domi-nate, showing a beautiful view of the Bristol Channel, and beyond it the Atlantic Ocean. The sun shimmers on the ripples of blue as they meet the horizon. We must be on the top floor of the build-ing, and across from the gorgeous view are windowed office spaces.

Dr Carpenter emerges from one of the rooms and offers a disarming smile. She thanks the orderly for escorting me and tells him to leave us.

When he releases his grip, the blood pumps back into my arm, but he gives me the most peculiar look, before turning and heading back towards the lift.

'Is everything okay?' Dr Carpenter asks me, oblivious to the force that has just been used to get me up here.

No, nothing is okay, I want to tell her. A moment ago, I was eating breakfast in The Butterfly Room, and I have no idea how much time has passed since that moment, nor why I have been summoned up here. If the spots in my memory are the result of sleepwalking, then they should just come out and tell me.

'I'm fine,' I tell her instead.

'Good. And did you sleep well?'

My eyes snap to her. This feels like a loaded question. If I tell her I slept fine, she'll know I'm lying because nobody would feel comfortable waking in a different room with no understanding of how they got there. I need to know whether she's really on my side.

'Why don't you tell me?' I say, turning the tables. 'You are the expert, after all.'

She takes a step backwards and waves her hand towards a long couch inside the room, encouraging me to sit. I oblige, allowing my eyes to take in the rest of the room. The back wall is lined with tomes of coverless books. I try to read some of the titles, but the print is too small.

'What is this place?' I ask. 'I thought your office was on the ground floor?'

'It is, but all the doctors here also have access to these therapy suites. It's where we bring our patients to talk. We find that the expansive view and airy feel helps relax most guests. I hope that's okay with you. My tiny office can be… overbearing?'

She sits in the desk chair across from me.

'I'd like to pick up where we left off yesterday,' Dr Carpenter begins, opening the notepad, and putting on her dark-rimmed reading glasses. 'We were talking about your childhood. You said you couldn't remember specific incidents of sleepwalking, and that – in your words – your childhood was *normal*. I wondered if you've had any further reflections on that?'

'Like what?'

She shrugs without judgement. 'Well, we're trying to establish if there are any triggers for your nocturnal behaviour, so has anything fresh come to mind from your childhood? Do you recall any specific traumatic experiences?'

I genuinely can't remember anything I would class as traumatic. My parents never beat or abused us psychologically. Sure, there were times when we would be disciplined, but on the whole, there was nothing harrowing. Max and I weren't particularly close growing up because he was that much older, and so we never shared any interests, but we've been closer since I finished school.

'I don't know what to say. I can't think of anything traumatic.'

She chews on the end of her pen. 'Okay, can I ask about your relationship with your mum then? Are you close?'

'Sure, I guess.'

'How often do you see or speak to her?'

'When I'm home we see her all the time.'

'Can you be more specific? Every day? Once a week?'

'I don't know. We don't have a regular routine if that's what you're asking. Lucy and I always said we wanted Sienna to spend as much time with her grandparents as possible, and so we try to ensure she sees her every week where possible, especially since Dad died.'

'And when you're not at home, how does your daughter react to not having you around?'

'It isn't my choice not to be home,' I snap.

She sits forward. 'I'm sorry, I wasn't accusing you of abandoning your daughter. I merely wanted to understand whether you or your wife noticed a change in her behaviour when you weren't around. As someone who rarely saw her father growing up, I understand how difficult that dynamic can be.'

'Lucy has never told me she acts any differently. She's a good kid, and I miss her dearly when I'm away, which is why I always try to make a big fuss of her when I'm back.'

'Must be hard, though, being so far away for several weeks at a time.'

'I compartmentalise, because I wouldn't be able to do my job if I allowed thoughts about my family to permeate my conscious mind.'

She continues to ask me questions about my relationships with Mum, and Max, even asking whether I have ever had any suicidal thoughts or diagnoses of mental illness. I sense she's pushing for something, but I can't quite see what. If Fahey or the court has asked her to push my buttons in the hope that I'll confess, it isn't going to work. I won't admit to something I didn't do, regardless of the sleepwalking.

'Talk to me about last night,' she says next.

'What about it?'

Her lips curl up slightly at the edges.

'Tell me what you remember about it.'

I have to assume they know I left my room. There is CCTV in all the corridors, so they will have evidence that I got up at some point and made my way to The Butterfly Room, but what's worrying me more is whether they also know I was almost caught by Brenda when I went into that other patient's room.

'I don't really remember anything,' I say cautiously, 'but I didn't wake in my own bed.'

Her smile widens; I've told her what she wants to hear.

'And do you remember any dreams you might have had?'

'I never remember my dreams.'

She closes her notebook and removes her glasses, her facial expression graver.

'It is my belief that you may be suffering from REM Behaviour Disorder, or RBD.' She pauses to allow the words to settle in. 'It is a parasomnia characterised by dream-enacting behaviour and loss of muscle atonia during REM sleep. Essentially, your body acts out your dreams, hence the walking. But there are two types of RBD. Symptomatic RBD is linked to a variety of neurological disorders, such as Parkinson's and dementia. The other kind is Idiopathic RBD, which has no apparent underlying cause but may be an indicator of future neurodegenerative syndromes.'

I don't respond because I don't know what to say.

She pulls her lips together, as if psyching herself to deliver the devastating news. 'Honestly, this condition does not necessarily mean you had anything to do with what happened to your wife. My primary objective here is to diagnose your exact condition, so that I can prepare a report for the court.'

'You only have until Tuesday, is that going to be enough time?'

'Now that we know what we're dealing with, your treatment can be targeted, so yes, a diagnosis with 90 per cent accuracy should be achievable by the deadline. We will of course run some diagnostic tests to see if we can identify anything neurological, but in the meantime, I am going to prescribe some clonazepam, which is generally used to control epileptic seizures and fits, involuntary muscle spasms, and sometimes restless legs syndrome. I will have Brenda give you a dose at bedtime.

'In addition to this, I'd like to work with you to better understand what specifically is triggering the movement while you're asleep. I want to know what you're dreaming about to see whether we can supress or reduce the dreams as a trigger.'

'I told you already: I don't remember my dreams.'

'That's a common belief, but most minds can be trained to recall even partial details. Given you were probably dreaming before you woke up in The Butterfly Room, can you tell me what you do remember?'

'I-I don't remember.'

'Anything, Jake. Any tiny detail will help build muscle

memory so that you'll be better able to recall dreams in the future. Have you ever kept a dream journal?'

I shake my head.

'I'd like you to start one. If I go and fetch a journal and pen for you now, will you try? That way we can start to talk about the nature of anything you do remember and identify causes.' She stands to leave but turns back. 'I know you're anxious not to discuss your military career, but I can assure you that anything you say to me during our sessions will be treated with the utmost confidence. My goal is to diagnose and treat, and nothing else.'

'Okay, I'll try,' I say.

She smiles and the relief in her face is clear. 'Good. I'll ask Brenda to provide you with the clonazepam. It should take about an hour to kick in, and then you will feel a bit drowsy, but that's nothing to worry about. I'll leave the journal beside the bed.'

14

Dr Carpenter escorts me back to The Butterfly Room. I ask whether I can use the phone to try to call Sienna again, and she promises she will see what she can arrange after I've eaten lunch. I'll need to phone Max as well unless he calls me first.

There is some kind of art class happening as I enter, with three people standing by the easels, each with a crude painting of a bowl of fruit on the canvases before them. I've never had any interest in art – whether in museums or attempting the craft myself – and so I steer clear but am disappointed to see the hot plates have yet to be lifted for lunch.

'We must stop meeting like this.'

I turn at the sound of Katy's voice. She seems more relaxed than when Dr Carpenter introduced us yesterday. The pyjamas hang from her tiny frame, but she looks less fragile somehow. Maybe it's because she's tied her sleek black hair in a ponytail, or because I'm the only other person she knows here.

'I take it that other guy isn't around, waiting to flip over a table again?' she continues.

'No, I haven't seen Sully since breakfast.'

I feel reluctant to engage with a woman I've known only for a few minutes, but with no sign of lunch arriving, and not wanting to get talked at by the artists in the corner, I agree to sit with her.

'It's Jake, right?' she asks, spreading her fingers on the table.

I nod, and she offers out her hand as if this is a formal introduction.

'Dr Carpenter introduced me as Katy, but I'm used to being referred to by my surname. I bet you're the same, huh?'

I nod again, wary of sharing too much information.

'It's Savage, by the way; Katy Savage.'

I don't provide my surname; in case she's read about what happened to Lucy.

'How did you sleep last night?' she continues, an air of mischief in her dark eyes.

Does she know I woke up in here? Does everyone?

Sully was the one that woke me, and while I don't picture him as a gossip, is it possible that others saw me and left me sleeping? I can't see that the staff would have openly told others, but if it was being discussed, could others have overheard?

'Well, I did sleep apparently,' I say, calmer than I'm feeling.

'So, you didn't sleepwalk last night then?'

The way she asks the question, there's enough innocence in her tone that maybe she doesn't know.

'How did you sleep? Have they cured the insomnia?' I say to deflect the question.

'Ha,' she scoffs. 'I think it's going to take more than a night, but actually I did sleep once I dropped off. It's amazing, the power of talking about things.'

Curiosity gets the better of me. 'Have you heard rumours about me?'

She also leans in conspiratorially.

'Like what?'

I shrug, not wanting to bait her. 'I don't know. Has anyone warned you about me, or mentioned the reason I'm in here?'

She doesn't seem overly worried, and certainly makes no attempt to get away from me.

'Other than Dr Carpenter mentioning your military service, no, I haven't been told anything. But to be fair, they do seem to try and keep a lid on things when it comes to privacy. Dr Carpenter keeps telling me that I shouldn't feel pressured to share anything I don't want to.'

She's saying all the right things, but I'm still not convinced I can trust her. I've seen enough crime documentaries to know that the authorities will sometimes plant informants when trying to extract a confession. Dr Carpenter introducing us yesterday, our shared military experience, and Katy approaching me today are all setting off red flags in my head, but then maybe I'm just being paranoid. I have two options: avoid her altogether or see if I can find whether there's an alternate motivation for suddenly appearing to be so open to talking.

'Apparently, I did sleepwalk last night,' I say after a moment, watching her reaction carefully.

Her eyes widen with excitement. 'Really? And where did you find yourself this time?'

I can definitely hear intrigue in her tone, but she could just be a good actor.

'I only got as far as this room apparently. Sully found me in here this morning.'

She looks around the room as if trying to work out what would drive someone to choose this as a destination, before fixing her gaze back on me.

'How does it make you feel? Knowing you're not in control of your body when you're asleep? I'm not going to lie; it would freak me out!'

'Honestly, I didn't know I was capable of it before today, so I'm not sure I've processed it yet.'

'Well, I hope for your sake they figure out what's causing your condition. I know my insomnia is PTSD. I've spent years denying I have a problem, but accepting is the start on the path to a cure; at least, I hope it is. But these doctors don't really understand, do they? I mean, how can they know what it's like to have seen the things we have? To have experienced those kinds of stressful, heartbreaking scenes? Being in a dogfight with another equally skilled pilot, knowing that it's you versus them, and only one winner... I'm not sure there's any way to come to terms with that. If talking about my experiences helps ease the burden enough, and medication can do the rest, well, then life can continue.'

I look over as Brenda enters the room. She claps her hands in satisfaction when she spots me.

'Your brother is here, Jake,' she tells me. 'Have you eaten yet?'

Max is here today? I was expecting him to phone, so does him arriving in person mean he's found something? I don't understand why else he would make the boat ride back.

'I'm not hungry,' I reply, standing and following her out of the room.

If Max is here, then he must have news, and I need to hear something – anything – positive, especially if it's going to help me get back to Sienna quicker.

Brenda leads me to the bank of lifts, and then we head down to the ground floor, and along to Dr Carpenter's tiny box room. The tiny window high up in the ceiling offers little illumination, and so Brenda switches on the light and says she will return with Max momentarily. There is a large unit of drawers just behind the door, and when I casually pull on the top one, I'm not surprised to find they are locked. I scan the titles of the books on the shelf, but they are all publications relating to psychology and neurology.

The room itself feels so oppressive. Despite the chaise longue and office chair, there are no obvious personal touches in the room. No photographs of a partner or family. No framed degree certificates on the walls. In fact, had she not told me so, I wouldn't even know this was Dr Carpenter's office.

Brenda returns with Max a moment later, and I move across to hug my brother, but the embrace is strained; the result of two brothers who simply aren't that close.

'What's new?' I begin. 'Have you found Lucy's killer already?'

Max unwinds the woollen scarf from around his neck and delicately folds it into four, before balancing it precariously on the stack of files on the old desk. He then removes his overcoat and hangs it on the back of Dr Carpenter's chair, before sitting in it and lifting his briefcase onto his knees.

I sit on the edge of the chaise longue across from him and try to still my rising pulse.

'Well?'

He extracts an A4 notepad and pen, and closes his case, resting both on top.

'I don't have any news,' he finally says.

My heart sinks.

'My team are reviewing the security camera footage the police collected from your neighbours, but nothing conclusive has been identified to date. Until I hear otherwise, you remain their prime suspect.'

I don't know why I was so hopeful that anything substantial would have occurred in the twenty-four hours since I arrived here.

'But presumably they will find footage of the person or people who broke into my house, right? I mean, even if they can't make out a face, the presence of figures in the vicinity should be enough to cast doubt on their theory, yes?'

I'm clutching at straws, but it's all I have.

'I would hope so. What would help more is if you could remember who else was in the house, why they were there, and why they attacked you both.'

'If I knew that, don't you think I'd tell you? I mean, it's the key to the whole thing, isn't it?'

'Well, is there anything new you can remember?'

I close my eyes and try once again to picture anything from that night, but there is nothing fresh, and the memories feel further away than ever.

'The last thing I remember is walking Sienna to school in the rain that morning. Then there's nothing until the moment I woke in the ambulance.'

My heart skips a beat as somewhere in the darkness I hear Lucy scream out. It's high-pitched and anguished, and it immediately puts me on high alert. It causes my skin to prick, almost as if a ghost has just passed through me. I can't see her screaming, can only hear it, but is that a memory from that night or something more distant that my clouded mind can't quite place?

If Max has noticed my change in temperament, he doesn't acknowledge it.

'The only way I can provide you with a proper defence is if you tell me everything, little brother.'

'What do you mean by that? Do you think I'm holding back?'

He doesn't answer at first, before finally letting out a heavy sigh.

'I just don't know. You're asking me to believe that someone broke into your house, killed Lucy and left you unconscious at the scene, framing you in the process. But you haven't offered a shred of evidence or even motivation as to why anyone would do that.'

I can't believe this is what he's now saying. When we spoke yesterday, I really felt like he was on my side. Is this why he's come here in person today? Has he decided that my case is unwinnable and is now washing his hands of me? Dad would be turning in his grave.

'Did you speak to Geraldine yet? Yesterday you said you were going to draw up a list of all her recent clients and look for motives there.'

'I have spoken to Geraldine, and she says there is nobody that she can think of who would want Lucy dead.'

I take a deep breath, trying to push my frustration down.

'So, what you're saying is you don't believe me?'

He puffs out his cheeks, and again I notice he doesn't answer the question.

'You should believe me because we're family, Max. You've known me my whole life, how can you believe that I could do something like this? Don't you think this is hard enough without you turning on me too?'

He buries his face in his hands, and I can see now I'm not the only one frustrated by this exchange. He eventually looks up, his cheeks pale.

'I'm not turning on you, Jake, but I need answers. You're not the only one who lost someone they loved.'

If he had any clue what Lucy really thought of him, I'm not sure he'd be so upset, but maybe I'm doing him a disservice. The age gap between us made it difficult for the two of us to be close, especially as he left home before I'd joined secondary school. Maybe he just has a difficult time showing how he really feels. But what I do know is that if I can't convince him, I have no chance of convincing the judge and jury.

I place both my hands on his knees until he meets my stare. 'I didn't kill her, Max. I swear to you that I'm not capable.'

'Well, then, you need to give me something, Jake. Blaming amnesia isn't going to sit well with a jury. The doctors at the hospital said the swelling in your head had reduced when they discharged you. I need you to do whatever it takes to remember what happened.'

I should tell him about last night's sleepwalking episode, but I don't want him to lose sight of the fact that Lucy's real killer is still out there. It could be that I was sleepwalking that night, and that's why I have no memory of what happened at the time, but my amnesia stretches longer than just the period where Lucy died. I can't have been sleepwalking all day.

'How were things between the two of you?' he asks next.

The question throws me. 'They were fine. We were good. We were happy.'

He raises a sceptical eyebrow. 'And in the bedroom?'

I snatch my hands back, offended by the insinuation. 'They were fine on that front as well.'

'I didn't ask to try and upset you, but when we return to court, the prosecution is going to use any means at their disposal to present your account as unreliable. I need to know in advance if there are any skeletons in the closet.'

'None.'

'You never strayed?'

'How dare you?'

'I'm only asking. Long periods away from home, a group of likeminded people in close proximity, sharing challenging circumstances... nobody would blame you if you succumbed to loneliness and sought comfort elsewhere.'

My cheeks burn with anger.

'Is that really what you think of me? That I would cheat on my wife?'

'I'm merely asking the questions that the prosecutor will put to you. There's no judgement here. Geraldine has already suggested to the police that things weren't as rosy as you've been describing, but I need to know if they're going to be able to find someone who casts doubt on your integrity.'

'Geraldine was envious of how strong our love was, and you shouldn't pay any attention to anything she is suggesting. I never once strayed from my marriage vows, and Lucy wouldn't either.'

I stand and squeeze my fists together, having to control my growing anger whilst desperately wanting to lash out at my brother.

'I need you to stop questioning me and start kicking over stones. Someone knows who did this, and you are the only hope I have of finding them. Pressure the police. Demand to see the CCTV footage as well in case they're trying to cover their ineptitude. Someone else was in my house that night and they're the one who killed Lucy. You find that person!'

15

SIX DAYS BEFORE THE MURDER

Jake is buzzing as he strides towards the tall office block, the shirt collar and tightness of the tie irritating his neck, but he knows it is something he is going to have to get used to as he takes a first tentative step into the corporate world. He'd been suspicious of the email when he'd first received it. The starting salary of twenty thousand to sit on a phone for seven hours a day, Monday to Friday, seemed too good to be true. So, he'd researched the company to check the legitimacy of the email, later discovering the recruitment manager who'd contacted him was an old school friend of Max's. His brother came through for him for once.

Jake spoke to the recruitment manager on the phone for an hour, being asked to give examples of when he had gone the extra mile for a friend or customer, had made key decisions, and when he has had to deal with difficult communication. He felt confident answering all the questions, based on his military service experiences, and this morning he received an email inviting him in for a chat.

He hasn't told Lucy about the meeting because he doesn't want to get her hopes up, but he hasn't felt this excited in a long time. The prospect of earning money again, and contributing to the bills, is what he's been hoping for. And once they've given him a start date, he's going to tell Lucy they should go out to celebrate. Ray agreed to pick up Sienna from school so Jake can attend the meeting.

He's nervous as he stands in reception waiting to be met by the recruitment manager, but he can see himself calling this new office home. He's never worked in an office before, but it can't be too hard if so many others manage to do it and hold down jobs.

He smiles when the recruitment manager, Colin, appears at the security barrier and invites him through. They ascend to the third floor and a secluded office in the corner of the floor.

'I'm sorry, Jake, but you didn't meet the recruitment criteria,' Colin says as soon as they're seated.

Jake just stares at him, certain he must have misheard, or that Colin is telling some kind of joke.

'I agreed to get the interview for you as a favour to your brother, but unfortunately, we have certain skills we're looking for, and you weren't able to demonstrate those with the answers you provided.'

Jake's breathing has become shallow. It feels like a bad dream from which he will wake at any minute. This can't be right.

'Why... why would you invite me all this way to reject me?'

Colin shrugs.

'Out of courtesy to Max. I thought it would be better to have this conversation face to face. I always find the telephone so impersonal.'

Jake doesn't know what to say; the wind knocked from his sails.

'Staff turnover in the call centre is pretty high, so we tend to have these recruitment drives every three months or so,' Colin continues, sliding a sheet of glossy paper across the table. 'This is a copy of the criteria we use to score applicants' answers. I shouldn't be giving it to you, but I want to help, so if you can go away and frame your answers to meet these criteria, there's no reason why you won't be successful next time.'

Jake's cheeks are blazing. He can't believe he's failed to secure a job in a poxy call centre. If anything, it's a role he's overqualified for. He was trusted to carry a weapon and assess whether to use it in combat situations, but he can't be trusted to answer a phone. He wants to turn and run out of the office and never look back.

'Your brother told me about your Victoria Cross for gallantry. That was another reason I wanted to meet you in person. I can understand how disappointed you must be, but I definitely think we would benefit from someone of your calibre here. I'd be more than happy to consider your application again in future.'

'So, that's it? There's nothing I can say or do to convince you to give me a job? Please, I'm desperate. I am willing to start at the bottom.'

Colin frowns empathetically.

'I'm sorry, Jake, but my hands are tied. We have to be transparent with our recruitment. The days of being able to give jobs to people we know or like is long gone. It's all based on set questions and answers have to meet a certain score to progress.' He taps the sheet of paper again. 'Work on your examples, and I'm sure you will have a happier ending next time. I'm happy to email you the next time we're recruiting.'

Jake snatches up the sheet, and stands, desperate to get out of the tie as soon as he leaves the building. Once outside, he tears the sheet of paper into bits and throws them in the nearest bin. Angry, he is tempted to find the nearest bar and drown his sorrows, but he only has twenty pounds left in his account, and that won't be enough. Ray's house is two miles away, and he decides to march in that direction, hoping the fresh air helps clear his mind.

He arrives half an hour later, the tie now stuffed in the pocket of his suit jacket, and the top two buttons of his shirt unfastened. He still hasn't managed to find the words he'll need to tell Lucy he's still unemployed. She's made it clear that he needs to find something soon or he'll have to ask his former Commanding Officer whether he can return to service. There are no guarantees they will reverse his resignation, and he really doesn't want to be posted overseas again.

Geraldine opens the door with a disgruntled expression.

'What are you doing here?' she asks.

'I've come to collect Sienna.'

'She's just started her dinner.'

Jake looks at his watch, trying to hide his frustration. The next bus home leaves the stop at the end of the road in five minutes, and it's a forty-minute wait for the next one.

'I didn't ask Ray to feed her.'

'No, well, she looked hungry, and I thought she could do with a wholesome meal for a change.'

Jake swallows down his anger at the insinuation, just wanting to get back home where he can open a can of beer and try to forget the day.

'I have dinner planned for her.'

'She can't survive on ready meals, Jake. I'd have thought with all your free time, you'd have been able to learn how to cook something decent for her. When was the last time she ate a meal with fresh vegetables?'

'She doesn't like vegetables.'

'So what? She needs a balanced diet, and that means she needs to eat plenty of fruit and vegetables. Besides, she always eats the vegetables I give her, so don't lie to me.'

Jake looks at his watch again.

'Just get my daughter for me, please. I don't have time for an argument.'

Geraldine stands firm, keeping the door just in front of her, as if primed to slam it at any second.

'No,' she says firmly. 'Sienna will eat the meal I've prepared for her, and then you can take her home when she's finished it. You look as though you could do with a decent meal inside you too, but I didn't make enough for you.' She sighs irritably. 'You can come in for a cup of tea if necessary, or you can wait on the doorstep, it's up to you. But there's no way I'm releasing her to you while you've got a face like thunder. Less booze and more sleep wouldn't be a bad idea either.'

He glares at her in disbelief.

'Oh, yes, she's told me all about the amount of cheap lager you're getting through every night. You need to pull yourself together, Jake, and stop taking your frustrations out on my sister. Oh, yes, I know all about the arguments too. Do you think Sienna can't hear the two of you going at it? The poor child would be safer living here with us until you two sort out your problems.'

His anger simmers over.

'She's my daughter, and you can't keep her from me.'

'If you were a real father, she'd be your priority, rather than a secondary thought.'

'How dare you? She is *everything* to me. And I would do anything for her.'

'And yet this is the fifth time in two weeks where you've relied on one of us to collect her from school for you. The only thing my sister has asked of you is to help take care of *your* daughter and you're screwing that up as well.'

Jake can hear Lucy's voice in Geraldine's words, and it's a scathing attack. He fought so hard to make it out of that desert alive, to get back here for them, and now he can't help thinking that it would have been better for them if he hadn't. He knows Lucy and Geraldine are close, so he shouldn't be surprised that his wife has been sharing her frustrations with her sister.

'I'm doing my best, and you'll forgive me if I don't pay too much attention to someone who doesn't have children of her own.'

Jake knows it's a cruel blow, but he's pleased to see Geraldine knocked off her perch; her hand shooting up to her mouth in shock.

'And what's that supposed to mean?'

'It's easy to stand on the outside and criticise but you have no real idea what it means to be a parent, so don't go judging me. If you're such an expert, why don't you have a child of your own?'

Her hand whips out so fast that he doesn't see it until he feels the slap across his cheek.

'Don't come here and speak that way to me in my own house. You should be grateful for all the support we've provided Sienna and Lucy while you've been off gallivanting.'

Jake has heard enough and knows the argument will continue in perpetuity if he doesn't leave.

'Get my daughter now, or I'm going to come in and take her.'

Sienna's head appears beside her aunt, and Jake realises now that she's been listening in to the conversation. She hugs and kisses Geraldine, before stepping out, carrying her coat and bag, her head bowed low as if trying to avoid her dad's wrath. It breaks his heart seeing her so afraid, and he wants to tell her that everything will be okay, but in that moment he doesn't know if things will ever be the same again.

16

I'm still grappling with the prospect that Max isn't convinced by my innocence, and for the briefest of moments I actually consider whether everyone else is right, and I'm wrong.

What if I did kill Lucy?

I slam the door on the thought the moment it appears. I know how much I loved – *love* – her, and there is no way I could have harmed a hair on her head. Even when we did argue, it was never violent. Bitter, yes. Heated, absolutely. But violent? Never.

Arguing with Lucy was always pointless. Three years at university plus two more at law school and she could debate with the best orators. It's what they trained her to do. It's why she was so good at her job, and why I never ever stood a chance of winning an argument.

And if Max is having doubts over my account of what happened that night, then how many others share that view?

I'm going stir-crazy in my room. It's not big enough to properly pace, even by pushing the bed up against the window, there just isn't the room. So, it's a relief when Brenda knocks on my door and asks if I still wish to use the phone. I practically skip out of the room, hurrying towards the lift shaft, desperate to speak to Sienna, hoping she's back from school.

Brenda doesn't move as quickly, and it's a struggle to maintain my calm when she eventually catches up and calls for the lift.

'I'll leave you a fresh pair of pyjamas in your room,' she tells me, while we wait for the doors to open.

'Thank you.'

'And Dr Carpenter said she's going to be prescribing you with some clonazepam. I'll bring the syringe to your room after dinner.'

My eyes widen.

'Syringe?'

'It's oral medication. The syringe goes in your mouth. More hygienic than a spoon. Less messy too. Have you ever taken clonazepam before?'

I shake my head.

'Okay, well, there are one or two potential side-effects you need to be aware of, but I'll explain those before you ingest it. Nothing major to worry about, but it can be a little unsettling if you don't know what to expect.'

The lift doors open and we enter, remaining in silence for the journey down to the ground floor. Brenda leads me through the web of corridors until we happen upon the small admin office filled with filing cabinets.

'Don't forget you need to dial nine for an outside line. Who is it you're phoning?'

'My daughter,' I say, my mouth naturally curling into a smile with the anticipation.

Brenda smiles back, then exits the room and closes the door behind her. It takes me a moment to recall the number for Geraldine's house, but I type it in, and listen to the dial tone. The phone is answered within two rings, almost as if she was expecting the call.

'Hello?'

'Geraldine? It's Jake. Can I speak to Sienna, please?'

There's a pause on the line, and I'm assuming she's beckoning Sienna over, until I hear Geraldine sigh loudly into the phone.

'You shouldn't be phoning here, Jake.'

'What do you mean I shouldn't be phoning you? I have every right to speak to my daughter.'

'Do you have any idea what all of this is doing to her?'

Sienna's innocent face fills my mind, and I close my eyes against the sting of tears.

'Honestly, no, I don't because nobody is letting me speak to her and explain what's going on. I imagine she's confused and drowning in her grief, but that's why I want—'

'She doesn't need to hear from you. I'm taking care of her.'

It worried me that Max was unconvinced of my innocence, but Geraldine seems certain I'm guilty.

'I didn't hurt your sister, Geraldine. You must realise that. You know how much I love her.'

'Oh, yeah, so many displays of your love and affection when you went off galivanting to one warzone or another. Where was your great love for her then? When she was struggling to get Sienna to transition from preschool to Year R, where were you then? When Sienna would be in floods of tears, every night asking where Daddy was. Sienna asking why Daddy didn't love them any more and had gone away. Have you any idea how tough that was for Lucy?'

Guilt scratches at my throat.

'Or when Lucy was so exhausted after a day in court only to return to an empty house and a daughter pleading for a bedtime story. Where were you then, Jake? Where was your great love for my sister and niece then?'

I feel ambushed and I don't understand where all this resentment is coming from. I've always liked Geraldine, and though I've doubted whether she ever thought I was good enough for her younger sister, I hadn't realised the animosity ran this deep.

'I know it wasn't easy for Lucy, but I didn't get to choose when and where I went. It was my job and she understood that.'

Geraldine scoffs loudly. 'You could have left the army whenever you wanted. How many times did Lucy beg you to resign your commission and find something closer to home?'

I can feel my own anger starting to bubble to the surface, and I have to close my eyes to maintain my calm.

'With all due respect, Geraldine, you have no idea what things were like between Lucy and me. I did what she asked and I resigned my commission, but I don't think she – either of you, for that matter – realise just how difficult it has been for me to find a new job. I don't have a university education, and the only job on my resumé is the forces. Not many employers are crying out for unqualified ex-military men.'

'There are plenty of companies that would have been open to recruiting someone with your background, Jake, and you're kidding yourself if you think I'm going to believe you even bothered looking for new jobs. Do you have any idea how much worse things were for Lucy after you quit?'

This is a blow to my gut, and I clench my jaw.

'She would phone me in the middle of the night telling me she couldn't cope any more. Your mood swings when you were back outweighed the loneliness she felt when you were away.'

'I don't know what you're talking about,' I say, but I can hear the lie in my voice.

She scoffs again. 'You think I didn't know about those? The

night terrors that had you screaming out in the middle of the night? She told me about those as well. She told me she didn't feel safe when you were back, and God, I wish I'd listened and forced her to move in with me. Maybe if I had, she wouldn't be...'

My frustration boils over.

'For God's sake, Geraldine! I did not kill Lucy. How many times do I have to keep telling you and everyone else this? Why won't you believe me?'

'Because I know how scared she was of you, Jake. And I've told the police as well. They have found her killer and I'm going to do everything to help them throw away the key.'

'I want to speak to Sienna now.'

'No chance.'

I can't contain my anger any longer.

'You have no right to keep me from speaking to my daughter, Geraldine.'

'I do, if it's for her own safety.'

I fall to my knees, barely able to keep hold of the phone.

'Please, I just want to speak to her and explain that I will be home soon to look after her.'

'Ha!' she scoffs. 'Have you heard yourself? You're a mess and in no state to take care of Sienna.'

It's like she's trying to push my buttons.

'I'm her father; I know what's best for her,' I say through gritted teeth.

'Ha! You might be her biological father, but you've been little more than a footnote in her life. The only reason she's as well adjusted as she is now is because of her mother's gene pool.'

My vision blurs as tears swell.

'That's not fair, Geraldine. I love Sienna and I have always made such a fuss of her when I'm back home. She knows how much I love her, and I demand you put her on the phone this second.'

'You say you love her, do you? Well, if you really loved her, Jake, you'd do the right thing and admit what you did. The sooner she can put all of this *and you* behind her, the sooner we can all move on.'

I've had enough of this, and grip the phone tighter.

'I swear to God, Geraldine, you'd better put her on the line now, or I'll—'

'Or you'll what, Jake? Are you threatening me? The same way you threatened my sister?'

The jab knocks me sideways.

'I never threatened Lucy.'

'She told me what you were like, Jake. She told me how dark your eyes would go when you got angry. How you would lash out at the wall because you couldn't control your temper.'

I see the plate splintering against the wall on impact.

'That isn't true. I-I never—'

'You mark my words: I will do whatever it takes to protect my niece from you.'

I don't understand why Geraldine is trying to paint me as this villain character. The Jake she's describing isn't me, but even I can see how monstrous he sounds. If this is how she's been describing me to Fahey and his colleagues, it's no wonder they're so adamant I'm guilty.

'Please, Geraldine, I just need to hear Sienna's voice.'

'It's not going to happen, Jake.'

'Please, Geraldine, don't do this. Lucy wouldn't want you to be keeping me from Sienna.'

'She was planning to leave you, you know. She'd been looking for a new house for just the two of them. Didn't know that, did you? That's how desperate she was to get away from you. She'd been saving up a little nest egg so she and Sienna could escape and never look back.'

It's another unprovoked punch to the gut. I know Lucy was getting frustrated with me being at home all day, but I would have known if she was keeping a secret that big from me, wouldn't I?

'This is the last time I'm going to say this, Jake: don't phone here again. The sooner you admit what you did, the better for all of us, but especially Sienna. She needs to hear what you did if she's ever going to be able to forgive you. Stop this charade now and tell her what she needs to hear. Just admit what you did.'

I open my mouth to challenge back, but she slams the phone down, and I'm left wondering whether things could have been worse than I ever realised.

17

I'm ready to give up trying to fall asleep. With no watch, I can't be certain how long I have been lying here, but it must be at least an hour. The sky is dark beyond the hanging blinds over my window, and there is an eerie silence filling the room. I can't stop thinking about who killed my wife.

But it's not just the question, it's the variety of cracks that stem from it that are like an unstoppable jackhammer inside my head, driving from one nerve to the next.

Why did they kill her? She was a sweet and kind woman, who loved her family and worked hard for her clients. She didn't have a bad word to say against anyone, so it is incomprehensible to me how her life could have been ended so quickly. Thirty-eight is no age.

Why didn't they kill me? I'm sure I would have tried to fight them off if we crossed paths, and maybe they thought they'd killed me with that blow to the head. Is there something telling in that fact? Was it an attempt to frame me, or does it reveal how amateur they were? But to what end? In my line of work, I don't collect enemies. Those I engage with overseas are generally faceless opposition, as I am to them, so I can't logically resolve that her murder is linked to my army career.

For the briefest second, a child's face flickers into my memory, his dark eyes pleading, but it just as soon vanishes. That has nothing to do with this. It can't; it's just my mind playing tricks on me.

And then there's Geraldine and her misplaced certainty that I killed her sister. Has someone got to her, and convinced her that I'm guilty? Has Fahey turned her into his star witness who will exaggerate the marital problems between us? That I can't figure out why she would change her tune so quickly is what is hurting my brain the most. She has taken temporary guardianship of Sienna and is keeping me from speaking to her, but what's her endgame?

But my recent confrontation with Max is what's troubling me the most. He's asking me to try and remember what my mind isn't allowing me, and despite vowing to search for the real killer, he spent half the day travelling to see me when we could have spoken on the phone. I am placing all my trust in him to defend me, but if he doesn't believe I'm innocent, then my trust is misplaced. I can't afford to find alternative representation, but if he doesn't come up with another suspect soon, this is something I'm going to have to look into.

I'm too hot beneath the thin sheet, and push it back, but the air is so still that there is no instant relief. I would give anything to be able to go for a walk outside in the gardens. I wasn't able to go out for exercise this afternoon, such was the ferocity of the wind and rain, so it feels like I'm a prisoner; I have cabin fever and need to reclaim my freedom. But the garden is out of bounds at this time of night and there are multiple secured doors and lifts between me and it.

I've never suffered with insomnia before, nearly always able to switch off my mind and get to sleep, but my brain just won't settle. It must have been at least two hours since Brenda brought me the clonazepam, in a plastic syringe like I'm a child unable to swallow and ingest tablets. She claimed it would take effect quicker, but here I am still wide awake with no idea how to feel about Dr Carpenter's diagnosis.

The term REM Behaviour Disorder makes it sound like I'm some kind of psychotic serial killer, lying in wait for my next unknowing victim. When Dr Carpenter reports this to the court, are they going to leap to the conclusion that Lucy was just the unwitting victim of me acting out some dream I don't recall? I can picture Fahey rubbing his hands together in glee, while the real killer lurks, watching it play out.

The most terrifying part is that RBD could be a sign of further neurological deterioration. Is that what my future holds? Slow degeneration until I'm nothing but a vegetable with a pulse?

Maybe that's the end I deserve for what happened in the desert.

I try to shake the thought away, but this time I picture myself, gun in hand, the man at my feet on his knees, pleading for his life.

Forcing myself to think of something else, I sit bolt upright. I need to find Dr Carpenter. Maybe Brenda gave me the wrong dose, and that's why I'm still wide awake, time ticking so slowly it's practically going backwards. Maybe, because of my athletic physique, I need a higher dose than others. Or maybe Brenda, with her failing eyes, misread what had been prescribed and gave me some kind of insomnia-inducing medicine, because I've never felt so awake. It's like I've been mainlining coffee all day.

Enough is enough. I can't just lie here with these voices in my head. I raise my right hand and scratch at a persistent itch between my shoulder blades. I push myself into a standing position but have to reach out for the edge of the bed as a wave of nausea sweeps over me, my legs unable to support my weight properly.

Have I underestimated the effect of the medication?

I fall back onto the mattress and stretch out, waiting for the jelly-like feelings to move up my body. I close my eyes and start counting silently. When I reach three hundred seconds, I allow my eyes to open.

I'm still in my room, the tiled ceiling and ventilation shaft where they always are. I lift both legs into the air, supporting them with my hands, my elbows pressed hard into the mattress. If I can get my legs above my heart, then maybe I can somehow get the clonazepam to flow back towards my head.

My arms and hands are both able to move freely, and when I sit up and stare at my feet, I can see my toes wriggling. I swing my legs back over the side of the bed again, this time planting them carefully, and maintaining my grip on the mattress just in case. This time there's no nausea or light-headedness.

I take a couple of steps forwards and backwards to test, but I have full feeling in both feet.

I make my way towards the door, a voice in the back of my head warning me to tread carefully in case the drugs suddenly kick in and I lose my footing again. The corridor beyond the door glows white, with no sign or sound of anyone. I don't know how I'm supposed to call for Brenda or Dr Carpenter if I need anything.

I step out into the corridor, and spot the ceiling camera, which I wave at frantically. Assuming someone is watching the feed, maybe they will see my waving arms and send someone to my aid.

'Dr Carpenter,' I call out, uncertain whether the cameras record audio as well as video. 'Brenda?'

My eyes fall on the big red door, and I freeze.

Dr Carpenter described it as the secure wing of the clinic, and when I pushed her, she said, not every patient who comes here is safe to be left alone.

I don't know why, but I feel drawn to the door, and don't resist as my feet move involuntarily towards it. There is no sign of a handle or locking mechanism. I press my hands against the wood, surprised at how warm to the touch it is, as if the Gates of Hell lurk just the other side. Now that I'm so close to it, I can hear sound. I press my ear to the grain, and am sure I can hear distant wails and screams coming from the other side.

I recall Brenda's words next: *I don't know how he got hold of a knife, but I've managed to sedate him and have removed the weapon from the ward.*

'Jake,' a voice whispers nearby.

I start when I see Sully standing at one of the closed doors that was previously locked. He must have heard me trying to get into his room and come out to investigate.

He waves a hand in front of my eyes, which I push away. 'I'm not sleepwalking,' I tell him firmly.

His round face breaks into a huge grin.

'Thank God for that. I was worried you might drag me into your psychosis.' He pauses and looks over both shoulders in case someone might be listening in. 'What you doing up, Bambino?'

'Couldn't sleep. Wanted to stretch my legs.'

'Well, I wouldn't let any of the orderlies catch you out of bed. One or two of them let the power go to their heads at times.'

He begins to move away, but I pull at his arm.

'Where are you going?' I ask.

He narrows his eyes as if trying to read my mind.

'What's it to you?'

It's a surprisingly blunt response, but I sense there's more to his being in the corridor than he's willing to let on.

'I was going to stretch my legs,' I say. 'Wondered if you cared to join me?'

His eyes narrow further to the point where he almost looks asleep.

'You're not one of the hospital's nursing staff working undercover, are you?'

I remember Brenda's warning about Sully's paranoia, but then I asked the same question of Katy, so I can understand his doubt.

'No, I'm a patient like you.'

'Because they do that, you know. They have nurses dress up as patients to get the inside track on things we won't tell the doctors. You swear you aren't one of them?'

'I swear.'

'No. Swear on something that means something to you. You got a kid?'

I picture Sienna's innocent face. 'A daughter.'

'Swear on *her* life that you ain't pretending to be someone you ain't.'

'I swear on my daughter's life that I am not a doctor, nurse or caregiver here.'

The tension in his face eases, and he slaps me hard across the shoulders.

'Then come with me. There is so much more you need to learn about this prison.'

18

Sully leads me through the brown door, past The Butterfly Room, along the corridor, through another brown door and into a second corridor. The walls are painted a neutral, pastel shade of blue, and look so identical that if I wasn't consciously aware of my surroundings, I could almost believe we'd walked back along the same corridor. He doesn't speak, and when I try to ask him where we're going, he presses a sausage-like finger to his lips before continuing. I feel like an errant pupil sneaking out of class, and I don't like the guilt-infused adrenaline that's pulsing through every sinew of my body.

What is Dr Carpenter going to say if we're caught sneaking about after hours? What if she reports this misbehaviour to Fahey's team and they pull me out of here before she's completed her assessment? I look back over my shoulder, but what I can see looks indistinguishable from what lies ahead. Did we turn right into this stretch, or left? How on earth am I going to find my way back to my room?

I have a bad feeling about this.

Sully suddenly grabs my arm and pulls me to one side, forcing me into the doorframe of a room, and presses a tentative arm across my chest, pushing me back until the locked door presses into my back.

'What the—'

Sully presses a second hand over my mouth to cut me off. We stand there in silence, my heart racing as my mind fizzes with possibilities for this sudden stoppage. I'm about to extract his hand when I hear the sound of footsteps and muted conversation. A moment later, two orderlies in white uniforms move past the end of the corridor, but much to our relief, don't stop to look up to where we're not quite hidden from sight. We both remain statuesque until the sound of footsteps ends, and Sully slowly lowers his hands from my face and chest. His crow's nest of hair is slick with sweat, and my own pyjamas feel as though they have been glued to my drenched body.

'That was a close one,' he says, with a chuckle, showing no sign of remorse that we were nearly caught.

'Maybe we should head back,' I say, looking up along the corridor, now pining for my bed.

'Nah, we're nearly there,' he says, grabbing hold of my wrist and pulling me after him.

He pauses when we reach the end of the corridor and he slowly peers out in the direction the two orderlies walked, and finding the coast clear, bends to the right, before opening what looks like some kind of storage closet.

I hear Brenda's voice in my head: *There's more going on there than just sleeping issues... Just steer clear if you can.*

I am suddenly conscious that I am alone with this man whom I know nothing about, and nobody knows that I am with him. What if he's a deranged psychopath who plans to murder me inside the closet?

Given what I stand accused of, the irony of the thought isn't lost on me.

He pulls me towards the open door, but I yank my arm back.

'I'm not going in there. I'm going back to bed.'

There's disappointment in his eyes when he looks back at me.

'Suit yourself. If you don't wanna know what's really going on here, then keep your head buried in the sand. That's your call.'

He begins to turn away, but I pull him back. 'What do you mean by *what's really going on here*?'

'Listen, Jake, I don't have all the answers, but I won't lie to you. If you wanna open Pandora's box then come inside. It's your choice.'

He disappears inside the dark room, and I suddenly feel like Neo in *The Matrix*, wondering whether to take the red or blue pill. I should just return to bed and forget any of this ever happened. Dr Carpenter will be reviewing the output of the sensors in this vest in the morning and she's going to wonder where I went and why. Staying out only risks irking her wrath further.

And yet.

Ever since we arrived on this island, I've felt like something isn't quite right. Sully could just be a loner with serious paranoid delusions, as Brenda has insinuated, or maybe he has the ability to help pull that thread at the corner of my vision.

I take another look back up the corridor, but I really can't be certain I'll be able to retrace my steps without Sully's help, so I step inside the room and, surprised at just how dark it is inside, stretch out my hands, searching for anything that resembles a light switch, but the door closes and the darkness envelops everything.

'Sully?' I whisper into the blackness, uncertain where he's standing.

There's no answer, and I am going to have to rely on my senses if he suddenly lashes out at me with an unseen weapon.

'Sully?' I try again, straining to hear the sound of his breathing.

'Over here,' he quietly calls back, further into the darkness than I'm expecting.

This is followed by the sound of something heavy and metallic scraping across the hardwood floor, and then the shuffle of boxes. I lower myself to my hands and knees, and crawl in the direction of the sound, allowing my eyes to adjust to the darkness. I find Sully on his bottom, his back pressed against some kind of shelving unit, his right arm pressed against a wall panel, which he gently knocks at three times. Two knocks are returned, and then Sully knocks five times in response. There is a cracking sound and suddenly the wall panel slides back, revealing a glimmer of light. Sully doesn't wait to explain, crawling through the gap, which is barely wide enough for him to fit through.

I follow, sliding on my chest, which reminds me of my forces training.

We find ourselves inside a room slightly larger than Dr Carpenter's own office. The light source is a torch in the hand of a gaunt woman with a shaved head. She blinds me with the beam of light, before demanding to know who I am.

'This is Jake,' Sully explains quietly. 'He's okay.'

I shield my eyes from the beam, as I adjust into a sitting position on the hardwood floor.

'You sure he's kosher?' the woman asks, her accent unmistakeably Bristolian.

Sully looks at me as if seriously considering the question.

'Yeah, I don't think he's one of them. You got the stuff?'

She keeps the torch trained on me for a few seconds longer, before finally lowering it, and standing it in the corner of the room, casting just enough light so we can see each other. I see now she is wearing what looks like a hospital gown, but it hangs from her tiny frame. She must be at least forty-five, and possibly older, with a nasty scar running from her left eyebrow down to her jawline. She reaches into the darkness behind her, before extracting a square-shaped bottle of something vomit-coloured, and hands it to Sully. He unscrews the lid and presses his nose to the top of the neck, inhaling the aroma, before taking a long swig and handing it back to the woman.

'Jake, meet Evelyn, one of the Lundy Clinic's oldest residents, and our very own brewer of forbidden hooch.'

She takes a drink from the bottle, swallowing it down without any reaction, and then nods in my direction.

'What is this place?' I ask, taking in the dimly lit room which doesn't appear to have any doors or windows, save for the crawl-space through which we just entered.

'It's the only place in the whole clinic where they can't find us,' Sully says. 'A structural phenomenon. This room exists in the blueprints, but because of an architectural screw-up, it has no access points. So, they pretend it doesn't exist.'

'In fairness, the current occupants probably don't even realise it's here,' adds Evelyn, scoffing.

'This place was a hotel before it was a hospital,' Sully explains.

'You mean *clinic*,' I correct.

Sully and Evelyn exchange knowing glances.

'No, he means *hospital*,' Evelyn says, taking another drink from the bottle. 'The clinic part exists just to trap you innocent incumbents, like rats.'

There's a bitterness to her tone, and I can't help but think of Brenda's words again: *all sorts of conspiracy theories; many of them sound so plausible.*

'Evelyn has been trapped here for over a decade,' Sully continues, reaching for the bottle. 'That's what they do, you see. They tell you they're gonna help with your mental health troubles, but then they make you sign various waivers claiming it's so they can give you medication—'

'But what you don't realise,' Evelyn interrupts, 'is that they make you sign away your life, so if you do try to leave, they won't let you, and can produce paperwork you signed saying you agreed to be sectioned for your own health.'

'I haven't signed any waivers,' I clarify. 'I'll be gone in a week.'

They exchange glances again.

'Once they have you here, that's when the experiments begin,' Sully continues with a wistful look in his eyes.

'They've got me on these pills at the moment that won't let me sleep,' Evelyn says. 'I've been wide awake thirteen days straight because they want to test out some new drug for some company that wants off-the-record human trials. All I want to do is go to sleep, but they won't let me. I'm so tired of it all.'

'But they can't keep you trapped here against your will,' I counter.

'Wanna bet?' Sully says. 'It's been years since I was last back home. Do you really believe I'm here by choice?'

Brenda said he was paranoid, and that's all this is.

'How many days have you been at the Lundy Clinic, Jake?' Sully asks next.

The hairs on the back of my neck stand. 'Um... two... no, wait, three. I think. Assuming it's now after midnight.'

'You sure about that?'

'Positive. I came over on the boat with my brother and...' My words trail off as I don't want to bring up Fahey and the real reason I'm here. 'And I've had two evening meals since I've been here, so this will be day three.'

'And have they asked you to sign any paperwork?'

'No, nothing.'

He considers my response, and offers me the bottle, but I decline.

'Doesn't prove they aren't messing with your head. Either way, if I were you, I'd start planning your escape.'

'My escape?'

'Sure, unless you want to wind up as just another vegetable, or permanently committed to an asylum. I had a friend in here who stole a knife and threatened one of the orderlies, but they overpowered him and now he's dead.'

I recall Brenda's panicked voice last night: *I don't know how he got hold of a knife, but I've managed to sedate him and have removed the weapon from the ward.*

I can't allow myself to get sidetracked.

'I need to get back to bed,' I tell them, turning, ready to crawl back through the hole in the wall.

'Watch your back,' I hear Evelyn calling after me. 'I thought I knew better and now I'm stuck. Don't make the same mistake as me. You can't trust anyone here.'

I make it back into the darkened room, and am a little annoyed that Sully hasn't crawled back through with me. But given what Brenda said about his mental health issues, maybe I am better off steering clear. I stand, before opening the door and I'm about to step out when I hear the sound of hurried footsteps and Brenda's panicked voice.

'What do you mean he's not in his room? Where the hell is he?'

19

FIVE DAYS BEFORE THE MURDER

Jake stands at the door, staring at his reflection in the glass panel in the door, checking that he doesn't look too hot and bothered. When he conceived today's plan, it had felt like the perfect way to reconnect with his mum and celebrate her birthday. But manhandling the large picnic basket on the bus wasn't as straightforward as he'd thought. He just hopes all the bashing and tipping of the basket hasn't spoiled any of the food inside.

He'd suggested Lucy and Sienna come with him, but Lucy wasn't prepared to let Sienna skip a day of school, even though it's her grandmother's seventieth birthday. And Lucy said she has too much on at work to take a day's holiday. He's told her countless times she needs to take a break, and that she'll run herself into the ground if she maintains the level of effort she's putting in. And *every* time she throws back in his face that she wouldn't have to work as hard if he secured employment.

She's made no secret of the fact she thinks he spends 'all day sat on his arse watching daytime TV', when he should be out hunting for jobs. But she doesn't understand how difficult it is in current market conditions. Most of the jobs not requiring formal qualifications either require employees to work at the weekend or in the evening, and he doesn't want to miss out on any more time with Sienna and Lucy. The whole point of him leaving the army was to spend more time with them, and working when they're at home is counterintuitive.

She wasn't happy when he broke the news about not getting the job at the call centre, and he only told her to prove he was at least trying to find something. She'd told him he should have better prepared and was naïve to base all his examples on his army experience. She's suggested he contact his former Commanding Officer first thing on Monday. He's made it clear he doesn't want to return to the army, but she's told him it's that or they're going to have to seriously consider selling the house and downsizing. He's got so much on his mind that he's becoming more dependent on alcohol to help him drift off to sleep at night.

He's hoping for a nice day with his mum, allowing him to temporarily forget all of his troubles. He adjusts the collar of his shirt as he sees the figure approaching through the panel of frosted glass and when his mum opens the door, she's taken aback to see him standing there.

'Hello, love,' she says, leaning in and kissing his cheek. 'What are you doing here?'

'Happy birthday, Mum,' he says. 'I've come to take you out for lunch, so put your shoes on.'

She spies the basket on the floor by his feet, and her eyes widen with genuine excitement. She leans back and grabs her anorak from the coat stand.

'I'm taking you to the park to feed the ducks,' he tells her, as they walk, arms linked, 'just like we used to when I was growing up. And I've prepared a few bits so we can have a picnic just like we used to do.'

He feels her squeeze his arm tighter and feels certain he made the right choice. He can almost imagine his dad following behind, narrating as he always did, sharing little anecdotes about the places they pass, even though they'd heard them a hundred times before.

The sun has vanished behind a large patch of cloud when they arrive at the park, and Jake purchases a box of duck food from the café that runs just inside the gates and they wander around the park, throwing the food in the direction of the few ducks they find. The grass is still damp with the morning's dew, but he hasn't seen his mum smile so much in as long as he can remember. He wishes he'd begged Lucy to come, even if just for an hour. The air is warm, and he would give anything to have her here with him, sharing in this precious moment.

They eventually find a free bench, and he invites his mum to sit down, while he opens the basket, and begins to pass her the cheese and pickle sandwiches he made, the sausage rolls he baked and cooled that morning, and the flask of tea. When they've finished that, he pulls out the box of cakes he bought at the shop after his attempt to make cupcakes failed, and plonks a candle in one, lighting it.

'Don't forget to make a wish,' he tells his mum as he passes the cake to her.

She closes her eyes, and her lips mumble, before she blows out the flame.

'I wished that both my children have happy lives,' she declares.

'You're not supposed to reveal your wish, Mum,' Jake warns her, 'or it won't come true.'

She shakes her head dismissively.

'I'm so proud of you and your brother,' she tells him. 'You've both found your soulmates, and little Sienna is a real credit to both you and Lucy.'

This triggers Jake's memory, and he pulls out the birthday card Sienna made for her grandmother, as well as the card Jake signed on behalf of him and Lucy after she'd gone to work that morning. He watches as his mum opens the envelopes, reads the messages, and clutches both close to her heart.

'I meant what I said,' she tells him, leaning closer so he'll be able to hear her lower voice. 'I do wish that both you and Max are happy, but I worry about you, Jake.'

'I'm fine, Mum,' he tells her, forcing a thin smile, and hoping she doesn't see through him.

'Your decision to leave the army was so sudden, and I worry that you'll regret it one day, if not already.'

His lips part in response, but she beats him to it.

'I know you probably left to pacify Lucy, and I'm proud that you would put your family first, but something just doesn't seem right with you at the moment, Jake. I mean, this – today – has been lovely, and I am so grateful that you've gone to so much effort for me, but there is a sadness to you that I haven't seen since you were a boy.'

'I'm fine, Mum, I assure you, and my decision to leave the army wasn't to pacify Lucy as you've suggested, but because I was missing my family too much. I just wish I could find another job, but something will turn up eventually.'

'Have you thought about asking Max if he can find you a role at the family firm?'

He doesn't want to tell her what Max's response to that request was.

'That's an idea, I'll be sure to ask him,' he says instead.

'Are you getting enough sleep, Jake? You look exhausted.'

Again, he doesn't want to tell her about the nightmare he suffers with every night. The kid's eyes pleading with him. She wouldn't understand how terrified he feels every night when his subconscious forces him to relive shards of that experience in the desert.

'I suppose you and Lucy are making up for lost time,' she says with a wink.

And he wishes she was right.

'Sienna must be loving having you back permanently.'

He nods at this.

'I walk her to school every morning, and it gives us the chance to talk, and she's growing up so quickly.'

'Maybe now would be a good time for a little brother or sister to come along.'

Chance would be a fine thing, he doesn't say. He still hasn't been able to pin Lucy down long enough to have that conversation but is still certain that another baby would bring them all closer together.

Jake suggests they return home for a fresh brew, and so they stand and make their way back along the same route.

Max's BMW is parked in the driveway when they make it back to the house, and he climbs out when he sees the two of them. He is carrying the biggest bouquet of flowers Jake has ever seen, and kisses his mum's cheek as he hands them over.

'Happy birthday, Mum,' he says, as he hands her a card as well. 'Catarina sends her love but is busy at the salon today. This is just a little token to show you how much we love you.'

She opens the card, and gasps as she reads the message inside.

'You've bought us tickets to the Royal Opera House in Covent Garden?'

He grins.

'Two nights in a slap-up hotel with dinner, and a night at the opera. It's the least you deserve for turning seventy.'

She pulls him close and kisses his cheek.

'Thank you, my darling boy.'

Jake's grip on the handle of the basket tightens, ashamed of the envy flooding his body in that moment. Where will Max's persistent game of one-upmanship end? It's been the same for as long as Jake can remember. Every time Jake would feel proud of an achievement, Max would pop up and spoil it.

His mum loops her arm through Max's and leads her first son towards the house, leaving Jake watching on, all thoughts of their lovely afternoon already a distant memory.

20

When I next open my eyes, I'm surprised to find myself sitting on the toilet inside my bathroom, but I've no idea how I got here, nor how long I've been sitting. Seconds ago, I was in the store cupboard, hiding from Brenda and presumably at least one of the patrolling orderlies.

Did I black out again?

The room is dark, which would suggest it's still night. When I stand, I'm surprised to see that my pyjama bottoms are still pulled up over my legs and behind, even though I have been sitting on the toilet as if in the throes of using it. I run a hand over the material to check I haven't wet myself or worse, but it is dry.

What do you mean he's not in his room? Where the hell is he?

Brenda's voice sounded panicked, but I suppose it's possible I wasn't the subject of her concern.

Instinct made me assume they were talking about me, but the 'he' was probably actually Sully, or maybe someone else out roaming.

Would I really have been able to sneak back to my room without them seeing me? Given how maze-like the corridors felt when Sully was leading me to the secret room, I have no confidence I would have been able to find my way back.

So, how the hell did I make it back to my room without being seen?

I suppose I shouldn't worry too much about the answer to that question, and just be grateful that I made it back. But could these blackouts have something to do with the degenerative neurological disorder Dr Carpenter was hinting at? Maybe if I tell her about these time slips or blackouts it will aid her investigation. I don't believe I fell asleep in that room and sleepwalked back here.

I'm about to head back to bed, when I decide I might as well use the facilities while I'm here. When I go to wash my hands, I'm surprised that the towel is no longer hanging from the hook behind the door where I left it. Instead, I find it hanging from the towel rail. Maybe Brenda moved it while I was asleep. I dry my hands, and check my reflection in the mirror. In the darkness, it's difficult to see much more than the dark bags beneath my eyes. I look tired, but I guess that's a result of the stress of my situation. I'm still no closer to finding out who murdered Lucy and left me to take the blame.

She was planning to leave you, Jake. She'd been looking for a new house for just the two of them.

Was Geraldine right? Had Lucy crossed the breaking point and I hadn't realised?

She'd been saving up a little nest egg so she and Sienna could escape and never look back.

I don't think she'd have been able to keep such deceit from me. I know my wife, and I know when she is lying. At least, I thought I did.

I hear Fahey's words from the interview next: *Lucy was feeling the strain of you being away from home so much.*

He didn't say it in so many words, but could he have been intimating that she was having an affair?

I quickly dismiss the thought. Not my Lucy. She was growing increasingly frustrated about my overseas deployments, and we had discussed me stepping away from the service, but she loved me, and wouldn't betray our vows.

You know, your sister-in-law had quite a bit to tell us about you and Lucy.

If Lucy was having an affair, the one person she wouldn't have been able to hide it from would be Geraldine. Did she tell the police that Lucy was cheating on me? Is that why they think I'm guilty?

I drop to my haunches, holding my head in my hands. It's like the walls of the bathroom are closing in on me, and I'm powerless to prevent them. These thoughts peppering my mind are fatigue-induced, and I know I'd be able to see how ridiculous they are if only I was more awake. What I need to do is get back into bed, and push it all away until morning. Maybe telling Dr Carpenter about the blackouts will help get to the bottom of what's going on.

I freeze as I open the bathroom door and see the shimmer of eyes staring back at me from the bed. There is a ghostly figure, wrapped in pale-coloured garments, sitting upright in the middle of the bed, the face unrecognisable against the darkness enveloping the room. A strange whisper floats to my ears, and I'm frozen with fear.

It takes all my willpower to duck back behind the door. I slap my face several times to wake myself from the nightmare. I don't believe in ghosts and monsters, yet I have no other explanation for the ghoulish figure staring back at me from my bed. I push the door closed with my foot in an effort to stop it getting in, even though that wouldn't stop a real ghost.

It's just a bad dream, I recite over and over, moving to the basin and running the tap, splashing handfuls of water onto my cheeks and rubbing at my eyes.

It's all in your head. There is nobody there.

I stare into the puffy eyes of my reflection.

I don't believe in ghosts and monsters.

It helps calm my mind, even if my hands are still trembling. I inhale deeply and hold the air inside my lungs until my chest feels like it will burst, and then I slowly exhale through my mouth. I repeat the process two or three times.

What if all of this is a dream?

It's the only thought that has any logic. I don't remember leaving the store cupboard and sneaking back to my room, so maybe I'm still there and have fallen asleep. I was tired and Brenda had given me that dose of clonazepam. Maybe it kicked in suddenly and I fell asleep. All I need to do is wake myself up and I'll be back in that cupboard.

I turn and face the door, taking another deep breath, before reaching for the handle and pulling it open. The dim purple light casts a shine over the figure's eyes as it stares back at me, but this time I remain where I am.

'You aren't real,' I say through gritted teeth, waiting for it to move or react in some way.

The figure remains upright on the bed. I take a tentative step forward, my gaze never leaving it. It begins whispering again, but I can't make out what it is saying.

I take another step closer, and another, finally releasing my grip on the door. On the fourth step, I realise the figure isn't a ghost, but a person. A woman. Her arm rises and her finger points at me, and in this moment, I realise what's happened: I'm not in *my* room.

The layout is the same, but the door is in the opposite corner to where mine would be.

I freeze.

What am I doing in this person's room? Did I sleepwalk and take a wrong turn?

The thought chills me, and I take a tentative step closer to the door. The woman continues to stare at me, whispering, but as I move past her feet, I realise she isn't staring and pointing at me, but at the bathroom door. Her eyes are wide open, but I think – no, I *know* – she is asleep.

I wave my hand in front of her face, careful not to make contact with her outstretched arm, but she doesn't see it.

Is this what I look like when I sleepwalk?

She's still whispering, but even this close to her head, I can't make out what it is she's saying, and so I decide to take my leave before I'm caught in another patient's room and all hell breaks loose. I step backwards, but a hundred thoughts are racing through my mind, with one in particular standing out: *How many times have I sleepwalked and not realised?*

Then a second thought hits and my shoulders drop: If I do still sleepwalk, does that mean I killed Lucy?

I step back again, but this time my heel catches on some kind of cable, and before I have time to react, a box falls from the overbed table above the woman's feet, and falls to the floor with an ear-splitting crash.

I look down at the smashed radio, and back up to the woman, whose head slowly turns in my direction like something out of a horror movie, but this time as she stares, she's wide awake. Her mouth drops and she bellows at the top of her voice.

I continue backing away, pressing my hands over my ears, while trying to shout over the din.

'I'm sorry. I didn't mean to wake you.'

I've barely made it out of her room when I hear the sound of footsteps on the tiled floor hurrying towards me. I begin to turn, ready to explain that I must have sleepwalked to her room, but I don't get the chance. Someone bigger and stronger than me ploughs into my side, and grabs both my arms, pulling them roughly behind my back.

I shout in resistance, but no matter how hard I pull and push, I can't break his grip on my wrists. He pushes me to the floor chest first, and continues to pin my arms. A moment later I feel the pressure of hands around my ankles, and then I'm being lifted back into the air, head first, towards my own room.

'It was a mistake,' I shout to anyone who will listen. 'I wasn't trying to hurt her.'

But nobody is listening, or at least nobody acknowledges my cries of pain. Inside my room, I'm forced onto the mattress, before being flipped over so I'm facing the ventilation shaft in the ceiling. I see now I'm being manhandled by two orderlies in white uniforms, biceps bursting out of the short-sleeved shirts they're wearing. Brenda appears at my side, takes one of my hands and pulls it to the side of the mattress, while the orderly replicates the motion with my other hand, and then they are fastening thick leather restraints around my wrists. The orderly then joins his colleague at the foot of the bed, and I stop fighting as they restrain my legs at the ankle.

'It's just a misunderstanding,' I say hurriedly to Brenda. 'I woke up in her bathroom, but I thought it was mine. I didn't mean to frighten her. I was heading back to my room when she woke.'

Brenda doesn't listen, instead looking at the orderlies and checking I'm secured. This level of restraint is so unnecessary, but as I'm trying to explain as much to Brenda, I feel the point of the needle that she stabs into my arm, and then the room blurs before fading to—

21

Suddenly it's like there's a herd of elephants tap-dancing on the inside of my temple. What did they inject me with? I tried to tell them it was a mistake; that I didn't mean to be in that woman's room, but they wouldn't listen, and now I can barely keep track of my own thoughts.

It's like I've fallen into a hole and now I'm freefalling into nothing. Nobody to save me, just a black hole of oblivion.

And yet there are voices. No, it's more than that. Somebody is shouting. Are they shouting at me? Or are they shouting *to* me? I strain to listen but can't make out a word; almost as if they're speaking in a foreign tongue.

Something is very wrong.

And yet there is something all too familiar about these noises as well. And as I try to stop myself falling, I realise now that I'm restrained; only it isn't the cuffs Brenda and the orderlies strapped me into. There is something holding me in place; something tight is pressing into my chest, and when I try to move my legs, they too are trapped by a dead weight.

The smell of burning flesh fills my nostrils, and in an instant, I know exactly where I am. I can picture the upturned Foxhound, the dry arid air. I can't open my eyes as blood flows in every time I attempt it. But I need to get free of the tangled frame of the now dead Foxhound, because I remember what happened the last time I was trapped here, and I can't go through that again.

I pull on the sleeve of my jacket and use it to dab at my face, allowing me to finally get one eye open. I'm flat out on what remains of the roof and I'm surrounded by burning grains of sand. The rear door to the left of us is prised open and I feel a pair of arms on my shoulders. The ringing in my ears begins to ease, and I can hear voices now. Angry shouts in a tongue I'm unfamiliar with. They must belong to whoever attacked us, and more alarming is how close they are getting. I need to get free of the Foxhound so I can help my team defend our position. When my eyes meet the person tugging me clear, I realise I've made a grave mistake.

We've all been briefed about the small pockets of resistance that continue to operate in the otherwise isolated desert. They don't take prisoners, and in this vulnerable state, we need to act fast.

The long, thick, jet-black beard is in stark contrast to the white eyes glaring back at me. Before I have chance to reach for my sidearm, it is yanked from the secure clip, and I am thrown to the sand face first, and peppered with kicks left and right, until all I can do is just focus on breathing. Coarse rope is twisted around my wrists, and I swallow sand as I am dragged across it, only yards from the enormous hole being dug.

I can see two of my team stripped down to just their boxers, kneeling before them. Their hands are tied behind their backs, and they are powerless to stop our captors wrenching the wedding bands from their fingers, and the dog tags from their bruised and bloody necks.

I want to call out to them, to tell them not to worry, and that I will do my duty and save their lives, but have to watch on as the flesh of their backs explodes to a chorus of semi-automatic gunfire. They drop from view like feathers in a gust of wind, and then two more bound bodies are being selected from the pile to my left.

With no identification and buried in an unmarked grave in the middle of nowhere, we'll never be found. I picture Lucy bawling at the news, trying to make sense of why I haven't returned home, and bearing the burden of having to try to explain to Sienna why I will never be there to read her a bedtime story again.

I try to break free of the rope binding my wrists, but it just cuts deeper into my skin and then I feel the barrel of a machine gun pushed against the back of my head. Grabbing a handful of sand, I roll onto my back and throw it in the direction of the guard closest to me. He drops his weapon as his hands fly up to protect his eyes, and I leap to my feet, elbowing him in the face as I grab the fallen gun, release the safety and fire blindly in the direction of the execution squad by the pit. They run for cover, but not before four of them fall. I bend and roll towards the dented Foxhound as retaliatory fire comes my way and misses. The moment it stops, I'm back on my feet and moving around the vehicle, discharging my weapon without hesitation, as I come across the next two before they can reload. To be sure, I fire a single shot into the back of each of their heads, before going to check on any signs of life in the grave. Four pairs of dead eyes stare back at me. I have failed these men who were under my command.

'Jake,' I hear a voice whisper, and that's when I see Tariq, lying prone on the sand where I'd been only seconds earlier, his wrists still bound and his legs a tangled mess of blood and bone from the RPG.

I cross to him, and crouch down, promising I'll do whatever it takes to get him to safety. His throat is charred and bloody, and I tear at my shirt to make a temporary bandage. The white material instantly turns a sickening shade of red, and I realise now that he will be another casualty of this war if I can't get him urgent medical attention.

But he isn't asking for my help, he's trying to warn me about the soldier I disarmed, who is now scrambling to his feet in search of a weapon. I use my foot to kick him onto his back, and gasp. He can't be much older than fifteen. I recognise the terror in his eyes. Keeping the sight trained on him, I look back to Tariq. There's no way he's going to be able to walk, which means I will have to carry him, but I've no idea where we are, nor how far it is to the nearest checkpoint. If I let this kid go, I don't know how long it will be until he makes it back to his camp and brings reinforcements to find us. Under the terms of the treaty, I should bring him with me as a prisoner of war, but I can't carry Tariq and keep him under armed guard.

It's an impossible choice to make, and yet I make it in less than a second.

His lips tremble as he begs for his life. My finger squeezes the trigger, and the single shot strikes him between the eyes and peace descends. His is not the first life I've taken, but it is the first time I've meant it.

And then I hear it. The sweetest, most angelic voice I've ever heard. She's calling to me. Sienna is calling to me.

22

I try to call back to her, but I can't open my mouth, and the words stick in my throat, sounding more like a gargle than speech. The overbearing heat and golden sands dissipate into darkness once more, and it's only when I try to walk forwards that I realise I'm horizontal.

There are other voices now, not just Sienna's. I take a deep breath and try to focus on the voices. Are they talking to me? No, I don't think so. There are three people: one female, two male. What are they saying? I concentrate harder, straining to hear.

'I think he's waking up. Be ready.'

I force my eyelids apart, and instantly recognise the white ceiling tiles and ventilation shaft of my room at the Lundy Clinic. It's a struggle to control my head, but I manage to lift it long enough to see that I'm spread-eagled on the bed in my room. I can't move my legs and arms as they're still held in place by the firm brown leather restraints.

I see Dr Carpenter: stern-faced and staring back at me from a chair at the foot of the bed. Behind her are the two orderlies, bulging arms crossed over their beefy chests. One is by the closed door to the room, and the other in the opposite corner. It is these men that Dr Carpenter has been talking to.

There is no sign of Sienna, and my heart sinks. I try to recall why I'm in restraints, but don't have to think too hard before Dr Carpenter stirs the memory to the forefront of my mind.

'You're not permitted to go into another patient's room.'

Her words cut through the fog of temporary amnesia, and I instantly remember waking in that bathroom, and the ghoul-like patient staring at me from her bed. She was asleep with her eyes open until my heel caught on an errant cable and sent her radio crashing to the floor.

How long have I been unconscious? What did they give me?

'Can you hear me, Jake? We found you in Wendy Tate's room. Can you tell us what you were doing in there?'

'I-I don't know,' I slur, my lips feeling as though they're not physically attached to my face.

'Wendy suffers with nocturnal lagophthalmos,' Dr Carpenter continues. 'It means she sleeps with her eyes partially open.'

I'm not sure she should be divulging this level of personal information, but if her intention is to make me feel guilty, it's working.

'I-I woke up in her room,' I say, my lips feeling as though they're twice the size as normal. 'One minute I was walking about and then I was in her bathroom. Check the CCTV!'

Dr Carpenter doesn't respond, and it's too much effort to lift my head again, so I remain where I am. She mutters something to the orderly closest to the door and he exits the room. The whole purpose of me being sent to the clinic was to assess whether I suffer from sleepwalking; surely the micro sensors will have picked up my movement?

The realisation hits me like a wrecking ball: I *am* sleepwalking, which means Max could be right. Did I kill Lucy?

'You gave us all quite the scare,' I hear Dr Carpenter say eventually. 'Given the reason you are here, finding you in another patient's room, and Wendy screaming hysterically... we had to be certain you weren't a threat to her.' Her shadow falls across my face, and when I open my eyes, she is standing over me. 'The restraints were for your safety as much as hers.'

I feel the orderly's fingers fiddling with the straps around my ankles, and then my legs are free. Warm blood rushes back into my ice-cold feet, and it's like my heels are being pricked with pins and needles. Dr Carpenter is gentler when she unfastens the bindings around my wrists, and then she helps prop me up against the pillows, raising them to support my back.

'You can leave us now,' she tells the orderlies.

'Just shout if you need us. We'll be waiting outside.'

They leave us, closing the door behind them.

'How are you feeling?' she asks.

'Groggy.'

'That'll be the after-effect of the sedative we gave you. I'd recommend you drink a lot of water to clear the dregs from your system.'

'I thought narcotics were prohibited here?'

She shrugs nonchalantly. 'As a general rule they are, but in certain circumstances we're allowed to administer whatever is necessary to aid a patient. You were wild when they found you.'

'I was fighting off people that were trying to imprison me.'

She doesn't argue, passing me a beaker of room-temperature water. 'You should feel right as rain within the hour.'

I sip and grimace.

'You said earlier you were walking in the corridor before you woke up in Wendy's bathroom. Can I ask where you were going?'

I need to be careful here. I don't want to get Sully into trouble, and I'm sure Evelyn won't appreciate me mentioning the secret room where they go to drink the contraband hooch she brews. I also don't want to influence her assessment of my apparent sleep-walking. But I can't cope with everything that's happening, and need to trust someone.

'I couldn't get to sleep,' I say, 'so I went for a walk. I heard a couple of the orderlies coming so I hid in a room as I thought I might get into trouble. And then the next moment I was in that bathroom.'

'You hid in Wendy's room?'

I could pretend, but that isn't going to help me figure out the truth of what happened to Lucy. I need to know if I'm responsible for her death.

'No. I was in some kind of storage cupboard and then the next moment I was in her bathroom. I have no idea how I got there. And it's not the first time either.'

Dr Carpenter sits forward, her interest piqued.

'Do you think you fell asleep and sleepwalked to Wendy's room?'

'I honestly don't know. I don't remember falling asleep, but there is this gap in my memory.'

'And you say it's happened before?'

I slowly nod.

'Did it happen the night that you... that your wife died?'

I frown at the insinuation. 'I can't tell you what happened that night as I have no memory of it whatsoever. The last thing I remember of that day is walking my daughter to school and then the next minute I woke in the back of the ambulance.'

'Do you think it's possible you had one of these blackout moments that night?'

'No, they didn't start until I arrived here.'

Her temple tightens with confusion.

'You've experienced those lapses while here?'

I nod. 'It's happened a few times. One minute I'm in one place and then the next I'm somewhere else with no idea how I got there.'

She sits back, staring off into the distance in quiet contemplation.

'I'd like to understand what's triggering these time lapses. When you were in the storeroom, can you remember how you were feeling? Were you stressed or worried in any way, for example?'

I think back to the fear that the orderlies would catch me sneaking about after hours, but I've been in much scarier places. That time in the desert when I was kneeling beside that pit immediately leaps to mind.

'I wouldn't say I felt stressed or worried. I was just keen to return to my room.'

'Very well, what about the other occurrences you mentioned? Can you remember what you were doing or where you were at those times?'

I try to remember, but already one day in this place is merging with the next, and I can't be certain.

'I was in my room shortly after I arrived here and you were escorting my brother out, then all of a sudden, I was standing at the door to the garden, and Brenda was holding the door open. And then, I was suddenly inside the administrators' office trying to phone my daughter.'

'Your daughter?'

'Yes, Sienna. She must be out of her mind with worry.'

'Were you thinking about your daughter when the time lapse occurred?'

'I honestly can't remember. I've been thinking about her and Lucy a lot. Maybe. Probably.'

'And of course, there was the morning you woke in The

Butterfly Room. The sensors in your pyjamas indicated that you may have sleepwalked there, and the footage from the security cameras supports that theory.'

She stands and straightens her white lab coat.

'There's something I'd like to try if you're willing?'

I nod, but there's a feeling of dread creeping through me.

'Once you've recovered from the effects of the tranquiliser, I'd like you to join me in the suites upstairs. I'd like to use hypnosis to attempt to unlock some of those time lapse periods and find out what was going on in your subconscious at the time. How does that sound?'

I need to be careful here as I don't want to appear difficult, but I cannot allow her to see what I did in the desert, or Lucy's murder won't be the only charge I'm facing.

23

FOUR DAYS BEFORE THE MURDER

Jake closes his eyes to try and silence the heavy drumming between his ears, focusing instead on his breathing, and trying to work out where he is and why he feels so rough. The pain behind his eyes is like nothing he's ever experienced. It's as if someone is driving an electric drill into the back of his skull. He shoots a hand up to his crown to check that isn't the case.

His last memory is of heading to the army base to meet his old Commanding Officer to try and ask to return to the service. With Lucy taking Sienna to a friend's birthday party, he was at a loose end, and when he'd left the house, he'd known what to say. But then he'd arrived on the base, and it had brought back so many bad memories of his last time abroad that he'd bottled it. Deep down, he knew he was only going to ask to pacify Lucy, even though the thought of being posted abroad fills him with dread.

Lucy was fuming when she showed up late last night, saying she'd had to spend her evening trying to calm Geraldine down after what he'd said to her when he'd collected Sienna.

'They were doing you a favour, Jake, and that's how you showed your gratitude? You know Ray and Geraldine tried all sorts to conceive, and it was not appropriate for you to throw that in her face last night.'

He tried explaining that he was only reacting to what Geraldine had said about him being a bad father, but Lucy wasn't listening. And the worst part is he knows she was right, and he shouldn't have taken out his frustration at the job rejection on Geraldine.

'You've no idea how much they've done for Sienna and me. I can't believe you would behave that way.'

Lucy went to her office with a large glass of wine, and he went to bed alone. She must have come up at gone midnight and was out running when he woke this morning.

'I'm taking Sienna to her friend's house, and I need you to pick her up at 5 p.m. promptly,' she told him matter-of-factly before heading out.

And with nothing better to do with his Sunday, he phoned his former Commanding Officer and asked for an informal chat. When he arrived, she'd immediately produced a bottle of her favourite brandy and he'd accepted a glass if only to summon the courage to ask her about his options. But she'd wanted to talk about his time in Basra, and one glass of brandy had quickly turned to two as he'd tried to avoid remembering what happened in the desert.

Now, lying on his back, he opens his eyes, having to squint because of the strong light hanging from the ceiling. He can see a thick sheet of glass about a foot to his left. It's a table of some kind. Scattered over the glass he can see squashed aluminium cans, and suddenly it's so obvious why his head feels as though it will explode.

His CO suggested they go back to her place, and for a moment he's terrified that something intimate may have happened between them, until he spots her fully clothed, dozing on the sofa across the room. She'd been so full of praise for how he'd saved Tariq's life and that his resignation was to the army's detriment.

He can't be sure whether he managed to ask her about coming back. He wanted to say he would return but in an alternative post. He is aware of other roles on the base, and would happily take a pay cut if it means staying closer to home, but for the life of him, he can't remember what her response was.

His head spins as he props himself up on his elbows.

He can't remember the last time he was so drunk that he passed out. Maybe the night of Max's wedding when several of them were determined to drink the bar dry because Max had made it open, and they figured he could afford it.

His CO groans on the sofa, before rolling onto her back and staring down at Jake. 'Jeez, did I fall asleep?'

Jake winces as he nods. 'We both did, I think.'

She laughs and then groans again. 'The room is spinning for you too, right?'

'We should probably try and eat something. Do you have any painkillers?'

'There's bread in the breadbin, and there is paracetamol in the medicine cabinet in the bathroom cabinet. If you're going to be sick, can you try and make it to the toilet?'

Jake hoists himself up on to the sofa, staring at the carpet between his feet to stop the room from spinning. He doesn't think he's going to be sick, but he definitely needs something to take away the pain in his head. He attempts standing, and feels like he might collapse, his feet shuffling to keep him upright.

His CO rolls off the sofa and crawls on her hands and knees out of the room, the door to the bathroom closing a moment later. Jake tries not to listen to the sound of her retching as he moves unsteadily towards the kitchen area. There are more squashed cans scattered along the countertop and an empty bottle of brandy.

He grabs four slices of bread from the breadbin and drops them into the toaster just as his CO returns from the bathroom. Her skin is pale, and her face is screwed in a ball of pain. She throws a box towards Jake, which he catches, popping out two pills, and filling a glass with tap water.

'Man, I haven't got that wasted in I don't know how long,' she says as she grabs two of the slices and butters them like she's laying cement on a wall.

Jake can only laugh as she takes a huge bite out of one and butter dribbles down her chin.

'Nor me. I hope your head is as sore as mine.'

She salutes this and retakes her place on the sofa.

'What were we talking about?'

Jake carries his toast over to the other sofa and bites into it. He has no appetite but needs something to soak up the alcohol.

'Hopefully, I was telling you about wanting to return.'

She snaps her fingers together as if remembering the conversation.

'That's right, you said something about your wife getting fed up with having you cluttering the place up.'

Jake doesn't remember saying this, but then he sees her laugh and realises she's just pulling his leg.

'Let me have a chat with Human Resources about what we can and can't do, and I'll let you know. Lord knows we could do with you back on the frontline.'

He doesn't correct her at this point, as he figures once he's back in he'll be able to look at other opportunities.

'They'd be mental not to accept an application from someone who's won the Victoria Cross for gallantry.'

Jake isn't so sure they'd be so open to his return if any of them knew what really happened over there.

'And I definitely think you ought to see someone about what you told me,' she concludes, finishing her first slice of toast.

'I don't follow,' Jake says honestly.

'The nightmares you've been having about what happened in Helmand.'

Jake has no memory of telling her anything about his sleep issues and is now paranoid about what else he might have let slip.

'Survivors' guilt is a common issue soldiers can suffer with. Given the ambush and fear for your life, it's highly possible you're suffering with PTSD, and that's why we have trained professionals all army personnel can talk to. I checked your record, and you refused counselling when you returned. If the army accepts your application to return, then I will insist that you speak to a professional. Is that clear?'

Wanting to avoid reliving what happened in the desert is one of the reasons he left so promptly.

He knows the counselling is offered because those who've seen conflict can often suffer mental health issues, but he doesn't want any such diagnosis on his record. Finding a new job will be even more challenging with that kind of label on his service record.

Jake swallows the last of his toast and tells her he should be getting back. He removes his phone to check the time and is alarmed to see a dozen missed calls from Lucy and almost as many messages. His eyes widen when he sees the time.

I need you to pick her up at 5 p.m. promptly.

'Shit! I had no idea it was so late.'

'It's barely six.'

'Yeah, but I was supposed to collect my daughter. Shit!'

Jake races to the front door, thanking his CO for her hospitality and apologising for leaving her with a mess to tidy. He hurries along the road to the command post and tries to phone Lucy while he waits in the queue to be seen. It is pouring and the wind whips the rain into his face. Lucy rejects his call instantly, and he begins to sense just how angry she's going to be. He can't believe he lost track of time, and what angers him most is the fact that he was once again trying to do a good thing that has ultimately backfired on him.

He plays each of her voice messages, the first demanding to know where he is and why he hasn't collected Sienna, until the fifth call where she tells him she's fed up with him letting her down.

It takes him almost half an hour to get home and he is drenched as he makes it in through the door. Sienna is watching television in the lounge and welcomes him when he takes off his coat and shoes, hanging both on the radiator. She tells him she had a good time at her friend's birthday party, and when he asks where her mum is, she tells him Lucy is upstairs showering.

Jake makes her a cup of tea to show her how sorry he is, and hopes that when he explains where he's been, she'll see that he was doing it to help their situation. But when he carries the tea upstairs, their bedroom is empty. Lucy is locked inside the bathroom, and when he puts his ear to the door he can hear her crying.

24

I don't know how long has passed by the time my heart rate has settled and I'm able to stand once again. My head is pounding, and my eyes feel overly sensitive to the light coming in through the blinds over the windows. So much so that I have to close them, just to be able to straighten. I wonder if this is a common after-effect of the clonazepam.

In my head, I hear Sully's paranoid rant about how the clinic lulls patients into signing away their lives so they can experiment on them. It's such a ludicrous claim.

And yet...

How can I be certain that what Brenda injected into me was a standard tranquiliser? What if it was something else? There must be a record of whatever she injected me with. I should ask Max to demand to see my records. But can I trust anything they've written down?

I try to focus on my breathing and quell the paranoia. But now all I can hear is snippets of what Sully and Evelyn told me in that hidden room.

Evelyn has been trapped here for over a decade.

I am only here to buy Max more time, I remind myself. If I was to phone and tell him that I don't want to be here any more and would rather face my day in court, he'd pull me out. Wouldn't he?

Once they have you here, that's when the experiments begin.

Nobody is experimenting on me, and Brenda warned me not to buy into any of Sully's paranoid ranting. And yet I have no memory of ever sleepwalking before I stepped foot inside this facility.

They've got me on these pills at the moment that won't let me sleep.

She didn't mention what medication she was taking, and I certainly haven't been given any pills, and yet the mouthful of clonazepam was administered to prevent movement but kept me wide awake. My heart rate is increasing again, and I physically shake my head to try and expunge the thought from my mind. I'm being paranoid, and it's just because I'm in a heightened state of stress. With not knowing who killed Lucy and the trial date looming ever closer, anyone would be freaking out in my position. That's all this is.

It's been years since I was last back home. Do you really believe I'm here by choice?

There's no reason anyone would want to trap me in a hospital or clinic. I am here to buy Max time. That's what we agreed. That's how he pitched it to me. I am here so he can find Lucy's killer.

My mouth is so dry, but the last jug of water Brenda brought in is now empty. I hobble to the bathroom, my legs still feeling uncertain beneath me, and clutch the edge of the basin when I get there. Dark bags hang beneath the eyes of the man in the mirror.

When did I get so old? I barely recognise myself. This isn't the face of the man who entered this clinic only three days ago. This man is dishevelled, face drawn, and stubble mounting on his chin.

What have they done to me? What if Sully and Evelyn are right in what they've said?

The man in the mirror shakes his head. Brenda warned me not to get sucked in by Sully, but that's exactly what she would say if she was in on it, isn't it?

Sully warned me not to sign any paperwork as that's how they trapped Evelyn, but I haven't signed anything.

A memory of Max and me standing at reception flashes through my mind. When they asked me to give up my personal belongings, they printed a list of the items and made me sign the page. Did I look at the page before I signed it? I don't remember reading any small print as I was too distracted trying to listen to what Coyle and Fahey were discussing.

I grip the basin tighter and close my eyes, inhaling deeply through my nose and releasing the anxiety through my mouth. It's a technique we were taught for handling the stress of armed combat, and after a few breaths, I finally start to calm down. I am allowing my imagination to run away with me. One thing's for sure: I need to stay away from Sully and his paranoid theories.

That said, I am worried by how exhausted my reflection looks. If I ran into this person in the street, I'd tell him to take a break and clear his mind, but I'm not going to be able to do that until I get out of here.

I switch off the bathroom light and make my way to my bedroom door. An orderly is waiting in the corridor and tells me he will escort me up to the therapy suites where Dr Carpenter is waiting for me. My mouth is still so dry, and I would give anything for a cup of coffee, but we head in the opposite direction to The Butterfly Room, towards the lift, and then up to the top floor.

I'd forgotten how bright it is up here with the floor-to-ceiling windows overlooking the sea. The sun is reflecting off the water, and practically blinds me as the doors part, though the orderly doesn't seem to be affected. I have to squint as we head out into the carpeted corridor, passing the other empty therapy suites. He tells me Dr Carpenter is waiting in the final suite, and then returns to the lift. I wait for the doors to close before moving forward, but when I'm only two suites away, I hear voices coming from the room.

'We're taking good care of him,' I hear Dr Carpenter say.

'One day you'll understand why things had to be this way.'

The second voice is one I would recognise anywhere, but how can I hear her? Unless she's here.

I burst forward, sprinting as evenly as my shaky legs will allow, already picturing Lucy standing in the therapy suite, revealing how the police made a mistake and it wasn't her they found dead in the kitchen. She'll tell some absurd story about how she'd nipped out to buy milk and then something happened that meant she wasn't able to return and reveal the truth. We'll laugh and the world will make sense once again.

'I'd better stop because he'll be here soon,' Dr Carpenter's voice carries, louder as I near.

Lucy's voice stops abruptly as I near the door, and when I look in through the tall windows, my eyes scan the entire room. My mouth drops as I see the side of her blonde hair at the desk, and I burst into the room.

'Lucy, you're ali—'

I stop myself as my eyes refocus and I see Dr Carpenter staring back at me from behind the desk.

'Jake, you startled me. I didn't hear you approaching. Please, do come in and take a seat.'

'Where is she?' I demand, entering the room, immediately scouring every corner, searching for where Lucy could have disappeared to.

'Where is who, sorry?'

'Lucy. I heard her talking and laughing. Where is she?'

Dr Carpenter remains behind the desk, her cheeks flushing as she closes the lid of the laptop.

I wheel her chair out of the way, looking under the desk, but there's no sign of Lucy.

My eyes dart to the triangular-shaped conference phone on the desk.

'You called her? Where is she? I need to speak to her.'

She stands and steps in front of me, forcing eye contact.

'I need you to calm down, Jake. I wasn't speaking to Lucy on the phone.'

'But you were talking to her. I heard your voice.'

There is pity in her frown.

'You're mistaken. I'm not even sure the telephone is connected.'

I stab a button on the device and hear a dial tone.

'You're lying to me, doc, and I want to know why. I heard Lucy speaking and I heard you reply to her. Is Lucy still alive? We need to tell the police. I need to tell my brother.'

She takes a step backwards.

'Jake, you're frightening me.'

I close the gap.

'I'm sorry, Jake, I can see this is causing you unease, but I assure you I wasn't speaking to anyone before you arrived.'

I can feel my anger rising, and suddenly realise I've balled my fists, and am digging my nails into my palms. No wonder the poor doctor looks so scared. I force my hands to unclench and move across to the couch, where I perch on the edge.

'I'm sorry,' I offer. 'I just... I know I heard her voice...'

She wheels her chair around the desk, so it is only a few feet from me, and then she drops back into it.

'The mind is an incredible tool that we still know so little about. Tell me, what did you hear Lucy say?'

The question throws me as I try to recall the specific words, but my mind is already starting to blank.

'Something about her being able to explain why things had to be this way. What did she mean? Please, if my wife is still alive, I need you to tell me.'

'How did hearing her voice make you feel?'

'Like all of this is just a bad dream and that a huge mistake has occurred.'

She considers my response.

'We all deal with grief differently. That's not me trying to sound profound; it's a fact. I cannot begin to imagine what you've been through, but I can empathise, having lost both my parents. There are times when we will dream about those we've lost, almost as if they're appearing to us from beyond the grave. I know it sounds a bit trite, but that's how I like to think of it. Maybe, with everything you're experiencing, your mind heard what it needed to hear.'

Is that what this is? Am I losing my mind? Dr Carpenter herself suggested my blackouts and amnesia could be a symptom of a neurological condition, so could hearing Lucy's voice be another symptom?

'What's wrong with me, doc? Are there any tests you can run to find out what's going on, because right now I don't know what's real and what's all in my head.'

She smiles empathetically, and in that moment, I want to believe that she genuinely wants to help me.

'Unfortunately, I'm not a neurologist, but there are a few basic checks we can do to see if further examination is required. Tell me, have you ever experienced any tremors in your hands or legs?'

I think back to my moving from the bed to the bathroom mirror less than ten minutes ago, and how uneasy my legs felt, but surely that was just the result of the tranquiliser or clonazepam.

'Not that I'm aware of.'

'Have you noticed any particular stiffness? I'm talking about first thing in the morning when you wake, or when you've been sitting for too long?'

'The mattress in the bedroom here is firmer than I'm used to, so I've been experiencing some minor twinges since I arrived, but prior to that, there's nothing I've noticed.'

'That's good, Jake. How about your handwriting? Has that changed in the last few months or years?'

I genuinely can't remember the last time I handwrote anything, as notes are usually typed into my phone, so I shake my head.

'Good. Well, aside from the time lapses you've been experiencing, I'd say the risk of you suffering with something like Parkinson's feels low at the moment. But as I said, I'm not a neurologist and it isn't my area of expertise.'

She pauses.

'How are you feeling now? I'd say you seem calmer than when you first walked in here.'

I nod at this, the tension easing in my hands.

'Good. And are you happy for me to still attempt to help you unlock some of those blackspots?'

'You still want to hypnotise me?'

'Hypnosis has a bit of a label as a means of tricking people into doing things they wouldn't otherwise consider. What I'm proposing is to help ease you into a settled and calm trance-like state that will then hopefully allow me to guide you through accessing some of the information hidden away.'

I'm convinced her efforts will fail, but I need to get beneath what actually happened that night, because although everyone is telling me Lucy's dead, I know what I heard.

25

Dr Carpenter closes the blinds to the office, and a dark shadow spreads across the carpet. She tells me to stretch out on the couch, but I suddenly feel vulnerable. She's my doctor and I should have total faith that she means me no harm, and maybe it's just this clinic, but something feels so wrong.

'I want you to try and relax, Jake,' she tells me, retaking her seat.

Her voice is softer now, as if she's trying to make it as soothing as possible; the kind of voice I would have adopted when Sienna woke screaming from a nightmare.

'When you're ready, I want you to rest your head back against the cushion, and slowly close your eyes.'

I can't let her inside my head. If she uncovers what I did in the desert, then she might tell my CO and I'll face a court martial.

My eyes snap open when I hear the sound of birdsong and a gently played harp.

'Just some background music to help us both relax,' she says, smiling, lowering the volume until it's just above the sound of my own breathing. 'Close your eyes and listen to the music.'

I do as I'm told, but my mind keeps flashing me back to the moment I heard Lucy's voice and laugh before I came in here. There was something so familiar about it, and now I'm trying to determine whether the sound was in my head; a memory breaking through the black hole of amnesia.

'I want you to imagine you are stretched out in a forest,' she continues. 'Beneath your body are crisp brown leaves, the kind that fall in the autumn, but it's a warm day. You can feel gentle humidity on your cheeks, and as you stretch your arms and legs you hear the light and playful rustle of the leaves as they crackle beneath you. You are in total control of this forest, Jake. The animals and trees are controlled by you. A gentle breeze is blowing, and it strokes the top of your head, cradling you as a mother would a child. You feel relaxed in this place, because you know you're safe and can come to no harm.'

I start when I realise all I can see around me is the leafless branches hanging above my head. I need to stay in control.

What was Lucy trying to tell me? Why that memory now? And why only the sound of her voice and not a visual to accompany it?

'In the distance you can hear the sound of a river running, the water splashing over the rock bed, but it almost sings out to you. I want you to stand and find the river, Jake. Listen carefully and the water will call you to it.'

Stop thinking about rivers! Concentrate on Lucy!

'You're beside the river now. The water's edge comes up to the bank and you sit down beside it, allowing your hand to dip into the cool, refreshing water, feeling it splash against your fingertips.'

Talk to me, Lucy. What do you want me to remember?

I try to think back to the night when my whole life changed. What did I do once I returned from walking Sienna to school? Did I see Lucy after we got back? No, she'd left for work before we went. I was on leave, so what did I do? It was raining, so I wouldn't have stayed out all day. Where did I go? What did I do?

'The river is flowing so freely that it's tempting to get in and swim, but instead what I want you to do is find the thought that is troubling you the most. The one thought that is keeping you awake at night. I want you to pluck it from your mind like you're plucking a hair from your head. I want you to hold it up to the light and see how harmless it is out in the open. It is lighter than a feather, isn't it? You see how harmless it is now that it is out of your mind. I want you to take the thought and push it beneath the forgiving waters of the river and then let it go.'

There are so many thoughts troubling me. Who killed my wife? Why didn't they take me too? I pluck them out as she's suggested and hold them both up to the bright sky. They look like bubbles, practically weightless against the gentle breeze.

'Have you done it yet, Jake?'

My mind snaps back to the harp-playing and the discomfort of the leather cushion beneath my body.

Concentrate! Don't listen to Dr Carpenter.

Somebody killed Lucy. That's what everybody has told me since I woke in the back of that ambulance. Fahey confirmed it. Max echoed it. Geraldine identified the body. Who killed her?

It wasn't me. I have to believe that I didn't sleepwalk that night and act out some nightmare that ended with her bleeding to death.

'Once you've released those thoughts, I want you to close your eyes again. I want you to shut out the bright sky, and just stare at the darkness in your mind's eye. I want you to listen to my voice and nothing else. I am your guide, and you will do as my voice instructs. I am going to slowly count backwards from ten, and with each number I want you to breathe in and slowly exhale, unburdening yourself of all your stress and anxiety.'

I stare into the darkness. Why would anyone want Lucy dead? Fahey asked me that question during the interrogation and I still can't answer it. Everybody loved Lucy.

'Ten...'

I breathe in and slowly release it.

'Nine...'

In and out.

'Eight... your shoulders are relaxing, Jake. Can you feel the weight of the burden lifting?'

In and out.

'Seven... Six... Five...'

My eyes are so heavy, and my head is starting to droop.

'Four... Three...'

I need to fight back, but I am so tired.

'Two... One. You are now in a peaceful state, Jake, and I am here to look after you. Nothing bad can happen to you. You are the safest you have ever been, and I will protect you at all costs. Keep breathing in and out and focusing on my voice. Do you understand?'

'Yes.'

'That's good, Jake. I want you to think about the happiest moment of your life. The moment when you felt truly blessed. I want you to picture a snapshot of that moment, like somebody is holding up a photograph in front of your face. Can you see it?'

'Yes.'

'Good, Jake. Tell me what you can see.'

'I can see Sienna.'

'What else can you see?'

'She is wrapped in swaddling, and her eyes are scrunched closed. Her mouth is open because she is yawning. I can see Lucy's hand holding her to her chest. She looks exhausted, but

I've never seen such love in her eyes as I do right now. Her lips are pressed to the top of Sienna's head.'

'How does it make you feel, Jake?'

'I am so in love with both of them.'

'Why did you choose this moment, Jake?'

'It was the day everything changed.'

'What do you mean?'

'My life was no longer my own. I made a silent promise that I would spend the rest of my life doing whatever it took to take care of them.'

'Okay, Jake, I want you to hold on to that feeling. Can you do that for me? I want you to put your arms around that feeling and hold it close to your heart. Have you done that?'

'Yes.'

'Good. Now close your eyes again. I want you to feel that special memory pressed against your heart, keeping you safe like an airbag. And now I want you to think back to the last time you saw Lucy.'

'I don't want to.'

'I know you might be scared, but I promise you no harm can come to you in this place. You have your wife and daughter's love keeping you safe. Nothing can take that away from you. Tell me where you are when you see Lucy's face.'

'I'm at home.'

'Good. Whereabouts at home?'

'Downstairs.'

'Where is Lucy?'

'She's in the kitchen.'

'Can you see her?'

'No.'

'Why not?'

'The door is closed.'

'But you know she's in there?'

'Yes.'

'Can you hear her moving about?'

'No.'

'How do you know she's inside then?'

'Because I do. I don't want to go in there. I don't want to see her.'

'Why not, Jake?'

'Because something bad happened.'

'Something bad happened to Lucy?'

'Yes.'

'What happened to her, Jake?'

'Can't say.'

'You're perfectly safe, Jake. You can tell me what happened to Lucy. You won't get into trouble. I want you to open that door and look inside.'

'No.'

'Why not?'

'No.'

'Tell me why you can't open that door. Do you know what happened inside?'

'Something bad. I can't go in. I won't go in. I don't want to see.'

'Okay, Jake. Calm down. Focus on your breathing and the sound of my voice again. You don't have to open the door right now. We can look at the door again later. Okay? Close your eyes and return to the darkness.'

'No.'

'Why not?'

My eyes snap open and I am relieved to find myself stretched out in the therapy suite. What happened to me? I feel like I was here and yet I wasn't in control.

'It's okay,' Dr Carpenter says from over my shoulder. 'Just take a few breaths to compose yourself. You're perfectly safe and we're still at the clinic. How do you feel?'

I can't answer because I don't want to fall under her spell again. I sit up instead and swing my legs over the side of the couch, blinking several times to vanquish the fatigue I'm feeling.

'You did very well, Jake. I think we should try this again tomorrow, because there's a chance that the key to unlocking your amnesia is buried deep inside your mind.'

I can picture the kitchen door from home and can feel the intense terror standing outside of it, knowing something bad lay beyond, but I'm unable to articulate exactly what that is. I genuinely can't see beyond the door, but it was more than just fear holding me back. It was like some invisible presence was there, holding the door closed, but I don't know who or what it was.

I hear Lucy's voice from before playing over in my mind again. Is Dr Carpenter right and it was all in my head? If so, what was Lucy trying to tell me?

'How are you feeling now, Jake?'

I ignore Dr Carpenter's question as the tiny voice in the back of my head continues to gnaw at my conscious mind. It's trying to push a thought through, but it's so ridiculous and unbelievable that I can't believe any sane person would even consider it. And yet there it is: Lucy isn't dead.

I want to burst out laughing at the stupidity of it. Of course she's dead. The police wouldn't be investigating her murder otherwise. Max wouldn't lie to me. Geraldine wouldn't lie to me. But then I think back to what Geraldine told me on the phone yesterday: *She'd been saving up a little nest egg so she and Sienna could escape and never look back.*

I know things weren't picture-perfect, but would she really go to the extreme of faking her own death and leaving me to take the fall? Were things really that bad between us?

26

As soon as I finished the session with Dr Carpenter, I demanded access to the phone to call Max. I need someone I can trust to dig into whether Lucy could still be alive. But the call didn't connect. After lunch, I'm relieved when Brenda tells me that he's waiting for me down in Dr Carpenter's office, but the sour look on his face tells me all I need to know about how little progress he's made with finding Lucy's real killer.

'I hear you've been sleepwalking,' is his opening gambit.

I hadn't realised the clinic would be keeping him informed of my situation, and it doesn't sit well with me that Dr Carpenter has so brazenly broken doctor–patient confidentiality. I know she's been sanctioned by the court to assess me, and I guess I always knew everyone involved in the trial would see her report, but I didn't think she'd be providing updates along the way.

'She's still investigating,' I say dismissively. 'But right now, we've got bigger troubles.'

He stares back at me with an air of indifference.

'Go on.'

'I think...' I begin, before becoming conscious of who else

might overhear, and moving closer to him, lowering my voice in the process. 'I think Lucy is still alive.'

He blinks several times, as if not certain if he misheard.

'I heard her voice upstairs,' I continue, suddenly aware of how batshit crazy the statement sounds without context. 'I was going to meet with Dr Carpenter, and I heard Lucy's voice. I *know* it was her. She was saying something about things making sense later, and I definitely heard Dr Carpenter say something back to her, but when I asked her about it, she denied all knowledge and made out like I was hearing things.'

He doesn't respond, just keeps staring at me.

'I'm not making this up, Max. I know it was her voice.'

He places his hands on my upper arms and squeezes gently.

'I believe you, Jake.'

It's not the answer I'm expecting him to give, but the words bring so much relief.

'You do? So, you think she's still alive too?'

He locks his eyes on mine, his arms still holding on to me.

'I believe you believe you heard her voice—'

I break free of his grip and throw my arms around his neck.

'Oh, thank God. I was starting to think I was losing my mind. So, we need to figure out how she did it. There was a body, right? So where did that come from? It was Geraldine who confirmed her identity, so we have to assume she's in on it.'

I snap my fingers together as another thought leaps to the forefront.

'That's why Geraldine won't let me speak to Sienna. Maybe Lucy is with the two of them now, and she's worried Sienna will let slip that Mummy is with her.'

'Jake, stop, I need you to calm down.'

'No, don't you see? This makes so much sense. The reason I

can't remember what happened is because I didn't kill her. Nobody did.'

Another light bulb moment in my head.

'Maybe it was Lucy that knocked me unconscious, before making her escape. She must have hidden out somewhere until the dust settled, and now she's working with Dr Carpenter to keep me here.'

'Jake, wait, please—'

'Geraldine said something about her squirrelling money away, so she won't use her accounts while the police are investigating. But we need to find her, Max. She's the key, don't you see?'

He stands and forces me to meet his gaze.

'Jake, you need to listen to me. I believe you think you heard Lucy's voice, but I know for a fact that she isn't alive any more.'

'No, she is, that's what I'm saying. She's made everyone think she died and that I am responsible. She's probably bribing Dr Carpenter into making me think I'm sleepwalking so that when we get back to the court the judge rules that I killed her in my sleep, and the case is closed.'

'Jake,' he shouts, almost knocking me backwards. 'Lucy is dead! I saw her body.'

Why would he say such a thing? He said he believed me, so why would he now contradict himself? My mind is racing so fast, it's a struggle to follow one thought before it leaps to another.

If Lucy faked her death and Geraldine has been helping her to steal Sienna away from me, would they let Max in on it? Lucy and Max were never that close, but would he be willing to sell me out for the right price? They'd need someone to help smooth things over with the court. And he was the one who first suggested sleepwalking. I've misplaced my trust in him; blinded by the fact he's family.

'Oh my God, you're helping them, aren't you? You're in on it.'

'I'm not in on anything, Jake. You're letting your imagination run away with you.'

'No, I'm not. I knew your knight in shining armour act seemed against character, but I was prepared to overlook my doubt, thinking you had my best interests at heart.'

'We all have your best interests at heart, Jake, but you need to focus on reality. Lucy is dead. You were found with her blood on your pyjamas and your prints on the murder weapon. All the evidence points at the fact that you killed her, and the only person who says you didn't is you.'

I shouldn't have trusted him. After how he stole the business from beneath Dad's feet, I should have known he would only be looking out for himself. I am only in this clinic because he made out it was for the best and to buy him time, but in the four days I've been here, what has he actually done for me? He's spent more time travelling to and from the island than he has looking for alternative suspects.

'I want a new solicitor,' I tell him, stepping away, the pain of his betrayal too much to bear.

'Don't be ridiculous. Another solicitor isn't going to help you at this point. I'm here to help you, Jake, but I can't do that – none of us can – until you start accepting the truth.'

'Don't talk to me about truth. How much are they paying you for your part in this charade?'

'Nobody is paying me anything to be here, Jake. I am here because you are my brother and I love you, and I want to help you find the truth.'

'Oh, really? Okay, so if you're here to help me, tell me what you've uncovered while I've been in here buying you the time you asked me for. Who is on your list of alternative suspects?'

He doesn't answer.

'Okay, let's try another one: why is Geraldine keeping me from talking to Sienna?'

Again, he stares back at me, incredulous.

'All right, how about one that my legal representative should be able to answer if he genuinely has my best interests at heart: what has Geraldine told the police? You must have had access to her statement so you can see the prosecution's case against me.'

'Statements. Plural.'

So, she wasn't bluffing when she said she'd been candid with the detectives.

'What has she told them about me?'

His head drops, defeated.

'She has said there were difficulties in the marriage; you had mood swings; you were having intense night terrors and then taking it out on her.'

'Lies,' I shout, 'things weren't that bad. This is all bullshit to fit their storyline. Geraldine must have got to Lucy, poisoned her against me.'

'She also suggested that Lucy was seeking solace with another man.'

I grind my teeth together at the thought of Lucy sneaking around behind my back. She couldn't; she wouldn't. And yet all I want to do is break down and sob.

My voice cracks as I try to speak.

'Who does she claim this man is?'

He runs a large hand over his chin, and his eyes tighten, as if he's trying to work out how to break the news.

'I'm not sure.'

I don't believe him. I think he knows exactly who and is acting ignorant in an effort to protect my feelings.

'Bullshit! Who is he, Max? Someone I know? Is that why you don't want to tell me?'

'Geraldine didn't give a name in her statement.'

'You're lying. You know who it is, don't you? Let me see the statement.'

'I don't have it with me, otherwise I would.'

'But you can bring me a copy, right? Tomorrow?'

He clenches his jaw, but eventually nods.

'Well, I want to see it. I deserve to know who they claim was coming between us.'

'I will see if I can dig it out, but I don't see how it's going to help. Ultimately, no matter what Lucy may or may not have been planning, she died that night, so it isn't going to help your situation. If anything, it only makes things worse.'

If he's part of the conspiracy, then it is in his best interests to make me think that I'm losing my mind. There is no point in me arguing with him because no matter what I say or ask, he will simply deny it if it doesn't fit this narrative they're painting.

What I need is to find someone I can trust to tell me the truth. I need to get access to Lucy's email account and bank statements. That will show whether Geraldine is just making up this story to throw the spotlight off them, or whether she's covering her tracks. I think Lucy's email was backed up to the cloud, and I think I know what her password is, so if I can get access to a computer, or my phone, then I'll be able to see what she's been up to and how long she's been planning it.

Max crosses over to me and blocks my exit from the room.

'I know you don't want to hear what I have to say, Jake, but you're my little brother, and I want to help you figure all of this out. Have you even allowed yourself to consider whether the amnesia you're clinging to is just your mind's way of trying to protect you from seeing what you did?'

I try to push past him, but he grabs my arms again, pushing me back against the wall and pinning me there.

'What if it was late and you and Lucy were arguing about your inability to find a new job, or about money, or your refusal to seek help for your PTSD? The argument becomes heated. Maybe Lucy slaps you or throws something against the wall. You're both angry and accusations fly. You're struggling to control your anger, and your hand instinctively reaches out for the nearest object it can find and suddenly there's a knife sticking out of Lucy and her blood is on your hands. You panic. You didn't mean to kill her; it was an accident. But you don't think the police will see it that way, so you bash your head against the floor so there will be evidence of a bump, and then you wait for the police to turn up. You're suffering a concussion, so of course they'll believe your claims that some mystery man struck you. Throw in a bout of amnesia which can't be proved one way or another and suddenly you're in the clear.'

'That isn't what happened,' I shout back, as the blood rushes to my ears.

'But you don't know that for sure. Until you can break through the amnesia, you can't say definitively what did or did not happen.' He prods two fingers against my temple. 'The truth is in your head somewhere, and the sooner you open yourself to the prospect that you could have killed her – accidentally, or not – the sooner we'll be able to establish the truth.'

I count to five in my head before speaking again.

'If you're so sure Lucy is dead, how did I hear her voice this morning?'

He throws his hands into the air in frustration.

'I've no idea! Maybe you just heard someone that sounded like Lucy. Or maybe it was a memory playing out that you thought you heard. Was anyone with you and heard it as well?'

I shake my head.

'They don't just rely on a family member to identify the body.

They will have seen her photographs in your house, they will have checked for fingerprints and DNA. They will have been 100 per cent sure they had identified the right person before inviting Geraldine to confirm. And I saw her body too. Have you any idea how ludicrous your claim sounds?'

I don't want to hear any more of his lies. He's trying to make me think I'm losing my mind, but I know what I heard, and I know the answers are out there. I just need to find someone who can help me uncover the truth. I push past Max and race out of the door.

27

THREE DAYS BEFORE THE MURDER

Jake isn't sure what wakes him at first, but as he turns over in bed, he finds Lucy's side empty, and when he presses his hand over the sheet, it's much cooler than he is expecting. Checking his phone, it's almost three in the morning, and he can only assume she is on the toilet, but after five minutes she still hasn't returned, so he gets up and heads to the bathroom himself. Finding it empty, he pokes his head in through Sienna's door. There's no sign of Lucy inside the room, but he heads in, adjusting his daughter's duvet, so that she doesn't get too cold, and gently running his hand against her cheek.

'I'm sorry for all of this,' he whispers. 'I will try to be a better dad.'

She stirs slightly, and he creeps backwards out of the room, closing the door fully, before returning to his room, but there is still no sign of Lucy. He can't hear any movement downstairs but can't think of any other logical place she could be. He doubts she is still awake working at this late hour but wouldn't put it past her.

He wonders whether she has decided to sleep downstairs because his snoring has disturbed her. It's also possible that he screamed during his sleep again. She's dropped more than a few hints at her frustration with his nightmares impacting her sleep cycles as much as his. They haven't discussed what is causing him such unrestful sleep, because he's afraid she'll judge him for what happened.

It isn't right that she should be the one to give up their bed because of him, and so he makes the decision to swap places with her. If he can carry her back upstairs, she can still get a few hours' sleep before the alarm sounds for her pre-work run. Shoving his pillows under his arm, he also collects his dressing gown from the peg behind the door and steps out onto the landing.

Switching on his phone's light, he creeps down the stairs, conscious of making too much noise and waking Sienna. There's no sign of Lucy working in the kitchen, so he continues along the hallway and into the living room. It is pitch black, and as he shines his torch around, he doesn't find her stretched out on either sofa. He checks the time again, curious as to whether she could have gone somewhere but unable to think of where that would be.

And then he hears a noise, and his eyes dart to the closed door of Lucy's office. He's sure he heard her voice, but who could she be talking to this late? He drops his pillows and dressing gown on the edge of the sofa and moves closer to the door, straining to hear anything further. There is a line of light reflecting off the carpet beneath the door, and a shadow moving about inside.

He tiptoes closer, but as he nears, the floorboard beneath his feet creaks, and a moment later the door to the office flies open. Lucy starts when she sees him, and confusion cloaks her face. Nobody else emerges from the room, and as he looks down at her hands, he can see she is clutching her mobile between them.

'Who were you talking to?' he asks.

She looks down at the phone, almost as surprised to see it there as he is.

'Oh, um, Mum,' she answers, almost too quickly. 'You were already asleep when I came to bed, so I climbed in next to you, but must have forgotten to put my phone on silent. It started ringing, and I saw it was Mum, and – you know what she's like – I thought I should answer it. I came down here so I wouldn't wake you.'

Jake knows all too well that since Lucy's mum moved into the nursing home, her failing memory means she can often phone at the oddest hours. She's been in the care home for over two years since her dementia became too much, and meant she wasn't able to take proper care of herself. Her body is still more than able, but her brain doesn't fire as once it did. The nurses at the home are pretty good at limiting her calls during the night, but Lucy tends to leave her phone on silent and then call her back in the morning. Nine times out of ten, Lucy's mum has no memory of ever placing the call.

Lucy finally looks up and meets his stare. 'What are you doing up?'

He studies her face for any sign that what she's just told him isn't a fabrication, but it's too dark to tell whether she's being honest. Instinct tells him she isn't.

'I was thirsty, and came down to get a drink, but I heard voices. How is your mum? What did she want this time?'

Her brow furrows with thick lines, until she sees the phone in her hand and seems to recall why he's asking.

'Oh, you know, nothing important. She was asking after Dad again, and I had to remind her that he died years ago. The nurse took the phone off her in the end.'

She steps forward and kisses his cheek.

'I'm going to head back up and try to get a few hours before work. Good night.'

He watches her leave but doesn't follow after. Instead, he sits down on the sofa, and replays the conversation through his mind. This isn't the first time they've both been woken by a phone call from Lucy's mum, but this time, something was different about her behaviour. She seemed guilty when he caught her emerging from the office, but she shouldn't feel guilty about speaking to her mum.

His eyes dart back to the office door, and something tells him he'll find the answers he's looking for inside.

28

The orderly escorts me back to The Butterfly Room, and I immediately approach Brenda, who is heading into the small administration office.

'I need to make a phone call,' I tell her.

'I'm sorry, Jake, but they'll be preparing to dish up supper soon. Maybe afterwards, eh?'

'I need to find a new solicitor. You need to let me use this phone now, or unlock my mobile from reception.'

A table tennis match is taking place over in the corner. The bounce of the ball reminds me of the Newton's cradle that my dad used to keep in his office. I would sneak in whenever he wasn't around and set the balls cascading into one another with perfect pace, until he would shoo me away. But the sound now grates against every nerve in my aching head, to the point where I stand and move to a table further away, but still the tapping sound continues.

'I'm sorry, but it will have to wait. I need to start preparing for my rounds.'

'Well, what if I want to speak to my daughter? Dr Carpenter promised me I'd be able to access this phone whenever I needed.'

'I can't comment on what Dr Carpenter may or may not have told you, Jake, but I'm telling you now, you'll have to wait until later.'

I hear Sully's voice in my head: *If you want to believe that they're going to let you make as many phone calls as you like, then who am I to dampen that hope?*

No, it's just a coincidence. Brenda has explained why I can't use the phone, and she hasn't said I can't use it later. I will just have to bide my time and remind her when she's finished her rounds.

'Oh, hey, I was wondering where you'd got to,' Katy calls from behind me, and when I turn to look, I see her sitting at one of the tables.

She pushes out a chair with her foot, and wanting to keep an eye on the administration office, I drop into it.

'This place is amazing, don't you think?' she says with more openness and positivity than she's shown in any of our previous encounters.

'Is it?'

'Yeah, I don't know what they put in the water, but man, I had the best night's sleep last night. Was asleep almost as soon as my head hit the pillow and got an undisturbed nine hours clean through. I can't tell you that I've ever slept so well.'

I nod in acknowledgement, but I'm not feeling the same level of enthusiasm.

Katy pulls her shiny dark hair back into a ponytail and fastens a band from her wrist to hold it in place.

'How are you getting on with your sleep difficulties?'

I don't know how she's expecting me to answer the question. I certainly don't feel any more convinced about whether or not sleepwalking has been a condition I've suffered with and nobody has ever noticed. And all these time lapses have to be a sign of something, but I still don't know why they're happening, nor what my body is doing when they occur. Is it a case that I'm blacking out and my subconscious is moving me from one place to another, or is it that my memory just isn't recording those particular periods? Either way, I don't know why it's happening. And more troubling is whether something similar happened the night Lucy died.

'Talking to Dr Carpenter has been so useful,' Katy continues when I don't respond. 'I mean, I was sceptical before coming here – you know, there's a stigma with counselling and mental health conditions – but I now wish I'd sought help so much sooner. She's so easy to talk to, don't you think?'

I think back to Dr Carpenter's reaction when I accused her of talking to my dead wife. She looked uncomfortable and anxious, but I can't tell if that's because she was worried about my state of mind, or because I caught her in a lie.

I shrug, in no mood to simulate conversation when I'd rather be left alone with my thoughts.

'I was reluctant the first day we met, but by the end of the session she had me feeling so relaxed that I was ready to tell her my deepest, darkest secrets. And by the end of yesterday's session, it felt like I was chatting to my oldest friend. I know I'm not allowed to reveal mission specifics with her because she's a civilian, but just talking about the emotions I've felt as a result of those actions has been so cleansing for my soul. I'm certain that's what allowed me to sleep. By confronting my trauma head-on, my subconscious can see it's not nearly as scary as it thought, and rest is my reward.'

It sounds like she's been brainwashed by one of those pamphlets in Dr Carpenter's office. If Mr Coyle is looking for a poster girl to advertise the clinic's benefits, he's surely found her.

'I'm pleased for you,' I say dismissively, hoping that will be the end of the conversation and she'll go and find someone else to share her news with.

'Have you opened up to her much?' she asks, eyeing me carefully. 'About your time overseas, I mean.'

What was it Dr Carpenter said when I arrived, about patients not having to share personal details with other patients if not comfortable to do so? Maybe it's because Katy sees me as a comrade of some sort because of our military backgrounds.

'Not really, no.'

'I understand it seeming scary to do – worried you might let something slip – but I don't get the impression that Dr Carpenter would go blabbing to anyone. Her goal is to cure whatever is causing our respective conditions, and it's also in our best interests.'

I look straight at her, not wishing to come across as rude, but keen to disrupt the interrogation. 'With all due respect, I don't feel comfortable talking about my history with you. It's nothing personal, but I don't know you from Adam, and—'

She raises her palms in a passive gesture. 'Hey, listen, I understand, and I'm sorry if I was being intrusive. I'm like a kid with a new toy, wanting to tell everyone about how cool it is, but I understand if you're not benefiting from the treatment yet. I'm sorry.'

Great. Now I feel guilty.

Lucy always used to be able to flip our disagreements in a similar way, making me turn from the wronged party into the apologist.

'Don't get me wrong,' I say with a weak smile, 'I'm pleased you're making progress, I'm just not there yet.'

She nods, and her eyes wander around the room, before

returning to the table. An awkward silence forms, and I'm hoping she either gets up and leaves me alone, or I'm going to have to go and find somewhere else to sit.

Her lips part as if she's going to say something else, but then she reconsiders and closes them again.

'Can I ask you one more question – and then I swear I'll shut up and leave you alone.'

I nod reluctantly.

'I'm assuming you were offered counselling for PTSD after each tour, right? I'm pretty sure it's standard practice for it to be offered to all serving personnel.'

I nod again, biting at the chipped nail on my right thumb.

'I always refused the counselling,' she says, wrinkling her nose in what I assume is shame. 'I think it's difficult for soldiers to admit when they're struggling. It goes back to that stigma thing with mental health conditions. You know? Like, we're trained to protect our country, and how can we do that if we have perceived flaws in our psyches? And yet ironically, the people who would probably benefit most from opening up and combatting their feelings are those exact same military personnel. Maybe it's unfair for me to paint all of us in that way. What I can say is that I always refused the counselling because I didn't want my team to think I was strug-gling; they need to be able to rely on me and I thought by ignoring my feelings that I'd maintain their faith in me, when actually all I was doing was slowly chipping away at that earned trust.

'On my last tour, I was involved in a dog fight with two enemy jets. I was over their air space and they engaged me. I was on my own, and it hit me like a ton of bricks when I realised it simply came down to them or me. I was paralysed with fear. I've never been so scared my entire life. I figured out of sight, out of mind. But I'd wake in the middle of the night suffering panic attacks, or just unable to switch off my brain. And it would be going over such mundane thoughts, so I didn't link it back to what happened in the Panther, but clearly that incident hit me harder than I realised.'

She shivers like a ghost has just crossed her grave, but all I can think about is that moment when I was watching my team being executed and dumped in that pit, and how terrified I was that I'd never see Sienna or Lucy again.

'You ever suffer anything like that?'

I want to tell her that yes, I know exactly how she feels, but I can't tell anyone about what happened. The only other person who knows what really happened in that desert is Tariq, and he's already made his feelings perfectly clear on the matter.

I carried him for what must have been three miles to the nearest checkpoint and when we got there, he made it clear he would never utter a word about what he'd witnessed. I tried to justify it in my head that I'd only done what the kid was planning to do to us, but I saw that fear in his eyes. He begged me for his life, and I swatted him like a fly. And rather than facing the punishment I deserved, they gave me a fucking medal.

'I swear you can talk to me if you need to,' Katy continues, sitting forward, her fingers splayed on the tabletop. 'We can go and find an empty room, so we're not overheard, and I promise you'll receive no judgement.'

What she doesn't understand is that what happened to me in the desert has nothing to do with why I am here. Sharing the truth about my war crime will not provide me with the obvious relief her own confession has brought.

I freeze: why is Katy so keen to know about my history?

I can't help but feel the hand of Dr Carpenter and her slimy boss Mr Coyle at work here. Have they put Katy up to this? Do they think that I'll be more likely to confess what I did to a sister in arms?

'We can go now. We could head up to one of those airy therapy suites if you want? Or your room? You can unburden yourself and I will just sit and listen. I want to help you, Jake.'

I don't appreciate how pushy she's being.

'No, thank you.'

An image of the kitchen door flashes into my mind's eye again, and I feel the same angst I felt when I was kneeling down beside that pit. There is something so bad behind that door.

'Let's go now, Jake, and you can tell me every—'

'No!' I scream, slamming my hand down on the table, and standing. 'Just leave me the fuck alone.'

I storm off, my palm stinging with the impact.

29

TWO DAYS BEFORE THE MURDER

Jake waits until Lucy has left and he's dropped Sienna at school before daring to venture into Lucy's office. He's spent most of the morning going back and forth in his mind as to whether it is right for him to go snooping through her stuff. A marriage should be built on trust, and aside from the 3 a.m. call this morning, she hasn't given him any reason to be suspicious. But then again, why was she acting so shiftily when he caught her in the office? And every time he tells himself that snooping is calling their marriage vows into question, another voice will pipe up and challenge why she's been away working so late every night, and why she's shown him no affection since his return. In the past, when he returned from overseas they'd struggle to keep their hands off one another, but he's barely spoken to her, let alone been intimate.

Something feels so off, and he is now justifying his action as searching for something that will prove he's wrong to be suspicious. But in truth, he doesn't know what he's looking for, because he doesn't know what he suspects her of. An affair? He doesn't want to acknowledge the possibility that Lucy could betray him in that way. But he also doesn't know what else she could be planning. It's his birthday in a couple of months, and it's possible that she's trying to organise something for that, and he knows he'll feel perpetually guilty if he spoils the surprise.

He knows the only way to calm the arguing voices in his head is to go into the office and see if he can find any clues.

He walks into her office and surveys the mess. Her desk is covered with various piles of paper and folders, with no obvious means of knowing what they relate to. Given her profession, he's assuming they relate to cases she's working on, and he knows he will be breaching more than her confidence if he reads any of it, so he ignores them initially. He slides out her chair and drops into it, pulling on the handle of the drawer directly beneath the desk, surprised to find it locked. He doesn't remember Lucy locking it before, and no matter how hard he tugs and jiggles it, there is no give. The drawer is only a couple of inches deep so he's not sure what she could be hiding inside. She always used to use it for storing odd pens and spare paper for the printer. He can't think of any reason she would feel compelled to lock away stationery, and it only heightens his suspicion. He wants to know what is inside. He jiggles it again, dropping to his knees and staring at the thin gap between the drawer and the desk, wondering if there's any way he could use something hard like a ruler or credit card to force the locking mechanism down. He wasn't even aware the drawer had a lock, so he has no clue where the key would be. There's every chance she has it with her, but he decides to search for it in case she keeps it hidden somewhere in the office.

He crosses to the large bookcase on the opposite side of the room. The tomes of law books are covered in dust, but she has nicknacks like picture frames standing in front of some of them. He lifts the lid of a ceramic pot, but it is empty. He lifts the wooden flowers out of the small plastic vase, but there is only dust in the bottom. There is nothing beneath the large scented candle, or in the small jewellery box Sienna made for her last Christmas. He drops back into the office chair and swivels it, allowing his eyes to take in the whole room. His gaze eventually falls on the large metal tin, standing precariously on top of the bookcase, but when he opens it he finds Lucy and Sienna's passports and a bag of euros left over from their last holiday. He's not sure why they aren't in the fireproof safe beneath their bed, but then his is still in the bag of his army gear he hasn't unpacked since returning four weeks ago. He assumes Lucy must have forgotten to put them away or has decided to store them down here and he's forgotten.

He returns the tin, and attempts to force the drawer open for a third time without success. He's about to give up when his eyes fall on the clothes peg on the back of the office door. He hadn't noticed it before, but there is a small keyring hanging from it, and when he slips the key inside the lock it's a perfect fit.

Jake slides the drawer open, and stops as his eyes fall on a mobile phone and charger inside. He knows instantly it isn't Lucy's phone, and it isn't boxed so he's pretty sure this isn't a gift that she's keeping for his birthday. The knot of tension in his gut tightens. He picks up the phone and switches it on, frustrated when it asks for a PIN. He tries Lucy's date of birth and then Sienna's but neither work. He's about to try the date of their wedding anniversary, but is worried the phone will lock him out if he gets it wrong again, and then Lucy will know he's been snooping.

It could be a work phone, the logical part of his brain tells him, but he doesn't know why she wouldn't have taken it to work, and why she would have it switched off and locked away in her office. It definitely isn't the phone she was holding when he caught her this morning, but he can't be sure she didn't lock this one away when she heard the floorboard creak.

He returns the phone to the drawer and locks it back up,

hanging the key back on the peg. He entered the office searching for something to allay his suspicions, but all it's done is heightened them.

30

I'm still fuming as I stalk back to my room and am relieved that I don't hear Katy hurrying after me. Just because we've both been in combat, it doesn't dictate that we have shared experiences. I still think Dr Carpenter is somehow involved in that little tête-a-tête Katy has just instigated. Katy isn't a medical professional, so why would she think I'd be willing to go with her and talk about my experiences?

I start as I open my door and find Dr Carpenter sitting in the armchair beside the window. Was this Katy's plan: get me back to my room ready to open up and then Dr Carpenter would step in? Seems too coincidental for her to be here otherwise. I'm almost expecting to hear Katy approaching, but the corridor behind me remains empty.

'Hi, Jake, I hope you don't mind me waiting here, but I wanted to check how you were feeling after our session? You were very quiet when you left the therapy suite, and I was worried that you might—'

'That I might figure out what you're up to?' I snap.

Her brow furrows instantly.

'I'm sorry, I don't follow...'

I step into the room and close the door behind me. 'I am not suffering with PTSD. Okay? The sooner you and your cronies get that into your heads, the sooner we can actually figure out why this is happening to me.'

She sinks back into the chair, her confusion fading into concern.

'Nobody mentioned PTSD, Jake, although it's a common condition for returning soldiers to suffer with.'

'That's as maybe, but the *only* thing I'm traumatised by is the fact that someone murdered my wife and I have no idea who! I know what you're up to; you and your minion, Katy.'

I'm not going to tell her that I now believe Lucy to be alive and that Geraldine, Max, and Lucy are working together to make me take the fall. If Dr Carpenter is also conspiring with them, I don't want to give her reason to make my time here worse.

'I don't understand, Jake.'

'Stop lying to me! Katy Savage was just quizzing me about my time overseas. Kept banging on about the PTSD she's suffering with, and how talking to you has magicked it all away and now she's sleeping every night like a baby. Do you really think I'm that easy to con?'

Dr Carpenter considers her response.

'I didn't put Katy up to anything. I'm thrilled to hear that she feels she's benefiting from the work we're doing, but I assure you I didn't ask her to speak to you about it. A person's history outside of the clinic is for them only. I haven't discussed you with any other patients, and that's why I won't discuss Katy's history, or our work. I would be in breach of my patient–doctor confidentiality oath.'

She's good, but I'm not convinced.

'Is someone paying you to do this? The military police,

maybe? Or is it Detective Fahey pressuring you to make me confess to something I didn't do?'

She holds her hands up, palms outstretched as if she's holding up an invisible shield.

'I have no interest in your military history, save for whether it's causing shifts in your sleeping pattern. I'm not working for anyone. My sole purpose here is to try to help you, Jake. Do you believe me?'

I ignore the question, because I don't want to see her disappointment when I tell her I can't trust her.

She lifts her right hand into the air as if swearing an oath.

'I am not working for the army or police, Jake. Cross my heart and hope to die. I am here solely to help you.'

I can see sincerity in her eyes and desperately want to believe her, but I don't know how I can. I can see now that something has felt so off about this place since I arrived. I tried to ignore the paranoia for as long as possible, but I can't cope with it any longer.

'I want all of this to just be over,' I say.

'I don't doubt the stress and trauma you're suffering right now. That may be part of the reason you've been sleepwalking here since you arrived. The blackouts you've been experiencing: I had our team look at the data collected by your pyjamas during the day, and it suggests you may have been sleepwalking at those times.'

The statement stops me. At no point has anyone told me they've seen me sleepwalking around this place. And if she's telling the truth, then it's possible I could have been experiencing bouts of sleepwalking and nobody realised or thought to tell me.

'That was another reason for me being here in your room, Jake. I have some of the results of the tests we've been running.' She pulls out sheets of paper from behind her back and offers them towards me. 'Here, please, take a look for yourself.'

I snatch the papers from her and hold them beneath the overhead light. The first page looks like some kind of printout. There are numbers in non-bordered cells in a table, but I don't recognise any of the acronyms, and there's no kind of code to explain whether the numbers are high, low, or normal. I flip to the next sheet; this time there are three charts with coloured lines, but again it isn't obvious what I'm looking at.

I pass them back to her in frustration.

'I don't know what any of this shit means.'

'Well, once you're feeling calmer, I'm happy to talk you through it all. But essentially, the charts show elevated levels of melatonin, which promotes healthy rest, and low levels of cortisol, which spikes when someone wakes. Given your heartbeat and blood pressure remain normal during the movements we've observed through the corridor cameras, I am certain that you have sleepwalked several times since your arrival. I cannot say conclusively that you did on the night of your wife's murder, but you are clearly prone to the condition, so it is not unreasonable to suspect it is possible.'

I fall to my knees, the weight of the news too heavy to bear. 'You're saying... that you think I killed Lucy?'

She slowly slides from the chair to make eye contact with me.

'No, that is *not* what I am saying. That isn't my place, and the truth is, without hard evidence, we probably will never be able to say for sure. That is, unless we're able to once and for all break through that door shutting out your memories. Medically speaking, there is no reason for your amnesia, other than it's your brain's way of trying to keep you safe in some way.'

'You're saying *I'm* causing the amnesia.'

'Not exactly. Sometimes the mind can dissociate things in order to be able to function and process. What I'm suggesting is that whatever happened to you that night was so alarming that your brain is forcing you to forget.'

I feel so tired. My brain physically aches from trying to figure out what is happening to me. It's a nightmare...

I freeze.

'Am I dreaming? Is that what this is? You, the clinic, Lucy's murder? Am I asleep right now?'

'Look at me, Jake. Give me your hands and place them on my cheeks. You tell me: am I real, or is this all just a figment of an overactive imagination?'

I don't move at first, but she takes my hands in hers and moves them to her face. Her cheeks are cold and soft, and for the briefest moment I remember holding Lucy's face in the same way on the day we got married.

My eyes open and I snap back to the room, and lower my hands from Dr Carpenter's face.

'You are not asleep right now, Jake.'

I allow my eyes to wander around the room. How would I know if I was asleep? I grab a handful of skin from my forearm and dig my nails in hard, until the pain is too much. I'm still in the room with Dr Carpenter. I take a step back and march into the bathroom, running the tap and splashing cold water on my face, but I'm still in the room.

If this isn't a dream, then could I still be under hypnosis? She put me in a trance-like state, but what if everything since then is all part of it?

I exit the bathroom and stop in front of her.

'Am I still under hypnosis?'

The look of confusion that now crosses her face is a relief; she doesn't look like she's been caught out.

'No, Jake, you were never under hypnosis. What we did earlier was a guided trance, but it isn't like those cheesy shows where thoughts are implanted to make unsuspecting victims cluck like chickens. I think what you're experiencing right now is a culmination of lots of things that are triggering your fight or flight response. You're breathing erratically and this is causing the adrenaline in your system to make you overreact to stimuli. In fact, I think you should sit down and just focus on your breathing.'

She forces me into a chair, and I've never felt so out of control. It feels so much like a nightmare, but I think that's because there are still too many unanswered questions. I don't know who I can trust, and I need to keep in mind that Dr Carpenter may be in cahoots with the others, so I shouldn't be listening to her.

And yet I need to regain my composure. I need to figure out a plan to get out of this place and back to the mainland. It's time I took back control of my life.

'I want to help you, Jake. I believe the answers you're seeking are buried deep in your subconscious, and if you let me help you, I think we can dig them up. I only want what's best for you, and I don't know what I can say to convince you of that. But, if you let me try, and we do manage to unlock whatever traumatised you that night, then maybe we will finally be able to get to the bottom of all this. What do you say? Will you let me try?'

If she's right, and I can finally access the repressed memories of that night, then I'll be able to see exactly what happened to Lucy, and maybe figure out why she set me up in this way. The only question is whether I can trust Dr Carpenter.

31

A blinding flash of light forces me to bury my face behind my forearm, and when I pull it away, the intense heat and arid air tells me exactly where I am. Instead of lying in my bed with Dr Carpenter talking to me, I am surrounded by sand. I can taste tiny grains between my teeth and try to spit them out, but my mouth is dry of all fluid.

Gunfire to my left is followed by the sound of dead weight collapsing into the manmade grave only yards away from me. I struggle with the coarse rope around my wrists and feel the pressure of the gun's barrel against the back of my head.

I know exactly where I am because I have been here before.

Remember, I'm right here with you, Jake. You are in control. Tell me what you can see.

I hear two of my men yell out as they are dragged over to the hole that's been dug, their camouflage jackets torn from their bodies. I need to help them, but I'm in no position. I try to push myself up but feel the pressure of the barrel against the back of my head. One of my men kicks out at one of the resistance fighters but then takes the full swipe of the gun's butt into his cheek and drops without any further fuss. Before I can yell out to him, the front of his face disappears in an explosion of blood and bone, and both of them tumble into the hole.

To my right, Tariq cries out as two pairs of hands pick him up off the ground. The moment I feel bony fingers on my arms, I hurl sand into their faces, grab the falling gun and open fire.

Four of them drop as they did before, but something feels different this time. I can't place why, but it feels more real than the last time I relived this experience.

You are in control of everything, Jake. Focus on your breathing. Stay calm.

It's like I'm no longer in control of my own movements and actions. The sound is muffled, as if playing out to me in slow motion. Bullets whizz by my face in retaliatory fire, and I spin and roll towards the upturned Foxhound, already pre-seeing what's to happen next. I'll remain where I am for several seconds before rolling and heading around the back of the vehicle to execute my enemy. And as soon as I hear Tariq calling out to me, I already know I will check on him and witness the kid trying to arm himself in a vain attempt at life preservation.

And then I have the kid on his back once again, staring up at me, eyes pleading for mercy. Without even considering the conse-quences, I raise the gun's sight to my eye line and take aim at his head, but my finger hesitates on the trigger as he whimpers at my feet.

What can you see, Jake? Are you at the kitchen door again? Are you ready to push it open?

Wait, why is Dr Carpenter talking about a kitchen door? Doesn't she realise where I am?

I continue to stare down at the kid, my own vision blurring as tears sting the edges of my sockets.

'P-please,' he stammers.

Saving Tariq has to be my priority, and under the terms of the treaty, I either need to bring this kid with me or let him go. If I bring him with us, we'll be slowed further. But if I let him go, then there's a strong chance he will notify his comrades of our position and what I've done, and they'll track us down. But I can't kill this kid in cold blood.

I lower the weapon slowly, a decision I instantly regret as the kid copies my earlier move and throws a handful of sand towards my face. I try to duck, but grains scratch at my eyes, and I drop the gun as I claw at my temple, trying to clean the brittle dust away.

Wait, this isn't how I remembered it before. I shot him, didn't I? Is this just my imagination plugging a hole in my memory, or am I seeing things clearly for the first time?

The ground bites up as bullets ricochet against the sand, and with no idea what's around me, I throw myself to where I hope the Foxhound will provide some shelter. It stings as I try to part my eyelids, but I need water to clear the grit scratching at my pupils. The echo of bullets thudding against the other side of the Foxhound has me instantly ducking my shoulders as I scrabble towards the rear of the vehicle where I remember recovering a water bottle. Fumbling around, I search for the small, hardened plastic canteen, until my fingertips brush against it. Pulling it free of its harness, I grope at the lid, struggling to unscrew it between my sweaty fingers. But then the lid is off, and I lean my head back and pour the water over my face. It takes all my strength to force my eyes apart as the lukewarm water splashes over them. I blink and will my sight to return, and as the fog clears, I see the shadow of the kid moving before me.

I attempt to duck for cover, but the gun rattles as his trembling hands raise it to his face, and he points it at my chest. I'm already too late.

Push open the door, Jake. Nothing inside can harm you. I am here to keep you safe.

'You don't have to do this,' I tell the kid, my throat hoarse. 'Let us go, and you will never see us again.'

I have no clue if he understands English, but his lack of response suggests he doesn't, and I have no idea how to beg for my life in Pashtu. Asking for directions and basic greetings and acknowledgements is all I've picked up.

'Please,' I try again, taking his lack of action as a sign that he might show me the same mercy I've shown him. 'I have a wife and daughter I love very much. I just want to go home and be with them.'

I can see Tariq trying to twist himself around on the sand just beyond the kid, but the nearest discarded weapon is too far for him to crawl to, undetected. If the kid decides to fire, the last thing I'll see is Tariq watching on helplessly.

'I have money I can give you,' I say, without thinking about the consequences of reaching for the small purse clipped to my belt.

He shouts something unintelligible, and I suddenly realise he must be thinking I'm reaching for a hidden weapon. I clamp my eyes shut as I wait for the crack of the rifle and the bullet to pierce my skin.

But all I hear is a click as the gun jams. I don't wait, leaping to my feet and charging my shoulder towards him, sending him crashing to the baking sand beneath us. He holds the rifle across him as a shield, and I grab hold of it too. We struggle and roll across the sand as I try to prise it from his fingers and gain leverage. If he gets free and can fix the jam, I'll be dead. I need to disarm him at all costs.

The overpowering sun glints from the silver blade now in his hand. He's standing a few feet away from me, the knife pointing in my direction. I was willing to let him go, but he seems intent on killing me. There's no way he'll come quietly.

'You want a piece of me?' I yell, unzipping and pulling off my camouflage jacket.

I wrap one sleeve around my right hand and do the same with the left, making a tight rod that may just about help me to butt his knife arm away.

'Come on then,' I yell again. 'If you think you're brave enough, kill me. Come on, what are you scared of?'

He stands, legs astride, his arm ready to strike, and yet I sense the uncertainty in him. Wanting to kill someone and actually following through are distinct, separate actions and doing one doesn't dictate doing both. A wet patch forms in the crotch of his loose-fitting trousers.

I lunge forwards to test his reaction and he takes an unsteady step backwards. The sun glinting off the blade is blinding me as his hand trembles in anticipation.

It comes down to this: him or me.

Pulling the jacket taut between my hands, I yell, and charge forwards, anticipating the upwards swipe of the blade and coiling the jacket around his wrist in one fell swoop. I turn my back towards him and use my momentum and shoulder to knock him off balance. He still has hold of the knife, but as I twist the jacket noose tighter, he soon lets go.

I don't wait to snatch it up off the floor and plunge it into his side.

'S-stop,' he yells out, the fight going from him, but I'm not falling for that trick again.

I thrust the blade forward again, and again, slicing through his flesh like a hot knife through butter. He drops to the sand, the blood drying instantly as it blots against the grainy ground. I turn him over to check for signs of life, but I already know he's dead.

I could have restrained him, and forced him to help me carry Tariq, but I know deep down that I wanted to see him suffer as a consequence of what his comrades did to my men.

A sudden brilliant white flash overhead has me scrambling to protect my eyes with my forearm again, but this time when I lower it, I'm no longer in the desert. Instead, I see Dr Carpenter shining the torch from her phone into my face, and I have to swat her hand away.

'Wake up, Jake,' I hear her yell, so loud that I have to protect my ears.

'I am awake,' I shout back at her, but as I train my gaze on hers, I realise why there is such heightened alarm in her voice.

I am no longer in bed, instead, standing in the doorway of the bathroom, brandishing a toilet brush. But it's the scene before me that makes no sense. The mattress is no longer inside the frame of the bed, the two armchairs are upturned, and the bed sheet hangs from a crack in the bedroom window.

What the hell happened here?

It's as if a bomb was detonated or two prize fighters have gone at it.

Wait, did I do this?

Dr Carpenter is still gripping her phone tightly, though the torch light is no longer pointed at me. She is sweating, her cheeks flushed, and panting tremendously as if in fear for her life.

'I'm sorry,' I mumble as I survey the damage.

But I don't wait for her to acknowledge the apology, instead dropping the brush and racing from the room.

32

I run as fast as I can, down one corridor and then along another. This place is a labyrinth and no matter how many times I turn onto a new corridor, I always end up passing The Butterfly Room. I need to get out of here, because my mind is racing, and I cannot control the barrage of thoughts and illogical conclusions it's jumping to.

There's no way Dr Carpenter could have trashed my bedroom like that single-handed. The only conclusion I can draw is that she's telling the truth and it was me who caused all that destruction. And if I'm capable of all that damage when I'm asleep, then what else am I capable of?

I want to be outside in the fresh air, but I can't use the lifts without a security pass, which means I need to find Brenda or ask for Dr Carpenter's help; and given how pale-faced the latter looked when I left her, I'm not sure she'll be letting me go anywhere near her again.

Being back in the desert felt so real. From the humidity to the unbearable heat and the dryness of the air. That was more than just a dream. Dr Carpenter said she would be taking me back to the night Lucy died and helping me break through the black hole in my amnesia, so how the hell did I end up in that desert scene? Unless she lied to me and that was where she intended for me to visit.

Katy was pushing me to explore my time overseas, and although Dr Carpenter claimed she hadn't put Katy up to it, it's possible she was lying. Maybe that's what all this has been about. They want me to admit what I did to that kid, in order to convince the jury that I was also capable of murdering Lucy.

Closing my eyes, I try to think of anywhere that isn't this clinic. I picture the morning I last took Sienna to school. I remember it was raining, and she was excited because I agreed that she could jump in all the puddles if she had her wellies on. She was wearing the yellow waterproof jacket my mum bought her for her birthday – what kind of five-year-old would want a coat as a birthday present? And I had a golf umbrella that Geraldine and Ray had given me the previous Christmas, in another attempt to get me to the driving range. The air was so cold that morning, a sign that winter was getting ready to strike. I'd planned to stop for a take-away coffee on the way, but we were running late so I'd had to forego it, promising myself a latte for the way home instead.

I slowly open my eyes, half-expecting to see my daughter beside my legs, and my heart sinks when I see I'm still in the same corridor.

I spot the male symbol on a door to my right, and I push through it. I barely make it into the cubicle before I throw up. I tear toilet paper from the roll and wipe my chin, before stumbling to the basin and staring at the blood-drained reflection in the mirror.

Dr Carpenter said she would take me back to the night Lucy died, but what if that's what she did do, and on that night, I was having a nightmare about what happened to us in the desert? What if I was also acting out that dream that night? What if my shouting and aggressive behaviour woke Lucy and she found me downstairs and tried to wake me? And rather than succeeding, my subconscious mistook her for that kid and when I believed I was stabbing him, I was in fact... I was in fact stabbing Lucy.

I clamp my eyes shut as tears fill them, and I don't want to see the look of realisation and acceptance in the mirror. It would explain why I have no memory of killing Lucy, would explain why her blood was found on my pyjamas and why my prints were on the murder weapon.

Surely if someone else was involved, Fahey and his team would have found them by now. And Max would have found someone – anyone – who could be involved. But they haven't – no other names have been mentioned. There was no sign of a break-in. No intruder footprints or fingerprints were found at the scene. And why would there be if I killed her?

It doesn't explain how I sustained a head injury, but maybe I woke and realised what I'd done and in a blind panic, I knocked myself out. I've always been good at compartmentalising – God knows how many times I've said that to Dr Carpenter – and what if that is precisely what my mind has done here? It created the amnesia so I wouldn't have to deal with my actions.

I never meant Lucy any harm, but will Sienna see it like that? Will she secretly suspect that deep down there was something that drove me to kill her mother? If Geraldine can, she'll spend the rest of her life pouring poison into Sienna's ear to the point where she turns her back on me.

I need to speak to Sienna. I need to tell her how sorry I am, and that I never meant for any of this to happen. I am ready to come clean about what I did in the desert, and maybe if I speak to

Dr Carpenter about this realisation, she'll be able to help me explain to the court that there was no malice intended.

I splash cold water onto my face, my eyes bloodshot from the vomiting, but for the first time in days I feel like I'm wresting back control. I now know what happened, and it's about facing the music and dealing with the consequences.

I exit the bathroom and head back towards The Butterfly Room, finding Brenda dishing out medication by the administrator's office.

'Are you okay, Jake? You look white as a sheet.'

'I need to make a phone call,' I tell her, swallowing down the nausea.

'Oh, I'm sorry, my love, but the phones are out at the moment.'

'What do you mean they're out? I need to phone my daughter. I must speak to her.'

She locks up the medication and escorts me towards the window and points out at the charcoal-coloured sky.

'Storm's due,' she says. 'Plays silly beggars with the dish by the lighthouse. They reckon we'll be cut off from the mainland for at least thirty-six hours.'

'But I need to speak to her. There must be another way. Can I borrow your mobile?'

'I'm sorry, it's against the rules for staff to provide personal communication devices to patients.'

'Please, you can be in the room when I make the call, so you know I'm not doing anything illegal. It's vital that I speak to my daughter and let her know how sorry I am. I think... I think I know what happened and she deserves the first apology. Please?'

'I'm sorry, but I could lose my job if anyone found out.'

'Nobody will find out. I won't tell anyone, and you won't so—'

'No, Jake. I'm sorry, but no.'

'What about my own phone? Can't I get it out of storage?'

'No, not until you leave here. I'm sure it can wait until the storm passes—'

'No, it can't,' I yell, losing my temper and thumping the window with my fist.

I instantly regret the reaction as Brenda takes an unsteady step backwards.

'I'm sorry,' I say, struggling to regain my composure. 'There must be some way I can speak to her. Are you sure the phones are definitely not working right now? It's not raining yet, so if I could just get five minutes with her.'

She takes another step back, apologising, before returning to the office.

This can't be happening. I've spent weeks trying to figure out who killed Lucy, and now that I know, I'm not allowed to...

A thought catches me. Sully's voice in the back of my head. The day he woke me in this very room, he said if the clinic staff ever denied me access to a phone, he had one I could use. I tear out of The Butterfly Room, once again stalking the corridors looking for him. I've completed three circuits of the floor when I find him back in The Butterfly Room queuing up for dinner.

'I need your help,' I say under my breath.

'Sure, Bambino, what do you need?'

'Your phone.'

His brow furrows and he stares back at me blankly.

'Sorry, pal, I don't have a phone. Mine's down at reception like everyone else.'

'No, but you said... when we met you said you had access to—'

'Oh, shit, did I? Sorry, pal, it's the meds they put us on in here; sometimes I say the wrong things. I'm sorry.'

'But I need to phone my daughter. It's an emergency.'

'You should speak to one of the staff. I think there's a phone in the administrator's office you can use.'

I pull away from the queue, frustrated. I don't know what else to do, or where else to go, and find myself walking back towards my bedroom, but I stop before I get there when I hear voices inside.

'Enough is enough,' I hear Mr Coyle grizzling.

'But I'm so close, Angus. This is just a sign of how near we are.'

'He could have hurt you.'

'He didn't know what he was doing. Don't you see? This outburst has to be a result of PTSD. I tried shaking him, I tried shouting out his name, but nothing would wake him. He was somewhere in his head, and nothing could bring him out of it.'

'And what happens if I let you continue fiddling about with his subconscious, and next time it isn't just his room that bears the brunt?'

They're talking about me, about what happened, but there's something implied between them that I can't quite figure.

'I just need two more days with him.'

'No, we can't risk it. This experiment is over.'

Sully's voice in my head again: *Once they have you here, that's when the experiments begin.*

What experiment are they talking about? Hypnotising me into confessing to the kid's murder so they can use that against me in court?

'Please, Angus, just give me two more days, and if I can't get him to admit what he did, then we end it.'

'And what if he figures out what's really going on here?'

I can't believe it. I was right. I want to barge through the door and confront them, but they're hardly going to come clean now. No, I need to be smarter. I need to figure out what to do next. They don't know that I know they're up to something.

I back away slowly. I'm heading towards The Butterfly Room

when I feel a hand on my arm. Turning, I see Sully standing behind me.

'You want to use my phone? Meet me at the hidden room once dinner's over, and I'll let you use it.'

'But you said—'

'I didn't know who might be listening. Keep it on the QT and meet me there.'

33

THE DAY BEFORE THE MURDER

Lucy has spent most of the night working in her office. Jake stationed himself on the sofa across the room, pretending to watch the live football on the television, but his eyes are glued to the door. He is certain she will figure he's been snooping about while she's been at work, and has been waiting for her reaction, ready to bombard her with questions about why she has a second phone locked in her desk drawer, and why she's making secret phone calls in the middle of the night.

But there has been no reaction from her so far, and although he keeps creeping over to the door every few minutes, listening out for her voice in case she is on the phone with someone, at no point has he heard her speak. The longer he sits here, the more time he has had to extrapolate from the limited information available to him; much in the way he was trained to do by the army.

Avoiding intimacy has felt like the biggest red flag, but the more he thinks about it, the less he can picture his wife embarking on an affair. With her working so much, she wouldn't have time for one thing, and she's given him no other reason to suspect she might betray their vows. What is far more likely is that her frustration at his lack of employment has made her less attracted to him. He can see the pressure she's under and as much as he wants to ease that burden, he's not been able to. He isn't living up to his vows right now because he's not giving her the support she deserves. No wonder she doesn't want him near her. This also explains why she's spending so much time away from home: she's working so hard to supplement his lost income.

Earlier today he was back in the office, attempting to figure the PIN to the other mobile phone, but failed again, so instead he read every document in the piles on her desk. He didn't understand half of it, but he did find a printed email from one of Lucy's clients that piqued his interest. From what Jake has been able to deduce, Lucy is fighting a custody battle on behalf of her client, a British national whose husband has taken their children against her will to his native Egypt. It seems Lucy has been having regular conversations with Interpol about locating the children and ensuring their safe return, but the email from the client is a warning to Lucy that her partner is a violent man, capable of dangerous acts. The client specifically warns Lucy to watch her back.

His conclusion is Lucy is in trouble and is keeping it to herself to protect him. She'll know that if she confides in him he'll want to protect her and will insist she drop the client, or allow him to provide her with personal protection. He's not entirely sure why this would lead her to have a second phone locked in the drawer, but maybe that's what she uses to speak with her client. He wants Lucy to tell him the truth, but he knows she won't come clean if he asks her directly about it, so he bides his time.

When she eventually leaves the office around ten, she is surprised to see him still up, but rather than confront her, he offers her a back massage, hoping his endearing side will help her to open up to him. She declines the offer and tells him she's only come out to get a drink, and that he should go to bed.

'I think we need to talk,' he says, sighing, the most painful words he's ever uttered.

'Talk about what, Jake?' she snaps. 'The fact that you took it upon yourself to put our future at risk? The fact that you quit your job without even thinking what it would mean for your daughter and me? The fact that I'm having to work all hours just to keep a roof over our heads?'

'I'm trying my best,' he replies, defeated, already wishing he hadn't said anything.

'Well, clearly your best isn't good enough, is it, Jake?'

'What do you want me to do? I've spoken to my CO about returning to the army. Is that what you want? You used to bang on at me to leave, but when I do, you're angry. I just don't know what to do any more.'

'You spoke to your CO? When? Why didn't you tell me?'

'On Sunday. That's where I was when I should have collected Sienna from the party.'

'And what did she say?'

'She said she'd see what she could do and let me know.'

'So that's it? You've decided to go back to the army without consulting me again.' She screams out loud, and hurls her dinner plate across the room. It collides with the wall and shatters into several pieces. 'What other secrets are you keeping, Jake?'

He loses his cool, shocked by her action.

'You're hardly one to talk about secrets. Who are you phoning in the middle of the night with your second mobile?'

Her eyes dart temporarily towards the office door.

'Have you been checking up on me?'

'And what about your custody case, eh? When were you going to tell me that your life might be in danger?'

Her mouth drops.

'You've been reading my case files? How dare you? How dare you go snooping around in my office?'

'You've left me no choice, Lucy! I know something is going on, and I wish you'd just be honest with me. I—'

He stops as the living room door opens and a tearful Sienna stands in the doorway, begging them to stop arguing.

34

Dinner is the blandest macaroni and cheese I've ever tasted, but I force it down, hoping it will distract me long enough so that time doesn't drag, but it's as if someone is deliberately slowing down the seconds. I stay in The Butterfly Room, sitting alone on one of the sofas, waiting for the view outside the window to slowly disappear into the darkness.

There's no point in me heading to the hidden room until Sully has left The Butterfly Room, so I keep one eye on him, checking for any kind of sign or hint that he's ready, but he ignores me, talking to anyone else who will listen to him. I want to grab his arms and demand he hand over the phone, but that won't serve either of us. Patience has never been a strength of mine.

He finally heads out when dinner has been cleared away, and most of the other patients have retired to their rooms. I watch him leave and count to sixty before slowly following along the corridor, not even certain I'd be able to find the hidden room again without him leading me to it.

Once we're inside, he pushes the boxes to one side, searching for the torch before lighting up the tiny box room. I'm relieved that Evelyn doesn't appear to be here, as I don't want an audience for what happens next.

Sully sits and stares at me, and I'm now wondering whether he's forgotten why we're here.

'Where's the phone?' I ask.

'All in good time. Before I locate it, tell me why you want to use it.'

'I told you: I need to phone my daughter and the clinic's phone is out of service because of the storm.'

'And nobody asked you to get this for them?'

Sully's paranoia may be worse than my own.

'No, I'm not working for anyone at the clinic. Please, Sully, you can trust me. I just need to use the phone.'

He considers my response, before asking me to look away. I oblige but I can hear him rummaging behind his back, and the next thing I know, there's an old-fashioned flip phone in my hand. No internet connectivity sadly, but two bars of signal.

My eyes widen.

'Jesus! Is that the actual time?'

Sully glances back at the device. 'Yeah, probably.'

It's after nine, so Sienna won't be awake, and if I phone Geraldine, she'll probably use that as an excuse to stop me speaking to her. But I don't have any other choice. I'm surprised when she answers the call.

'Geraldine, don't hang up the phone. It's really important that I speak to Sienna now. I think... I think I might know what happened that night. The doctor here, she—'

'Jake? I told you not to call here again.'

'I know, but listen, I need to speak to Sienna.'

'What for?'

'I think I'm maybe starting to remember what happened, and I want to tell her how—'

'You're ready to admit what you did? You're ready to confess to killing Lucy?'

I don't know how to answer that question. My mind is so muddled with questions. On the one hand, I am ready to accept that I am prone to sleepwalking, and having seen what I did when Dr Carpenter had me in a trance, then it's clear I am capable of acting out whilst in that state.

But then I think back to what Coyle was saying about experiments, and it casts doubt on that other theory.

And then I think about hearing Lucy's voice earlier on. I can't decide if I imagined it and everyone else is right and I killed Lucy, or whether I did actually hear her and all of this is part of some elaborate scheme to see me imprisoned for a crime I didn't commit.

'I just want to speak to my daughter,' I say, avoiding Geraldine's question.

'If you ever want to speak to her, you need to tell the police what you did.'

'I will, I just want to speak to her first.'

'No. You admit the truth and then you can speak to her.'

'Please, Geraldine? I'm begging you. I've been here for days, and I desperately want to hear her voice. You have no right to keep her from me. I am her father and I demand you let me speak to her right now.'

'I can't. She isn't here.'

I freeze. It's after nine and Sienna is too young to be out anywhere on her own.

'What do you mean she isn't there? Where is she?'

'You're still at that hospital, right? Once I hear word that you've confessed, I will put you in touch with Sienna.'

She hangs up the call.

Why is she acting so cagey? If Ray has taken his niece out,

then why wouldn't she just say that to me? Her responses are setting alarm bells ringing in my head.

One day you'll understand why things had to be this way.

I hear Lucy's voice crystal clear in my head. That's what I heard her saying when I thought I heard her talking to Dr Carpenter. Why am I hearing that voice now? It has to be my mind's way of telling me what's going on. My subconscious is connecting the dots before my eyes. Of course, Sienna isn't there because she's with Lucy. That's why Geraldine won't let me speak to her, because Lucy is still alive and they're worried Sienna will let it slip, and then I'll have proof of their conspiracy.

I can feel Sully's stare burning into me. I refuse to meet his gaze, in no mood for small talk.

Eventually the silence becomes too much for him.

'Your kid's mom keeping her from you, is she?'

'Not exactly.'

'If you need to get to her, there may be another way.'

I look over to him.

'I'm planning to escape from this place tonight. I've had enough of them experimenting on me. The only way to stop them is to get out and expose them.'

Something begins to stir in the back of my mind.

'And how exactly do you plan to get out? Unless you've forgotten, lift access is restricted, and we'd need an access pass to use it. On top of that, there are orderlies and security guards all over the place.'

'Don't you worry. I have a plan that avoids all of those obstacles.'

I shouldn't be listening to him. Brenda warned me about his paranoid delusions, and this is probably just another.

'How do you know all of this?'

'Before I was a patient here, I was... I worked here as a janitor.'

He shakes his nest of grey hair. 'They were going to let me go but said I could make more money if I agreed to become one of their volunteers. If I'd known what they were planning to do...'

It's not what I'm expecting him to say, but the way he's frowning with such shame, I believe every word.

'And what do you intend to do *if* you make it off the floor? The main foyer is also protected by security guards, and the whole place is covered in cameras.'

He smiles mischievously.

'There are some places the cameras don't go, and I intend to use those.'

'Okay, so you somehow make it outside the clinic, then what are you going to do? We're on an island, and the only transport to and from here doesn't run at night. There's no way you'll manage to get off the island without being seen. Swimming would mean certain death.'

'I have a plan for that as well, but not one I'm about to share with someone who could blab it all to the quacks in this place. You sure you're on the level with me here?'

If he knew the real reason I'm being assessed, he wouldn't be questioning my legitimacy.

'I'm not lying to you,' I say instead.

'So, do you want in on the escape?'

Staying in here isn't going to help me get back to Sienna. Lucy, Geraldine, and Max won't be happy until they see me behind bars. My only chance is to get out of this clinic and catch them in the act. If I can find Lucy, I can show the police that all of this has been a miscarriage of justice.

But I need to know where Lucy is staying and for that I'm going to need help. I just hope he still has the same number.

I type in the digits and press the device to my ear. I'd rather Sully not be privy to this conversation, but he might not be so willing to let me use his phone if I ask him to leave. The phone rings and rings and I'm about to hang up and try again when the phone is answered.

'Tariq? Is that you? This is Lieutenant Jake Meredith. Zero four, zero nine, nine zero. Do you remember me?'

I wait for him to type his response into the machine he now uses to communicate, following the loss of his vocal cords during the attack on the Foxhound.

'How could I forget the voice of the man who saved my life? It's been a long time,' the robotic voice replies.

Second Lieutenant Tariq Farid is the only other person in the world who actually knows what happened that day in the desert. I can't think of anyone I would trust more right now.

'I'm sorry to call out of the blue like this, but I need your help.'

'You never need to apologise to me if you need help. Tell me what I can do.'

I'm so relieved, though in the desert I only did what anyone in my position would have done.

'I'm in a bit of trouble here, and I desperately need to find my daughter. I think her aunt knows where she is, so I want you to go to her house, and follow my sister-in-law. I need to know where she goes and when. And if you see a kid with blonde hair with her, follow her instead. Can you do that for me?'

'Send me the address of the house,' the robotic voice agrees.

'Thank you, my friend, I will call you back when I can tomorrow.'

I end the call and send him the address via a text message, before passing the phone back to Sully.

'What time do we escape?'

35

At Sully's suggestion, I return to my room, but he's promised he'll come for me when the time is right. He said I won't know when, but to stay awake. The bed is back in place, and Dr Carpenter isn't here, but I sense they'll be keeping more of an eye on me tonight.

I've only been back for five minutes when Brenda stops by and hands me a small plastic cup containing two white pills.

'Dr Carpenter has prescribed these for you to take,' she says in her matter-of-fact Welsh voice as she fills a beaker of water from the jug.

'What are they?'

'A sleeping pill of sorts. Should ensure you have a restful night's sleep.'

'I don't want to take these,' I tell her, attempting to pass back the small pill cup.

'Why not?'

I can't tell her it's because they will prevent me staying awake long enough for Sully to collect me.

'I just don't want to. Are they mandatory?'

She glances back over her shoulder as if conferring with someone, but the corridor behind her is empty.

'No, you can refuse to take them, but given... given what happened the last time you were asleep, Dr Carpenter is concerned you might hurt yourself. These will help control any involuntary movements.'

She pushes my hand back towards me.

If I don't take them then there's a chance they'll tighten security around my room, and that's the last thing I need. I toss the pills into my mouth, securing them beneath my tongue, before making a show of swallowing them.

She passes me the beaker.

'I need you to wash them down.'

I guess she's not so easily misled. I suppose it was naïve to think that with all her experience I would be the first to try to pull the wool over her eyes. I try to keep my tongue as low as possible, and take a sip from the beaker, hoping they don't dislodge.

'And raise your tongue, please,' she adds as I'm about to swallow the water, forcing me to swallow the pills.

I open my mouth wide and raise my tongue for her to see, and once content, she leaves the room and closes the door. I don't hesitate to rush into the bathroom, where I place two fingers on the back of my tongue and painfully expel the pills. I return to my room and open the door to check Brenda isn't there eavesdropping, but there's no sign of her. Hopefully, she'll now tell Dr Carpenter of my compliance, and I can wait for Sully in peace.

* * *

I start awake to find someone aggressively shaking my arm. I don't remember falling asleep, but that's clearly what happened. Did I not manage to expel the pills quickly enough and some got in my system?

'You awake, Bambino?'

'Yeah, I think so,' I reply, overcome with exhaustion.

'Good, well, it's time for us to make our escape, unless you've changed your mind?'

I think back to Geraldine's admission that Sienna wasn't with her, and the lies Max has had me believing, and shake my head.

'Just tell me what you need me to do.'

Sully enters my bathroom and searches inside.

'Where's your chair?'

I look over to the window where the chair once stood. I hadn't noticed when I'd returned to the room, but they must have taken it out.

I shrug pathetically.

'Come here,' he says, returning to the bathroom. 'I need you to give me a boost up to the ventilation shaft. Come on, scooch over so I can climb onto your shoulders.'

This is his plan? To escape via the ventilation system? This must have been what he meant about some areas of the hospital not being captured by video surveillance. It doesn't explain how we'll get down to the ground floor, but the window for our escape is narrowing by the second.

He signals for me to crouch down, and I obey. His first leg is like a dead weight as it bashes against my ear, before he hoists the other onto my left shoulder. I reach out for the countertop to steady myself, before wrapping a protective arm around his shins, and straightening. I can see his hands ferreting around the ceiling's slatted vent cover via the reflection in the mirror.

He gets it free and passes it down to me carefully. 'Once we're in, you'll need to put this back in place.'

He counts down and then pulls himself up off my shoulders,

scurrying inside the hole in the ceiling, his feet quickly disappearing from view, before his face pops back through the hole, where he's somehow turned around. 'Decision time, Jakey boy, you coming or not?'

If I'm right and Lucy and Geraldine have set me up for something I didn't do, then staying means they'll get away with it. If I'm wrong and I am responsible for Lucy's death, I need to be the one to tell Sienna. Either way, staying here achieves nothing.

I look around the bathroom for anything I can leverage so Sully doesn't have to pull me up, but all I see is the edge of the basin. It'll have to do. Clambering onto it, I try to straighten my legs, and tell Sully to get out of the way. It takes me two attempts to get my arms through the gap, but there's not enough room for me to crouch on all fours, so I have to lie flat. It's so dark; the only light coming up through ventilation shafts directly ahead and behind us.

I replace the vent over my bathroom and begin to crawl forwards. If it's a tight squeeze for me, it's worse for Sully ahead of me, and we make slow progress along the narrow tunnel, which is cold to the touch.

I'm not convinced the shaft will support both of our weights, and it's difficult to manoeuvre along. I'm having to press my palms out to the sides, and kind of drag the rest of me a little at a time. Claustrophobia has never been something I've felt before, but what happens if we get stuck in here? If nobody figures out we came up here, we could be trapped for years. Or what if I have another blackout?

I need to not think about it. I'm here, I'm awake – I think – and former janitor Sully is going to lead me to safety.

My left palm brushes against something sharp, and when I study it in the dim light cast through the occasional slatted cover, I see what resembles an arrow scratched into the side of the metal wall. It's pointing in the direction we're headed, and I soon notice another and then another.

'Hey, Sully, what's with these arrows?' I whisper, uncertain he'll hear me.

'This isn't the first time I've tried to tunnel out of here,' he pants back breathlessly.

'You, okay? You don't sound good.'

'I'll be fine. We're nearly there. Keep quiet now, we're about to pass over the orderlies' station. If they hear us, we're busted.'

I freeze. I hadn't even thought about our bearings in relation to the rest of the clinic. We move forwards unsteadily, and I'm now overly concerned about every slip and slide noise that is echoing around the chamber.

Is it too late to go back?

My brow is soaked through with sweat, as is my top, causing it to squeak against the metal floor every time I slide further along.

Surely the staff can hear us up here?

I reach the next slatted vent cover and pause to look down. Below I see a small box room, a panel of monitors covering one wall. A pair of feet are crossed and resting atop a wooden desk, leading to a pair of legs, which I see belong to a dozing guard in his black uniform of combats and polo shirt. When I look back to Sully's feet, they are no longer in sight. In blind panic, I grip the sides of the metal walls and pull and drag myself as fast as I can. Up ahead, I see one of the slatted vent covers is no longer in place, and I hover at the edge, daring to look down, certain that I'll see Carpenter or Coyle staring back up at me.

Instead, I see Sully peeling off his yellowing, sweat-stained pyjama top.

'Will you hurry up?' he says in a loud whisper.

I move past the hole, allowing my feet and legs to drop through, before swinging down.

We're in a similarly sized room to the guard station next door, only there is no panel of monitors or napping guard in here. Hanging from a rail against the wall directly in front of me are white orderly uniforms. Sully has stripped out of his sodden pyjama bottoms, and is reaching for one of the uniforms, his eyes encouraging me to hurry up and change too. I find a Medium and pull off my own damp garments. There are no shoes for us to change into, so our sandals will have to do for now. I guess we'll just have to hope nobody we pass looks down at our feet.

There's no mirror in here, so I run a hand through my shaved hair, trying to shake off any excess sweat.

'Being dressed as orderlies should allow us to avoid being identified on camera,' Sully tells me. 'The whole clinic is locked down, but nobody will be expecting us to try and escape.'

'How are we going to get through the doors? We don't have a security pass.'

He smiles at this.

'That's going to be more of a challenge, but I have an idea on where we can get one.'

He moves to the door and cracks it open, peering out into the white corridor beyond. He's about to step out when I grab his shoulder and pull him back.

'I need to know the rest of the plan. I've followed you this far, but if I'm caught trying to escape, it could mean real jail time for me. How are we getting out of the clinic, and once we're out, how on earth do we get back to the mainland?'

'There's a restroom just around the corner. We'll head there now and hide inside one of the cubicles. When an orderly or guard comes in to relieve himself, we jump him and steal his pass.'

My mouth hangs open as I stare back at him. 'That's your plan? Kill a guard?'

'No, not kill,' he snaps back, his face pained with hurt. 'I meant we'd knock him out somehow. Jeez, who do you think I am?'

I really don't know.

He crosses back to the door and peeks out, before quickly closing it as footsteps and voices approach. I don't breathe as the rumble of steps reaches a crescendo, but they don't stop, and are soon fading into the distance.

Sully holds his thumb up in my direction, before cracking open the door again, and slipping out. I quickly follow, keeping two steps behind him.

'No, next to me,' he whispers, and I hurry to catch up. 'Remember, as far as anyone is concerned, we're just a couple of orderlies and we're supposed to be here. Try to relax and walk with confidence. If anyone stops us, let me do the talking. Capiche?'

I've not known terror like this since being on patrol in highly fortified areas of Afghanistan; but at least there I had a weapon and means of defending myself. I'd give anything to be back there now.

Sully directs us to the end of one corridor, then left, then right, and then left again. He moves with such certainty, but I'm already lost and probably wouldn't be able to find my way back to the orderlies' station without a map. We turn left again, and this time I see a secured door at the end of the corridor.

My eyes widen as it begins to open. Somebody is coming.

36

THE DAY OF THE MURDER

Jake blows air into his hands, and then rubs them together. It's far colder than he'd anticipated, but it's too late for him to return home and collect his gloves. He's been standing behind the bus shelter for hours now, and desperately wants to nip to the local café to use their facilities and purchase a takeaway coffee, but he dare not move from his position.

Across the road stands the office space Geraldine and Lucy rent and use to run their firm. He knows Lucy isn't there, because her secretary said she was out visiting a client, when he called. Lucy's office faces the street, and he hasn't seen her moving about inside, so he's pretty sure the secretary isn't lying to him.

He needs answers, and Lucy has made it abundantly clear she won't be providing them; at least not directly to him.

He was back in her office this morning as soon as he got back from taking Sienna to school. He re-read the notes relating to the overseas custody battle, searching for any more information to allow him to assess the threat. Eventually he used Lucy's computer to search for the names of the claimant and her ex. But there was no mention of either of them and this has left Jake even more frustrated. But it's what he noticed as he was leaving her office that has put him on edge now: the small tin containing their passports and the bag of euros is no longer on top of the bookcase in Lucy's home office.

They were definitely there when he first searched her office a few days ago, and when he checked in the fire-retardant safe in their room, on the assumption that Lucy had finally got round to returning them, they weren't there either. He has checked every nook and cranny of their house in search of the tin or the passports themselves, and he couldn't find them anywhere.

Lucy hasn't mentioned needing to go abroad for work, and it won't be half term for another couple of weeks, and Lucy isn't the sort of parent who would willingly allow Sienna to miss school. He hasn't been able to stop thinking about it, but no matter how many theories he hypothesises, he can't figure out why she would have taken the passports with her to work. Unless...

No, he chases the thought away. Lucy wouldn't take Sienna away from him. It's purely coincidence that she's reviewing the case notes of a custody battle where one parent abducted the children and took them overseas. Even when he allows his mind to process the thought, he ends up laughing at just how ridiculous it sounds.

But why else would she be keeping the passports with her?

As much as he doesn't want to doubt her loyalty, he is no longer certain that she wouldn't cheat on him. And that is why he has come here today. He can't just outright accuse her of cheating and trying to steal Sienna away. He needs proof of what her intentions are. If he catches her with another man, that will all but confirm his worst fears. And then he can speak to Max and find out what he can do to keep Lucy from stealing Sienna away.

But only if it comes to it, he reminds himself.

He knows he hasn't been sleeping well, and that the sleep

deprivation is intensifying his paranoia. His CO warned him about the dangers of PTSD, and he can't say for certain that some of his recent decisions haven't been influenced by the trauma he suffered on his last tour. But he also feels sound of mind. There are too many hints that Lucy is up to something to ignore: the second phone; the locked drawer; the passports and euros; all the late hours she's been working; avoiding spending any time with him.

His patience is rewarded, when just after lunch, he spots Lucy turn the corner onto the road a hundred or so yards away. He'd know that smile anywhere. But it's the man whose arm hers is looped with that catches his attention. He's taller than Jake, dapper, dressed in a charcoal-coloured suit, the top two buttons of his white shirt unfastened. He has a strong jawline, and a mop of thick, shiny black hair. He has film star looks, and Jake can imagine he's turned plenty of heads in his time. Lucy is laughing at whatever he's just told her, and Jake can't stop the voice in his head telling him that they're laughing at him; at how well they've kept their affair a secret.

Jake pulls out his phone, ready to snap a picture, when he sees them stop outside the door to the office, and look into one another's eyes. Her body is open and facing him, and she's resting both hands on his arms. Jake is too far away to hear what they're saying, but he can see the sincerity in Lucy's face, and he doesn't want to see the kiss that he senses is to follow.

He pockets his phone and charges across the street. Lucy's eyes widen in shock when she sees him, but Jake isn't interested in confronting her. Instead, he takes a swing at the other man, catching his jaw with his fist, and instantly regretting it as a hot pain shoots through his knuckle. The man barely moves with the impact, and shoves Jake so hard that he topples backwards, crashing to the pavement.

'Jake, what the fuck are you doing here?' he hears Lucy cry out, but he isn't prepared to let this man beat him.

He leaps back to his feet, and charges towards the guy again, and this time it's Jake who receives a punch, but to the midriff, and it knocks the wind from him. He doubles over, desperately trying to suck air back into his lungs, barely able to breathe.

'Jean-Claude, I am so sorry about this. This is my husband Jake, and I have no idea what he is doing here.'

'Catching you with your lover,' Jake spits back.

'My... oh, Jesus, Jake, no. This is Jean-Claude, one of my clients. He is an old friend who asked me to look over a contract for him.'

Jake studies the man's face, looking for any sign to confirm what she's saying.

'Jean-Claude is looking to buy the old Post Office building and convert it into one of his restaurants. Given our financial situation, I agreed to have a look at it for him.'

'But you practise family law, so what do you know about reviewing contracts?'

'Well, if you ever listened to anything I ever tell you, you'd know I've been studying up so we can diversify the firm.' She points up at the sign above the office. 'We are now Family *and* Contract Law specialists.'

Jake's cheeks blaze, as he realises he may have made a mistake with this Jean-Claude character, but it doesn't explain all her other suspicious behaviour.

'Jean-Claude, thank you for lunch. I will look over the contracts today and brief you ahead of your meeting on Monday.' She pecks his cheek, adding, 'I am so sorry about my husband.'

He checks whether she wants him to stay, but she tells him she'll be fine, and he walks away, glancing back over his shoulder to check on her until he disappears back around the corner. She stares at Jake, hands on hips.

'I'm waiting for an apology,' she says firmly.

Jake straightens and composes himself, pointing his finger at her.

'I know something is going on with you. Why do you have a second mobile? Where are yours and Sienna's passports? What are you up to?'

She raises her face to the sky, and stares up at the clouds for several seconds, before meeting his gaze again. Her eyes are watering.

'I can't do this any more, Jake. Your paranoid delusions are beyond the pale.'

'I found your second phone. Don't tell me I'm being paranoid.'

'The phone is for work, okay? I use it to make international phone calls, and it gets charged directly to the business. I keep it locked in the drawer so I don't confuse it with my own phone. There's no conspiracy here. Can't you hear how crazy you sound? You seriously need to get help, Jake.'

He doesn't believe a word she is saying.

'You're lying to me, Lucy. I know something is going on, and I am going to prove it one way or another.'

She shakes her head and a tear escapes and rolls down her cheek.

'I can't deal with you right now. You should book an appointment with a counsellor, because you're losing it. In fact, I'm worried it may already be too late for that. I need to go back to work.'

She turns to head back inside, and he grabs her arm.

'Don't turn your back on me. I'm not going to let you take Sienna from me. Do you hear me? I will fight you with all my strength.'

She glares at his hand until he releases her arm.

'We'll talk about this when I get home, but you should have a long hard think about what you really want, Jake, because what we have right now: this isn't a marriage. I have work to do. Go and sort yourself out.'

And with that she heads inside her office, leaving him staring after her.

37

Sully grabs my arm and drags me towards a door to our right, which opens, and he pushes us through. The room is so dark, I can't see anything in front of me, and panic, my foot colliding with a bucket and a mop handle, which comes crashing down against my head.

We are standing in what must be a supply cupboard. As my eyes gradually adjust to the darkness, I can see a cart in one corner stacked with bottles of luminous liquid, cloths, and sponges.

I can barely see Sully, but as I take a step closer, I can now see that he has his ear pressed to the wall. The low rumble of voices appears to be coming from whatever room is beside us, and when I press my ear to the cold plasterboard, I immediately recognise Mr Coyle's Northern Irish accent.

'Where do we go next with him?' he asks.

And if there's any doubt about who he's referring to, it's quickly diminished when I hear Dr Carpenter reply. 'I think he's close to a breakthrough.'

I pat Sully on the shoulder, ready to point out that I recognise the voices, but he shoves a fat and clammy hand across my mouth, slowly nodding; he already knows.

'A breakthrough or a breakdown?' Coyle asks next.

She doesn't answer, and it kills that I can't see their facial expressions and body language. I wanted to trust her, but I know I heard her talking to Lucy, and she outright denied it to my face. Whether she's actually conspiring with Lucy and Geraldine or is an unwitting pawn in their game, it's hard to know whose side she's actually on. The blood is boiling in my ears, and it's difficult to hear anything over the thundering of my heart.

'This is unprecedented treatment for someone like him,' Dr Carpenter says. 'We knew we were taking a risk with his psyche when we started, but I'm certain we're getting closer to the truth about what really happened.'

'But we're running out of time,' Coyle fires back, his voice raised. 'Detective Fahey is expecting results, and if we don't deliver there will be no second chance.'

My shoulders sag to hear my worst suspicions confirmed.

'I'm aware we have a deadline, but I don't think we're going to get the answers we need unless I can convince him to go back under.'

'We can't risk him lashing out again,' Coyle cuts in. 'It's too dangerous. Not just for you, but also the other patients and staff.'

'With all due respect, nobody has ever attempted something as complex as this before, but if we're successful this could be the biggest breakthrough in the treatment of PTSD and mental health disorders for decades.'

My legs feel like jelly, and I have to press a hand to the wall to prevent myself from collapsing to the floor. They're looking to prove that my experience overseas is what led to Lucy's death, but Dr Carpenter knows she's still alive, so their logic is flawed. And what does any of that have to do with the treatment of sleep disorders? It sounds more like they're psychiatrists than sleep specialists.

That must be why she kept asking questions about what went on overseas; why she paired me up with pilot Katy – if she even is a patient here. For all I know, Katy was a plant, like Sully thought I was, but how can I even be certain Sully is who he says he is? I look at him in my periphery. All that talk about this being a hospital, rather than a clinic; him introducing me to Evelyn, who he claimed had been here for over a decade. Was any of that true, or just misinformation to keep me off the scent of what they were trying to uncover?

I try to pull Sully out of the way of the door, ready to confront them and finally bring an end to this slippery slope into madness, but he won't budge, pinning me back against the wall, a sausage-like finger pressed against his lips.

And then my mind connects the final dot when I hear a third voice on the other side of the wall.

'I agree with the two of you,' Max's deep brogue says. 'This isn't working. He needs to admit what he did once and for all.'

Although I've had my doubts about Max's involvement in the conspiracy, there was a tiny part of me still clinging to the prospect that I'd mistakenly lumped him in with Lucy and Geraldine. But even he wants to see me prosecuted for something I didn't do. The betrayal cuts deep.

It certainly explains why he hasn't yet found Lucy's real killer. Of course he was in on it; how else would they have convinced me to come to this place? Whatever this place actually is. A sleep clinic? I'm beginning to have major doubts. Looking back on it now, the clues have been there all along. The requirement to give up communication devices, the requirement to walk around in pyjamas where it's impossible to hide anything. Sully and Evelyn even told me it was a hospital and I dismissed them as kooks.

It was Max who told the police I had a history of sleepwalking, and even though I had no recollection, he pushed his agenda, and I went blindly along with it in the belief I was just buying him time.

How did Lucy and Geraldine get to him? What did they promise him in exchange for betraying me and escaping with Sienna? I know we weren't close growing up, but I still would have thought he would choose family over them. Unless they're blackmailing him to buy his cooperation.

The sound of the door opening and closing echoes around the small chamber and then the footsteps move back out and along the corridor. Sully releases my arms and gives me a look that's a cross between I told you so, and pity.

'This fricking place, man,' he concludes, with a shake of his head. 'Now do you believe what I told you? We're stuck in a mental hospital, not a sleep clinic. I told you you couldn't trust nobody here.'

I should have listened to him sooner. The only reason I didn't is because Brenda warned me not to. But of course she would say that, because she's probably in on the loop as well. That's why she's been denying me access to the telephone, and for all I know she's been slipping medication into my food.

'We need to get down to the ground floor,' Sully tells me, 'and to do that we need to access the elevator shaft.'

He pulls over the cleaner's cart and applies the brake directly beneath the slatted ventilation cover in the ceiling above us.

'You want to get back into the vent?'

Before he has time to answer, a deafening alarm sounds overhead.

'We don't have a choice,' he calls out over the din. 'They now know we've escaped. If you want to get out of here and get your life back on track, we need to stay out of sight.'

The alarm grates at every nerve in my body, shredding any sense of who or where I am. Clamping my palms over my ears does little to dull the onslaught. I hear someone calling my name, and when I look up, I can see Sully's face poking out of the ventilation shaft overhead. His lips are moving, but I can't make out what he's trying to say.

An arm shoots out beside his head, and I see now he's pointing at something on the wall. I tilt my head to look at what he's indicating and notice a large roll of blue toilet paper on the cleaner's cart. I don't understand and look back at him, to see he's now holding a small, round wad of something blue which he proceeds to push into his ear drum.

'Takes the edge off,' he says, his voice muffled.

Forcing myself up, I move across to the paper and tear off a wedge, scrunching it into a tiny ball, and then twist it into my ear. As I repeat the process, I can still make out a clamouring sound, but it isn't nearly as brain-splitting as before.

'Come on,' Sully shouts. I can hear him better now that I can concentrate. 'We need to get out of here before they figure out how we got out of your room.'

His head disappears back into the darkness like a tortoise retreating into its shell.

I hesitate. 'We're on the fourth floor. How are we going to get down to the ground floor? What about your plan to steal a security pass?'

He raises his eyebrows. 'That was before they figured out we'd gone. They'll be scouring every camera, stalking every corridor, checking every ID. We're safest up here, out of sight.'

'I'm not jumping out of any bloody window, Sully. I need to know how we're going to get out.'

'Get your ass up here and I'll tell you. Hurry up, before they start going door-to-door on this floor.'

His face moves back into shadow, and against my better judge-ment, I hoist myself up and into the shaft again. One benefit is the alarm isn't nearly as loud up here, the metal casing offering some protection from the ringing, so much so that I discard my balled-up tissue ear defenders.

He's already shuffling on ahead of me, moving at a much quicker pace this time. I don't understand how he can know where he's going as I've lost all sense of direction. It's been that long since I saw the sky that I don't know whether we're pointed north, south, east, or west. If I get left behind, I may never find my way out of this maze of tunnels again.

'Sully, where are we going?' I call out, and he instantly stops and stares back at me, placing a finger to his ears.

'You don't need to shout any more,' he whispers, 'but we don't want to draw attention to ourselves.'

It's a fair point and not one I'd considered.

'All the ventilation shafts lead to one place on each floor,' he continues. 'The elevator shaft. Inside we'll find a ladder down to the ground floor, and then it's back into the ventilation pipes from there.'

'Wait, if we make it to the ground floor, why can't we just prise open the lift doors, and make a run for it?'

'Because there are secured doors and orderlies, between the elevator and freedom. We need to drop into a room where they're not expecting us, and go from there.'

I don't know this guy from Adam, and yet I'm putting my trust in him implicitly. But why? I'm never usually so trusting of strangers.

'You okay, Bambino?' Sully calls out, and when I look up, I see he's further along the tunnel. 'You don't look so good.'

'Tell me again what happens if we make it out of the clinic?'

'When we make it out, we get down to the coastline. Patients have been escaping this place for years. Once we're out, we'll find some of them.'

I start moving along the pipe, finding a steady rhythm with my knees and palms, until I'm right behind him again. My arms and legs are aching from the constant shuffle of hands and knees, and I can't remember when I last had a drink. My mouth and throat feel so dry. I'm about to ask him if we can find a drink somewhere, but misplace my hand, not realising I'm over one of the slatted covers. It shifts beneath my weight, and then I'm falling through.

38

It's a miracle that I manage to land on the end of a bed, though my legs aren't quite as well coordinated, and they clatter into the overbed table. I freeze, looking to see who I've landed on, but am relieved to find I'm in a vacant room. My heart is racing from the fall, and as I look back up at the vent, I see Sully poke his head through.

'You okay, Jakey boy? You alive?'

'I'm fine,' I shout back as my ears pop, and I realise the paper has fallen out of my ears. My head once again fills with the overbearing sound of the alarm, and I search for where the tissue might have fallen, but there's no sign of it on the bedspread.

Has anyone heard me crashing through the vent? It's hard to tell, but I know I can't hang around down here for too long. Sully has already shuffled off, presumably expecting me to jump back up, but the vent here is much higher than where we climbed from his room. In fact, as my eyes adjust to the darkness, I realise this looks very different. There is no medical equipment stationed at the head of the bed for one thing, and for another, there's a bowl with two goldfish standing on the windowsill.

There's a television hanging from the wall. And picture frames standing on a chest of drawers, though it's too dark to make out any figures.

Is this someone's personal quarters? What did Coyle say about residents on the island?

The alarm here is so loud that it's tough to string coherent thoughts together. I suppose it's possible that some of the staff have rooms on site given the lack of transportation back to the mainland.

Maybe whoever's room this is has left their mobile phone in here, and I can try to call Sienna again. Or better still, maybe their security pass is here somewhere. I pull open the top drawer in the chest and rummage around inside but withdraw my hands when my fingers brush against bra straps. I move down to the next. Here there are vest tops and T-shirts, and the bottom drawer is loaded with jumpers.

I'm about to move to the windowsill when the door to the room bursts open, and I start.

'Jake? What are you doing here?' Katy shouts over the din. Her eyes fall on the upturned overbed table and gaping hole in the vent above it. 'You were in the ceiling?'

What is she doing here?

She glances back towards the door, and I immediately sense her discomfort. This is her room, which means I was right to suspect her intentions towards me. But she's on her own, and as much as I don't want to hurt her, I can't have her telling the rest where I am.

I pull her towards me, shutting the door in one quick motion.

'I'm not dangerous,' I shout over the din, in an effort to reassure her. 'Despite what they're saying, I didn't murder my wife. But if I don't get out of here tonight that's precisely what they're going to claim. I can't let my daughter fall for their lies. I need to save her. Please, I don't want to hurt you, but I will if you don't help me.'

I'm not expecting her to agree, so I flick on the light switch, and I begin scanning the room for anything I can use to tie and gag her. I'm not going to be able to get back into the vent on my own here, but maybe if I could get back to Sully's room, or back to that cleaners' room. I won't know exactly which way Sully has gone, but I remember him saying he was heading for the lift shaft, so if I head in that direction there's a chance I'll catch up to him.

'You'll never make it out of here on your own. There are guards all over the place. I can help you get out.'

My instinct tells me she's lying, but the way she spoke before about combat, I can't help thinking that wasn't all bullshit. Maybe she was in the RAF before she started working here.

'Give me two minutes to use the facilities,' she says, 'and I'll show you the quickest way out.'

I nod and she ducks into the bathroom, closing the door behind her. I return to the bed, again hunting for anything to plug my ears. But no sooner have I found a box of tissues on the windowsill than the alarm stops. The relief is palpable, but I pocket a couple of tissues in case it sounds again. With the air no longer polluted by the cacophony, I can hear the rain scratching against the window, and stare out into the darkness. The moon is hidden behind a blanket of dark cloud, and I can just make out trees being attacked by the storm Brenda mentioned earlier. I guess she wasn't lying about that. They're certainly not clement conditions for an escape, but I know from my military experience how good a friend the darkness can be when trying to move undetected.

I look back at the bathroom door. Katy is taking too long, and as I march back to the door, I hear her whispered voice beyond it. I kick the door open with all my force, to find Katy standing beside the shower cubicle, a finger pressed to the device in her ear.

'You need to get here now,' she yells out. 'He knows.'

I stare at her in disbelief. Yet another person so comfortable with lying to my face about their true intentions. That's why the alarm stopped. She must have told them where I was, and now they're on their way. I need to get out of here before they get here.

I pull open the door to the bedroom, the corridor here as white as all the others, but I charge forward, following the bend to the right until I come to the end, and then choose to turn left rather than right. I can hear Katy giving chase behind me, narrating my movements to whomever is listening on the end of her radio.

The corridors in this place are all so similar that I have no idea if I'm heading back towards the lift or racing in the opposite direction. I call out Sully's name at the top of my voice, hoping he'll hear and be able to show me the way, but as I take the next right, I'm immediately rugby tackled to the ground by a bear of an orderly. I kick, and punch, and try to break free of his grasp, but another arrives, and grabs both my arms, stretching me out, while the other one replicates the move with my legs.

'Let go of me,' I yell at them both, trying to free myself of their grip. 'You have the wrong man. I didn't kill my wife. She's still alive. They're setting me up.'

All I see is overhead fluorescent light boxes as they carry me along the corridor.

'This place isn't a real clinic,' I shout out in the hope that one of the other patients might hear and come to my aid, but then another thought slams into my head like a locomotive.

This time it's Sully's voice: *Because they do that, you know. They have nurses dress up as patients to get the inside track on things we won't tell the doctors.*

What if every 'patient' I've met in here is in fact a member of staff or actor paid to play along with the charade? Is Sully real? Is Evelyn? Or was it all part of their act?

I'm carried into the lift, and we descend. I allow my limbs to go limp, no longer putting up a struggle, but I'm just trying to lull them into a false sense of security. As soon as those lift doors open, I plan to break free and get out once and for all.

But when the lift doors do open, Max is standing there beside Dr Carpenter, and I know there's no escape.

'You fucking turncoat,' I yell at him, trying to pull my arms and legs free, but these two are far stronger than I've given them credit for.

'Enough, Jake,' he says, clearing his throat and shaking his head. 'It's time to face up to reality.'

'I didn't kill her, Max. I know what you're all up to. I know Lucy is still alive, and once I'm out of here, I will track her down and get my daughter back.'

He shakes his head again and looks down at Dr Carpenter.

'I thought you said he was close to a breakthrough.'

'He is,' she says, tilting her head, and looking at me with an empathetic frown. 'I think it's time we told him the truth about why he's here. Can you bring him to my office, please? There's a lot he needs to hear.'

39

I am forced onto the chaise longue in Dr Carpenter's office, my arms held firmly by the two orderlies while Mr Coyle tries to fasten leather restraints around my wrists.

'Those won't be necessary,' I hear Dr Carpenter say meekly, but nobody is listening.

'I'm not leaving you at his mercy,' Max replies without looking up. 'You don't know how he's going to react.'

It's like I don't exist. They're handling me like a piece of furniture and talking about me as if I have no voice of my own.

I glare at Max until he meets my gaze, but he isn't brave enough to hold it, quickly looking away.

'How could you do this to me?' I grizzle at him. 'We're family: you should be fighting for me, not against me.'

He opens his mouth to reply but thinks better of it and takes over fastening the second restraint.

'You're breaking all sorts of laws right now,' I call out to Dr Carpenter, hoping to appeal to her bedside manner. 'You're holding me against my will when I've done nothing wrong. You can't prove what did or didn't happen on that night, and I will never confess to something I didn't do. You won't get away with this.'

She busies herself with papers on her desk, refusing to look over at the four of us. Max pulls the restraint tight and fastens the buckle, before stepping back and running a hand over his bald crown. His cheeks are red and puffy; years of daily nightcaps taking their effect.

'Just tell me why you're doing this,' I say to him. 'Surely it's nothing to do with Dad and the family business. You forced him out, but I've never had any interest in the firm. If you want me to sign papers to that effect, then give me a pen. You didn't need to go to these lengths.'

He ignores me, and whispers something to Dr Carpenter.

'What has Lucy promised you in return for my incarceration?' I try again. 'If it's money then you won't get much. Her life insurance policy was only enough to cover funeral costs. I'm worth more dead than she is.'

They continue to whisper and ignore me, but at least the orderlies have released their grip on my arms. Not that it will do me any good. I have no way of getting out of these restraints without help. I can only hope Sully is aware of what has happened and that he's coming to my rescue.

Max approaches and hovers over me.

'It's time to stop all the lies, Jake. We all care about you, but it's time to finally tell us the truth. Admit that it was you who stabbed Lucy.'

I don't understand whose benefit he's saying this for, given Dr Carpenter has already spoken to Lucy herself. Unless she doesn't realise that's who she was speaking to. The thought hits me like a slap across the face. No wonder she's been thinking I'm losing my mind. Maybe Lucy gave her a false name or was claiming to be someone else. If she isn't in on the conspiracy, then maybe there's a way to convince her that I'm not crazy and that the others have been working against me from the start.

'You almost sound like you believe your own lies, Max,' I say loud enough that she has to be able to hear. 'You're the one who should admit what they did!'

He gives me a curious look, as if I've triggered something in his mind, but he looks over at the orderlies and ushers them out of the room. They leave with him, closing the door, leaving just me and Dr Carpenter. I pull on the restraints to test for weakness, but they are firmly attached to the chair.

My options are limited: either I need to convince her that I'm not crazy and that Lucy and Geraldine are behind all of this, or I need to convince her to release these restraints, take her hostage and use her as a human shield to get to the front door and out into the night.

She carries over a folder and sits down in the chair a metre or so away from me. Although my legs aren't restrained, I can't reach her.

'I really didn't want it to come to this,' she begins quietly, gripping the thin paper folder by the edges. 'I really thought we were making progress, and that maybe one more guided session would help you get through that door and access those memories you've kept locked away for so long.'

'Please, Dr Carpenter, you have to believe me when I say I didn't kill my wife. The woman I heard you speaking to earlier, whatever she said her name was, that was Lucy. I know I sound crazy when I insist that she's still alive, but that's who I heard you speaking to. I think my brother is working with her to make everyone think I killed her, but I didn't.'

'We all have your best interests at heart here, Jake. You may not believe me, but I promise it's true.'

'Then help me get out of here. I think Lucy has my daughter

now, and if you let me go I'll be able to find them and prove once and for all that they've been lying.'

She removes her glasses and catches a tear as it escapes, before sliding them back onto her face.

'Before we go any further, Jake, please trust me when I say your wife Lucy *is* dead. I can understand why you'd want to believe she's still alive, but I can assure you she isn't.'

'I know what I heard and being here, unpacking everything that happened in the weeks leading up to that night, I've come to terms with the fact that things between us weren't as rosy as I previously believed. Geraldine said she was having an affair and was planning to leave and take my daughter with her. For some reason, she must have changed her mind and decided to frame me instead.'

While I'm speaking, I allow my gaze to wander the room, searching for anything I might be able to use as a weapon or means of escape.

She opens the paper folder and lifts out an item, holding it up for me to see. I resist the urge to look at first, but finally allow my eyes to focus on it. The photograph is glossy, and it takes me a moment to realise what I'm looking at.

'That's my kitchen.'

She nods, lowering the image and lifting a second from the folder. This one is a picture of Lucy, stretched out on the kitchen floor, her pyjama top a bloody mess, her eyes lifeless. There are crime scene markers in various locations in the background. Dr Carpenter doesn't say a word as she lowers the image and lifts a third, and then a fourth.

'Why are you showing me these?' I demand, each more painful to see than the last.

'Because you need to accept that Lucy died that night in your kitchen in Camberley. She was stabbed seven times with a chef's knife and bled to death.'

'I can see why they'd want you to believe that, but those photographs could have been staged. I didn't kill her.'

'Police and crime scene investigators combed every inch of your house, and they concluded that the woman found stabbed to death in your kitchen was Lucy Meredith, aged thirty-eight. DNA confirmed it.'

'And I'm just supposed to take your word for that?'

'Why would I lie?'

'Because maybe you're in on it as well, and you want to make me admit to something I didn't do. I overheard you and Coyle talking about trying to prove some theory about PTSD and mental illness. You're using me as a guinea pig to prove some half-arsed theory.'

Her brow furrows, maybe wondering how I overheard what she, Coyle and Max were discussing.

'And what makes you believe that this is all a sham? Why are you so convinced your wife is alive?'

'Because I heard her when I came up to see you in the therapy suites earlier today. You denied you were speaking to her on the phone, but I know what I heard.'

Dr Carpenter's eyes narrow.

'I see. You're right that I lied to you this morning. What you heard was me listening to an old family movie of you and Lucy.'

'No, you're lying.' But as I say this, I remember how guilty she was looking when she closed the lid of her laptop. 'Why would you have a video of me and Lucy?'

'Your brother Max sent it to me. He thought it might help to access your trapped memories. It was footage of your daughter's fifth birthday party.'

She stands and crosses to her desk, opening her laptop and

fiddling with the cursor, until she finds what she's looking for and then turns it to face me. A video file plays, and it's one I know well. I see Sienna in a party dress seated at the end of our table, her face a picture of pure joy as Lucy carries over a chocolate cake in the shape of a dog. I remember Sienna initially being disappointed that she hadn't received an actual dog for her birthday.

'One day you'll understand why things had to be this way,' Lucy tells Sienna, stroking the top of her hair.

Dr Carpenter pauses the file.

'I'm sorry that you mistook that for something else, Jake. I probably should have admitted what I'd been watching.'

'But I heard you speak back to her. You said—'

'We're taking good care of him,' she says, and the hairs on the back of my neck stand. 'I was talking to the screen, just letting the ghost of her know that I wouldn't let anything bad happen to you.'

I blink several times, unsure whether I believe her story. She sounds genuine, but I don't understand why she would be speaking to the screen.

She holds up the folder. 'I also have photographs from her postmortem, but I wouldn't recommend you look at them.'

I don't know what to say. She certainly sounds convincing, but if Lucy didn't fake her death, why is everyone – Max especially – so convinced I killed her?

'What do you want from me?' I ask, defeated.

'I want to help you remember what happened that night, Jake.'

'You want me to admit I killed her? To what end?'

'I just want to get the truth once and for all.'

'Once and for all? You make it sound like it's been years, rather than weeks.'

She doesn't respond, watching me instead.

'I've told you countless times that I don't remember what happened. My memory of that day and night is gone.'

She removes her glasses and fixes me with a direct stare.

'What year is it, Jake?'

'What?'

'What is today's date?'

I shrug. 'I can't be sure. What day is it today? Monday? If so, then Monday, 12 October.'

'What year, Jake?'

'It's 2009, of course.'

'Would it surprise you if I told you you're wrong? Today is actually Monday, 28 October 2024?'

'Ha!' I scoff.

'It's true, Jake. It's been fifteen years since Lucy died in your kitchen.'

What is this nonsense? Does she really expect me to believe I'm going to fall for that?

She opens an internet search window and types 'Today's date' into the search bar. Monday, 28 October 2024 appears on the screen.

'You could be faking that,' I challenge.

'But I'm not, Jake. Do you really not remember any of what happened after the police arrested you?'

There's no way she's telling the truth. It's barely three weeks since I woke in the back of that ambulance with no memory of what happened. I remember Fahey arresting me; I remember the judge at the court commanding I attend this stupid clinic; I remember Max and Fahey escorting me across here on the boat.

'Let me fill in a few of the blanks for you. In October 2009, you were sent to be assessed at a sleep clinic in London, but after a week of tests, they concluded that you didn't suffer from the condition. You returned to court and were sentenced to serve your term in a mental health facility. You've spent most of your adult life in a drug-induced state in one facility or another, until you were transferred here. There have been previous attempts to access those memories, but whenever they cleaned you up, you became paranoid about people being after you, and attempted to escape. Tonight isn't the first time you've tried to break out of here.'

This is so surreal. I don't know what she's expecting me to say, but there's no way I've lost fifteen years' worth of memories.

I see a flash of me looking at my reflection's tired and blood-shot eyes when I woke in that other patient's bathroom. I couldn't explain why I looked so old and tired.

'I begged for the chance to try and finally get through to you by creating this experiment. We've been managing your medica-tion through your meals to keep you conscious and the paranoia under control. Everything you remember from the moment you stepped off the boat with Max and Detective Fahey has been our attempt to help you feel secure enough to smash down the walls you've put up around your memories of that night. I believe the amnesia you suffered was self-inflicted because you couldn't process what you'd done, but previous attempts to convince you of this have failed. It was my hope that putting you back in that year would succeed.

'We were so close the other day in the therapy suite. You took me as far as the kitchen door, further than you've ever taken anyone before. But we need to push through that door, Jake. We need to know what's on the other side so we can once and for all know the truth.'

No, this is all too unbelievable, and yet the voice in the back of my head isn't arguing against what she's saying. I don't want to believe any of what she's told me, but it sure does explain some of the oddities I've noticed while I've been wandering this maze of white corridors. I can't just accept her at her word.

'That's some story, doc, and you tell it in a pretty compelling way, but it's going to take a lot more than showing me a date on a computer screen to convince me that we're now in the year 2024.'

She flicks through the paper folder again, and lifts out an image of Sienna, laying it on my legs. I recognise the photograph instantly as one that hangs in our bedroom. But she then places an unfamiliar image on top of that. This one is Sienna, looking fractionally older, feeding some ducks in a pond. Then there's an image of her wearing an 'I'm 7' badge. And then an image of her, much taller in a bridesmaid's dress; another of her taller again, holding hands with a now grey-haired Geraldine. My daughter ages year by year before my eyes until she's wearing a graduation robe with a mortarboard hat.

40

I stare at the graduation picture for what feels like eternity. It's my little girl as I've never seen her before. She is as beautiful as her mother, and that proud look in Geraldine's eyes isn't something that could be doctored. As impossible as it seems, I've no doubt that this photograph is my daughter.

How could I have been so oblivious? How have I allowed myself to miss out on my little girl growing up?

Dr Carpenter passes me a tissue and encourages me to wipe my eyes.

'I appreciate it's a lot to process,' she says, 'but our work is only just beginning.'

I don't look up from the photograph. 'Does she... does she know I'm in here and what I did?'

'Your daughter? Yes, she knows you're in here.'

What must she think of me? I suspected that Geraldine would be poisoning her against me following my arrest, but I dread to think what fifteen years of negative comments will have done to Sienna's opinion of me.

'Can I speak to her? I need to tell her how sorry I am.'

'What would you tell her? Imagine she's here right now. What would you say?'

'I'd... I'd tell her how much I love and miss her.'

'What else?'

I focus my gaze on the girl beneath the mortarboard hat. She has Lucy's smile, but my bright blue eyes.

'I'd tell her I'm sorry, and that I wish I could turn back time and undo everything that's happened. I'd ask her if she's had a good life, and if she can ever find it in her heart to forgive me for not being there for her.'

There's a brief silence before she speaks again.

'I have more photographs of Sienna if you'd like to see them.'

I look up at her, though my eyes are blurred with tears. She passes me a photograph of the now adult Sienna in Paris with the Eiffel Tower prominent in the background. She's smiling broadly at the camera. Does that mean she's found a way to put her nightmare upbringing behind her?

'Is she happy?' I ask, barely able to get the words past the lump in my throat.

'She has been, but there's something troubling her, and that's why I'm here, trying to resolve your amnesia.' She pauses, taking a deep breath. 'The thing is, Jake, Sienna wasn't five years old when her mother died. She was twelve.'

My eyes snap up and meet hers. 'No, she was five.'

Dr Carpenter shakes her head gently.

'You've been adamant about Sienna being an infant since your arrest back in 2009, but she was in fact much older. It's the oddest part of your amnesia. It was like your mind wiped out seven years of your life. But ask yourself this: what is your daughter's date of birth?'

'It's 7 March 1997.'

My eyes widen. The date rolled off my tongue so naturally that

I know it's correct, but that would mean when I was arrested in 2009, she would have been twelve.

I shake my head. Something is very wrong. This is like a nightmare I can't wake from. How could I have fabricated so much? Why have I been lying to myself for so long?

'That makes her twelve when Lucy died. Don't you see, Jake? I'm not trying to trick you in any way. There's so much more that you've been running away from, but I feel like tonight is the night we can finally confront whatever it is that has been chasing you.'

'Where's my brother? I want to speak to him. I don't want to believe any of this, and I need to hear it from someone I trust.'

She nods.

'I can ask Max to come in here and corroborate what I'm saying, but I think you know deep down that I'm telling you the truth.' She reaches out and presses a hand against my knee. 'I appreciate it's a lot to take in, and Mr Coyle said I shouldn't be wasting my time. He thinks you're beyond redemption, but I firmly believe that the truth is buried inside your head. And that with my guidance, we can find the key to unlocking it once and for all.'

'I'm not saying another word until I speak to someone I know and trust.'

She stands and crosses back to her desk, opening a drawer and rummaging about inside, before returning and retaking her seat. She gives me a piece of paper, laying it on my lap. It's a handwritten letter, addressed to Mr Coyle. My eyes scan over the words: the tone is professional, and the content is about me. The references to 'Mother and Father' would suggest Sienna is the author. It provides detailed background on my arrest, trial, and failed appeals. It talks about my incarceration in multiple mental health facilities and ends with a plea that Mr Coyle considers taking on my care at the Lundy Clinic. But it's the signature at the bottom of the letter that throws me most.

I look up at Dr Carpenter, wiping the tears from my eyes, and trying to focus on hers. It can't be.

'You signed this letter.' It's more of a statement than a question. 'Your name is Sienna Carpenter?'

'Carpenter is my married name. I was born Sienna Ann Meredith.' She stops and bites her lip. 'Dad, it's me.'

I look back at the graduation photograph and compare the girl in the image with the woman sitting across from me now. How didn't I see it before?

'Sienna? Is it really you?'

A single tear rolls down her cheek as she nods.

I try to move closer to her, wanting to pull her into an embrace, but the leather restraints keep me from moving. She watches my efforts but doesn't offer to untie me.

'Why didn't you say something sooner? Why keep your identity a secret?'

'Because I need to know the truth about what happened that night. We thought that if you knew who I was, you would try to hide me from the truth; to protect me. But I'm an adult now, and I deserve to know what happened to Mum.'

'But I don't remember,' I plead. 'I still can't see beyond me walking you to school...'

My words trail off as I realise the futility of them. That memory of me walking her to school in the rain was from when she was five, not the actual day of the event. No wonder Detective Fahey had such issues believing my story.

Why did I go back to that moment, some seven years before Lucy died? What else has my mind been protecting me from?

I hear Geraldine's words in my head: *She was planning to leave you, Jake. She'd been looking for a new house for just the two of them...*

That's how desperate she was to get away from you. She'd been saving up a little nest egg so she and Sienna could escape and never look back.

I thought she was saying it to be spiteful, but how much has this wall of amnesia been protecting me from? My memory is of a loving relationship. Yes, we had arguments, but no more than any other couple. But was it worse than that? Is there more truth in what Geraldine was saying about Lucy feeling threatened and needing to escape? Was the PTSD far worse than I ever realised?

She told me how dark your eyes would go when you got angry. How you would lash out at the wall because you couldn't control your temper.

How bad were things between us? I still don't believe I could be capable of killing Lucy. She was the love of my life, but is that what the amnesia is protecting me from? Am I the monster I've been running away from all this time?

'When we tried the hypnotic session, it brought you to that kitchen door, Jake. I want you to let me take you back there and try again.'

'No. I don't want to see what's beyond that door... what I *might* have done.'

'Don't you see that's exactly why we need to try? This is our last chance to learn the truth. Mr Coyle allowed me to work with you because I pleaded for the chance. He's ready to keep you drugged up for the rest of your life unless I can make a break-through.'

'But he can't do that.'

'He can and he will. I had to call in so many favours for him to even consider this little experiment. I sold him on the idea that if we could take you back to 2009 that you would be ready to open up. But after you trashed your room and then tried to escape *again*, he won't let me back here after tonight. It really is now or never.'

'Surely there's some board or judge you can refer my case to? You can see I'm not a violent man. I tried to escape because I needed to speak to my daughter, and I didn't know you were here under my nose the whole time. I have no reason to escape now.'

She stands and crosses to the closed blind behind her desk and doesn't turn back to face me.

'It's too late for all that now. Tomorrow I will be gone, and you will be returned to a vegetative state, and I'll never learn what really happened.'

Everything is moving so quickly. I don't want to let her down, but I equally don't want to go through that door and see what I did; what I caused. I've been fighting to get my daughter back, and now that she's here, I don't want to frighten her off.

'I have these dreams, Dad. Well, they're nightmares really. In the dream I am back in that house and it's late. The curtains are drawn and it's dark outside. You're standing over me, outside the kitchen door, and there's blood on your hands. I have an intense feeling of fear and anger. I am terrified, and you're there telling me to go back to bed. I try to look past you, but you block my view, telling me everything will be okay. The dream is splintered. Like there are moments where we're downstairs talking, and then the next second, we're upstairs.'

Did she wake after what I did? My poor girl.

'I keep having the same dream, Dad. Every day. That's why I did all of this. That's why I wrote to Mr Coyle and pleaded for the chance to try and break through your amnesia. I need to know. Will you try? For me?'

I've been running from the truth for so long that I've managed to convince myself that the world is against me. And in all that time, Sienna has stayed loyal, fighting to get the answers she deserves. She has built a life for herself without my help, and there really is only one thing I can provide that nobody else can.

'Okay,' I say. 'I'll do it.'

I hear the sound of water lapping at the shore, and realise she's put on background music. I am ashamed that I failed to see who she was all this time, and yet also proud to see she's managed to achieve so much despite everything that occurred while she was growing up. It seems the apple fell far from this tree and it's a huge relief.

'As before, I want you to lie back, and close your eyes,' Dr Carpenter – I mean Sienna – tells me.

Once again, she tells me to relax and asks me to imagine myself on a beach; perfectly at peace.

41

I start awake, slowly opening my eyes, but the room is in total darkness. I can no longer hear the sound of waves, and rather than stretched out on a beach, I am sitting upright on a sofa, rather than a hardened chair. My hands are free of restraint, but as my eyes slowly adjust to the darkness, I am no longer in Dr Carpenter's office. I can no longer hear her voice, and yet there are voices approaching.

My eyes dart to the doorway as the door opens and Lucy marches in, slamming her hand against the light switch on the wall, and the room fills with light. I want to rush over and embrace her, but I'm not in control of my actions.

'I've had enough, Jake,' Lucy says, and as I look closer, I can see her cheeks are red and puffy. 'I'm tired of having to manage everything on my own, and then having to sacrifice everything the moment you walk back in the door.'

'So, what are you saying?' I hear my voice say, but it isn't me using it, more like an echo from the past that I can't prevent.

'I'm saying that I can't go on like this. It isn't fair on me, it isn't fair on you, and it definitely isn't fair on Sienna.'

'You want a divorce? That's what you're saying?'

'I'm sorry, but yes. You must be able to see that this isn't work-ing. I used to blame it on the fact that you'd be away for over half the year, but since you left the army, even though you're here more, we still barely speak. I have no idea what's going on in that head of yours, but I hear you screaming out as the nightmares chase you.'

'There's a reason I don't talk to you about what happened overseas. You wouldn't want to know what I've seen.'

'Maybe not, but that shouldn't be just your choice to make. When we stood in front of that registrar, we signed a contract saying we would be equals in our marriage, and we haven't been on a level footing for too long. Enough is enough.'

How couldn't I have seen how strained things had become? It's almost as if I'm hearing her words for the first time, but I know it's because I'm actually listening this time.

'And you really think that's fair on our daughter?' I hear myself say.

'Ha,' she scoffs. 'I'm not sure Sienna would even notice a difference. When was the last time you sat down and asked her how she's doing?'

'What are you talking about? I speak to her whenever I'm back.'

'No, you ask her about school and her subjects, but when was the last time you asked her about *her*? Did you know she's skip-ping meals because some girls in her class called her fat?'

I feel all the anger I did the first time when I hear Lucy say this. Children can be so spiteful at that age, and I instantly want to leap to Sienna's defence.

'What? She isn't fat.'

'I know she isn't, but at that age girls can be particularly cruel.'

'Have you reported these bullies?'

'I'm handling it, but you're missing my point: you're oblivious to these things.'

'So why haven't you told me about them before?'

'What would be the point? What could you have done to help from whatever secret basecamp you were in?'

I take an involuntary step closer to her.

I want to tell her I'm here now. That this is why I quit the army: to give her the support she needs. But I'm unable to control my voice.

'That's hardly fair, is it?' I say instead. 'I work hard to provide a home for this family, and if you knew half the shit I've protected you from, you'd maybe be a little more forgiving.'

No, you jerk! That's the wrong answer. Why couldn't this version of me see how upset she was? Why couldn't I see she was at the end of her tether?

She shakes her head, wiping a fresh tear from her cheek.

'I think you should sleep down here tonight.'

'Why are you doing this? Is there someone else? Are you having an affair?'

There's the slightest dip in her head, and she quickly denies the accusation, but given what Geraldine told me recently, I can read the guilt in her face.

'Sleep down here, and in the morning when we've both calmed down, we'll talk again,' she says with a finality that shakes the seat beneath me.

The room grows dark again, and when I next look up at the clock, I can see it's now after midnight, and I don't know why but I am compelled to stand and head out of the room. A feeling of dread passes over me, as I see the closed kitchen door, a thin trail of light escaping from beneath.

I know exactly where and when I am, and I don't want to move any closer to that red door. This is precisely how I felt the first time Dr

Carpenter led me through guided therapy. This time I can't hear her voice, but deep down I know it is her controlling my movements, like a puppet master.

I force my eyes to close, willing my mind to take me away, but as I dare to squint, I am now right outside the red door. I don't want to open it. I don't want to go through.

But my trembling hand stretches out, and lowers the handle, pushing it open. I try to keep my eyes closed so I won't have to see what lies beyond it, but I am no longer in control.

Lucy's bloodstained body lies at an odd angle on the kitchen floor, her eyes open in a lifeless stare.

Oh God, no; not again.

I drop to my knees, and shuffle closer to her, ignoring the crimson puddle as it soaks through the knees of my pyjamas, the liquid surprisingly cold already. I press my fingers to Lucy's neck, desperately feeling for any faint trace of a pulse.

God, please, no. Don't take her from me all over again.

I don't understand what has happened. I didn't see myself picking up the knife and stabbing her. The last thing I saw before I opened the kitchen door was Lucy forcing me to sleep downstairs. Is this still the amnesia blocking out my actions?

I close my eyes again, willing my mind to show me even a glimpse of me stabbing Lucy, or the argument that triggered such a response, but there's nothing.

My heart tremors as I think about all the other recent times I've woken somewhere unfamiliar with no recollection of how I got there. Does this mean Max was right about the sleepwalking all along? I refused to accept the possibility for so long, but I have no other explanation for how Lucy has ended up this way, and I have not a single flash of what happened. Maybe she found me sleepwalking downstairs and tried to wake me, and for some reason my subconscious felt threatened and grabbed the knife.

This must have been how it played out originally. I woke in the living room unaware that I'd been sleepwalking and become violent with Lucy. I must have come into the kitchen and found her like this and panicked. My mind must have concluded that someone had broken in and attacked her.

I pinch Lucy's nose, and part her lips, attempting mouth-to-mouth, but although her chest rises fractionally, bubbles of blood emerge from her chest where the knife must have punctured her lungs.

I start at a creak on the stairs, and suddenly I'm aware that I'm not the only person up and moving about in the house.

A tiny voice in the back of my head tells me that despite what everyone else has said, there may have been an intruder, and that's who I can hear creeping about.

I wipe the tears from my eyes and move towards the half-open door, straining to hear any further sound from beyond.

I need to see their face. I told the police I was attacked but couldn't describe my attacker because of the amnesia. But maybe this is my chance to unlock the memory, and then when Dr Carpenter brings me back I'll be able to tell them exactly who did it.

Another creak, this time definitely on the landing overhead.

I need to see their face. I need to commit it to my long-term memory. If I don't recognise who they are, I'll need to be able to describe what they looked like. I need to look for head shape, hair colour and length, any scars or birthmarks. I need to retain as much detail so they can pull together a sketch and finally track down this man. It's my last chance to clear my name.

I creep out from behind the door, tiptoeing towards the staircase and treading ever so gently, avoiding the second and third steps where the floorboards usually exhale under my weight. There is no light on upstairs, and as much as I want to turn it on, my hand remains by my side.

I continue around the bend in the stairs, until I'm on the landing, but I can no longer hear anything. But then I spot that Sienna's door is open. That must be where he is. I must keep Sienna safe at all costs. I charge forwards, ready to attack whoever it is, and slam my hand against her light switch, but the room is empty. Sienna's unmade bed is empty as well.

I turn, and gasp as I see Sienna standing, half-asleep in the frame of our doorway, her hands covered in blood.

42

'Dad, what's going on?' she asks, unable to stifle her yawn.

I can't take in how old she looks, and it feels like this is the first time I'm seeing my daughter aged twelve, and yet deep down I know it isn't.

I can't keep my eyes off her blood-covered hands, and for the briefest moment I try to convince myself that she must have had an accident, and that what I can see has absolutely nothing to do with the scene downstairs. But I know I'm lying to myself.

Oh, God, she must have heard the fight and gone down to investigate and discovered Lucy's body before I did. My heart breaks for my poor, beautiful girl. No wonder she's been having nightmares about this night. Seeing a corpse at any age is a traumatic experience, amplified when it's a loved one, and probably magnified tenfold at such a young age.

I don't know what to say to her. I'm in shock, uncertain whether what I've just witnessed is real or part of a hideous nightmare. With Sienna standing half-asleep in the doorway, I can't be certain I'm not still asleep. I know I need to get her cleaned up and put her back to bed. It is too early in the morning to be trying to explain what has happened. I need to gather my own thoughts and call the police. I can't hear any other movement, and my last hope of an intruder swiftly diminishes as I realise the footsteps I heard up here belonged to Sienna.

I move her to the bathroom, and she doesn't struggle as I run warm water and soap over her hands. There are splashes of blood on her pyjama top as well, and I ask her to remove it while I fetch a fresh top. She must have tried to help Lucy as I did, but I can't get over how different her trauma response is to my own. My head is all over the place, but she is docile. There is no fear or confusion.

I wave my hand in front of her eyes, but she barely registers it.

'Sienna?'

She doesn't answer, still staring into a void. I'm about to gently shake her arms when the penny drops.

She's sleepwalking.

Is this what it's like when I'm sleepwalking? Semi-responsive so people wouldn't necessarily realise I'm not fully conscious, but not really in control of my actions? My thinking the apple had fallen far from the tree may have been premature.

I continue to watch her, taking her hand and escorting her back to bed. She lies down, and I tuck her in as if nothing has happened, and she doesn't question any of it. Her eyes close the instant her head hits the pillow.

That explains why she didn't scream out or come and tell me what she'd discovered. If she was sleepwalking herself, she wouldn't know what was happening and would have virtually no memory of it.

I wait until I'm certain she's asleep before leaving the room, ready to head downstairs, when a fresh thought hits, but the idea is so ridiculous that I instantly dismiss it. But a voice in the back of my head keeps asking it on repeat: what did she do?

I can hear Dr Sienna Carpenter's own words in my head: REM

Behaviour Disorder, or RBD... is a parasomnia characterised by dream-enacting behaviour. Essentially, your body acts out your dreams.

I have no memory of stabbing Lucy; there was no blood on my pyjamas until I entered the kitchen and attempted mouth-to-mouth; the blood on Sienna's hands and pyjamas. Could she...?

No.

No.

It's ridiculous.

My daughter isn't capable of such an act.

But as I turn back and look at her room, something glints on the carpet just inside the doorway. I move closer, unable to believe my eyes, but then I see the bloodstained chef's knife, by the skirting board.

There's only one way the knife could have made it up here, and that's if she brought it up here.

That doesn't mean Sienna killed Lucy. The other version of me is leaping to this conclusion, and I can now understand the actions that must have followed this realisation. My instinct has always been to protect my daughter.

I collect the knife from the floor and carefully wrap it in her pyjamas, and then I carry the bundle downstairs, placing the knife on the floor beside the body and the pyjamas in the sink. I search in the cupboard beneath until I find the brown bottle of hydrogen peroxide. I pour some on a washing-up sponge and scrub at the stains on her pyjamas. I've had to do this with my camo gear so many times overseas that it is second nature. I then place them into the washing machine along with the other wet laundry I forgot to empty earlier today.

I keep my eyes away from Lucy, not wanting to look at her, but I keep seeing imagined snatches of what might have happened. I don't want to even consider the possibility that it was Sienna that killed Lucy. There has to be another explanation.

I was the one sleepwalking, having a nightmare about what happened in the desert, and when Lucy tried to wake me, I lashed out. Then, having returned to the lounge, poor Sienna came down and discovered her mother's body. Yes, that has to be what happened.

But why would she have picked up the knife, let alone carried it back to bed?

I don't want to think about the other possibility, but as impossible as it sounds it's the most obvious answer: I wasn't the one who was sleepwalking and stabbed Lucy.

I hear a creak on the stairs, and race out of the kitchen, pulling the door closed behind me, not wanting Sienna to disturb the scene any more than she already has.

'Hey, sweetie, I think you're sleepwalking again,' I say gently. 'Let's put you back to bed.'

'What? I'm not sleepwalking. What's going on, Dad? Why aren't you in bed?'

Shit. She's awake. And I'm standing here with bloody kneecaps.

'Where's Mum?'

Her words are like a dagger to my heart. I can't bring myself to tell her.

'Mum's loading the washing machine,' I say. 'Don't worry about it for now. Just get yourself back to sleep. School in the morning.'

I'm expecting some kind of resistance, but instead she returns to her room, closing the door behind her, and I fall into the wall. I know what I have to do to keep her safe. I won't let her be blamed for a condition she inherited from me.

I can already foresee what is about to happen, and I don't regret the choices I made.

I pick up the knife and coil my fingers around the handle. I need to make sure the police only ever have me in the frame for what has happened here. There can be no momentary doubt about Sienna.

I feel the blade's handle beneath my skin, squeezing it tightly, making sure my palm print is the only one that will be recovered from the weapon. I crouch down beside my wife's lifeless body, and I plunge the blade into her gut, making sure her blood spatters against my wrist.

'I am so sorry, my darling. You deserved so much better than me,' I say.

For added effect, I place my hand in the pool of blood that is blotting into my pyjama bottoms again, and smear some across my top.

There can be no doubt about who is responsible for this crime. I will accept full accountability to protect my little girl, who is merely an innocent victim in all of this.

I stand and reach for the phone, ready to call the police, but the phone isn't in the charging station. I have no idea where it could be.

I cross to the opposite side of the kitchen, checking under the pile of unopened mail, beside the microwave, and even behind the fruit bowl, but there's no sign of it. I'm about to venture out of the kitchen, when the ground moves beneath me, and I'm flying backwards. It's like everything is in slow motion as my vision shifts involuntarily towards the ceiling. I catch a glimpse of the puddle my foot has slipped on, but no amount of waving my arms will correct my descent. And just as I'm bracing myself for the impact of the floor on my back, I feel something hard strike the back of my head, as my skull connects with the edge of the counter.

And then the darkness comes.

43

I open my eyes and find myself staring into the innocent blue eyes of Sienna, staring back at me in her white coat, the name badge still referring to her as Dr S. Carpenter.

'Hey,' she says, an edge to her voice. 'I lost you there for a bit. You were telling me about an argument you and Mum were having and that she banished you to the sofa, and then nothing afterwards. Can you tell me what happened once you went through the kitchen door?'

I watch her face, trying to determine if this is the truth, or whether she's now expecting me to say the words aloud. In the memory, she woke and saw me with blood on my pyjamas, so she must be able to remember that, but I can't be sure she remembers any of the sequence leading up to that.

I'm not even sure what I believe at this point. In the cold light of day, back in this room and with both arms still restrained, I don't know what to make of it. I'm not sure I'll ever be able to forget Lucy's lifeless eyes staring back at me, or the way the blood bubbled from her chest when I tried to resuscitate her. Now that the memory is out, I wish there was a way to put it back in Pandora's box.

I continue to stare at her face, looking for any tell she might subconsciously give away; a tic of some sort; something that tells me whether she knows she was the one who killed Lucy.

'The way your head was rocking and your eyelids blinking,' she continues, pressing me for answers, 'I'd say you were in a REM state of sleep, but you became otherwise unresponsive. What did you see?'

As far as I can determine, she either has no idea about what happened, in the same way I did before, or she at least suspects what may have happened. She said she's having nightmares about that night, but I can't be sure there isn't more behind that claim. For her to admit what she did would be to throw a spotlight on both of our lives, and whilst it would eventually see me cleared of the charges that have stalked me for the last fifteen years, it would also see her facing charges of her own.

'Please, Dad, I need to know what you saw. Was I there? Did you see me?'

I continue to stare at her as my mind tries to process the crime I just observed. Lucy was spread out in the kitchen, just as she was in the crime scene photographs Sienna showed me before she put me under. I can't escape the possibility that everything I just observed was more akin to a dream, peppered with gaps filled by my imagination. The scene I saw in the kitchen could have been inspired by the photograph; my interactions with twelve-year-old Sienna stimulated by her admission to nightmares of her own.

You're standing over me, outside the kitchen door, and there's blood on your hands.

But unlike a dream, this felt so real. Although I wasn't in control of my actions or words, there was a familiarity about the motions, as though I had lived through the events before but hadn't seen them again until just now. I need to know whether she remembers doing it.

'The red door in the corridor,' I say, my mind all over the place. 'It's the same shade as our—'

'Kitchen door,' she finishes. 'I had it painted to try and trigger your memory. It worked, didn't it? You broke through the amnesia?'

'I saw your mother,' I say quietly, struggling to get the image of all that blood from my mind. 'She was dead in the kitchen.'

'And before that? Did you see... did you see who killed her?'

I can't tell if she's asked the question this way because she suspects me to be the killer and doesn't want to outright accuse me, or because she suspects herself and doesn't want to put words in my mouth.

'No, I just saw the body. I didn't see her die.'

I study her face, expecting to see a glimpse of relief, but she's devoid of emotion, and I feel like I'm letting her down with my succinct answers.

'What do you remember of that night?' I say, reversing the interrogation.

She sits back, and her eyes dart to the wall over my shoulder before she speaks again.

'I don't know, to be honest. It's hazy, and I can't tell what parts are actual memories, and what are things I've imagined or dreamt since.'

I inhale deeply.

'Explain it to me.'

Again, she averts her gaze before meeting mine.

'It's as I said to you before. I see myself upstairs in the bathroom with you one second, and the next I'm at the bottom of the stairs and you're there and there's something dark on your hands and pyjama bottoms, like you've been painting or something.

You tell me everything is okay and that I should return to bed. And then I'm woken by a policewoman telling me I need to come with her and to keep my eyes closed when I go downstairs.'

I can't help feeling like she's holding something back, and I don't want to force her into saying the wrong thing. She said that for years various doctors had been trying to coax me into admitting what I did, and I can't help but feel that is the purpose of my role here. I remain silent, allowing the awkwardness to grow.

'The thing is, when I'm standing at the bottom of the stairs, and you're talking to me, it's like my entire body is in shock. I don't know how else to describe it. There's this fear, but more intense than I've ever experienced. It's like I'm standing on the edge of a cliff, and I know I'm about to fall over the edge, but there's something just about holding me up.'

I want to press my hands to her face and tell her everything is going to be okay, but the leather restraints bite into my wrists. If I continue to take the blame for what happened, I'll spend the rest of my days under heavy sedation, and I won't ever be able to speak to her again.

I think she suspects that she was the one who killed Lucy, and it's a suspicion I share. As much as I don't want to admit it, the realisation is sinking in that I wasn't the one who killed Lucy.

'The thing is, Dad, I sleepwalk as well,' she says, so matter-of-factly that it catches me off-guard.

I picture her in the trance-like state in the bathroom when I was washing her hands.

'Where yours might have been brought on by PTSD, I don't know the cause of mine, but I've spent the last two years terrified that I've been prone to sleepwalking for longer than I realised. I think... I'm terrified that it was me who...'

She can't finish the sentence as her eyes well up with tears.

I want to protect her and tell her that she's mistaken, but I don't want to lie to her any more.

I tell her what I saw, and how I was prepared to cover it up and take the blame, and but for my slip and concussion none of this would have happened.

She wraps her arms around my neck, and I rest my head on the top of hers. She unfastens the restraints, and my heart fills with love as I'm finally able to hug my daughter after all this time. I've spent the last few days desperately trying to get back to her and she's been here supporting me the whole time.

'I'm so sorry you had to go through all of this, Dad,' she whispers into my ear.

'You have nothing to be sorry for. None of this was your fault.'

I don't tell her that I deserved far worse for what I did to that kid in the desert.

'What happens from here?' I ask.

She wipes her eyes on the shoulder of my pyjama top, and stares into my eyes.

'We need to tell the police so that your case can be retried.'

I'm in no state to be released into the world. I can't begin to imagine how much has changed in the fifteen years while I've been under sedation. There will be no evidence that Sienna was responsible, because I did a good job of covering it up, but the only way she can clear my name is to take my place in the frame. I can't let her throw her own life away.

'Before you do anything, can you get Max for me? There's something I want to speak to him about.'

44

She stands, reluctantly, and heads out of the room, leaving the door ajar.

I rub at my reddened wrists, but remain where I am. There is no point in me trying to escape now. The world I was yearning for is a lifetime away. I'm too late to put things right and give Sienna the life she deserves.

Max appears in the doorway, standing there motionless, staring at me, but I see now how much older he looks than I remember. He's had no hair since an alopecia diagnosis in his thirties, so I guess had I seen greying hair I would have realised sooner how much time has elapsed since that night. The skin beneath his eyes is drawn and bloodshot, and his cheeks droop as Dad's always had. If fifteen years really has passed, is my mum even alive still?

That he is here now, supporting his niece and her last desperate attempt to uncover the truth, tells me more about him than I've probably given credit for. I guess, despite our differences before, he is doing the brotherly thing. But there's one thing he can tell me that Sienna can't.

'Hey,' I say to him. 'I need you to do me a favour.'

He comes in and plonks down on the chair Sienna vacated.

'I'm pretty sure you're out of favours, if I'm honest.'

'Is she happy?'

'Who?'

'Sienna. She looks well, and it can't have been easy for her to qualify as a medic, but what else can you tell me about her?'

He fixes me with a long and cold stare.

'Hey, listen, this might be the last time either of us speaks again, so cut me some slack.'

He considers me for a moment before responding.

'She has her mother's drive and ambition.'

'And how are you, Max? Are you even still practising law? I feel like with fifteen years missing, I know nothing about you. How is Catarina?'

'She remarried and now lives in Australia. She barely speaks to me after what happened.'

I feel my brow furrowing. I had no idea what kind of repercussions that night would have on those around me.

'I'm sorry, I had no idea you'd separated.'

He gives me a sceptical look, like he doesn't believe me.

'And Mum?'

'She passed twelve years ago. She suffered a stroke after your second appeal failed, and she went swiftly downhill after that. She never stopped believing that you were the unwitting victim in all of this.'

He's not saying it directly, but he blames me for her poor health, as well he should. If only I'd known the truth sooner, I could have made everyone's lives easier. I won't ask after Lucy's parents. That Geraldine clearly still bears a grudge tells me everything I need to know.

'There's something I need to tell you, and I don't want you to discuss it with Sienna until you've told the police.'

He sits forward, unable to hide his intrigue.

It takes all my willpower to utter the next words.

'I was the one who stabbed Lucy.'

There is no look of surprise on his face.

'You're finally admitting it then?'

I force myself to nod, worried that Sienna might be just outside the door and will rush in and force me to stop. Wherever she's gone, I sense it won't be long before she returns, and that means I need to convince Max and have him relay the message to Fahey, or whoever is now looking after Lucy's case.

'The amnesia was genuine,' I say. 'I guess my mind repressed it to protect me in some way. Sienna took me back and helped me break through it. Lucy and I argued that night and I accused her of having an affair. She asked me for a divorce.'

'And that's why you killed her?'

I could tell him it is more complicated than that, but there's no point. The sooner he believes me, the sooner Sienna can close this chapter of her life. I will not allow her to throw away everything she has achieved despite the mess I left her life in.

'I guess so. It's no excuse, but I think that everything that happened on my last tour... you could say I was suffering from PTSD. I think I still am if I'm being honest with you. I did things over there that I couldn't forgive myself for, and I think a combination of the stress and guilt, and then the shock at what Lucy told me—'

'Wait, she told you? You've known all these years and you never said anything?'

I freeze, uncertain why he'd phrase the question in that way. What does he think I know about, if not Lucy's divorce request?

'I'd forgotten she'd asked for a divorce, and I guess the bump to my head must have blocked that bit out as well,' I reply, watching him closely, desperate to read his mind.

He sits back and places his hands together over his lap.

'When I first arrived at the hospital, I was convinced you'd be off with me, and wanted to tear your head off, but you looked so frightened. And when you said you had no memory of what had happened, I was convinced you were lying, and that as soon as we were outside, you'd attack me.'

My mind is racing once again, a fresh picture appearing before my eyes, and I don't want to believe it. Lucy made no secret of how much she despised Max, but could that have all been a pretence to throw me off their scent? Geraldine hinted that Lucy was having an affair and planning to leave me but wouldn't admit who the culprit was. All those nights when she'd had to drive back to Geraldine's to work on cases for the following day, I'd taken her at her word. The second phone that she claimed was for international calls. The fact that she had hers and Sienna's passports with her. And she was so angry when I told her I'd quit the service and would be at home more, and I see now it was because I was disrupting her routine. I can hardly bring myself to say the words.

'You and Lucy were having an affair.'

It's his turn to look perplexed.

'Yeah, that's what she told you that night, right? That's what pushed you over the edge.'

I feel sick to my stomach. Until this moment I'd assumed Geraldine was only saying those things out of spite. Did she know Lucy was carrying on with Max? I have to assume that's the real reason Catarina divorced him. I can't help wondering whether Sienna knows as well.

'Even when I suggested you be assessed at that sleep clinic,' he continues, a wry smile on his face, 'I kept thinking you'd finally come clean to me. I figured you couldn't keep up the pretence forever.'

I want to rebuff his claims to an affair; that the Lucy I loved wouldn't do that to me, but the red mist descends, and before I know it, I'm off the chair, my hands immediately reaching for Max's throat, and the satisfaction of feeling my palms pressing against his jugular.

We fall from the chair, writhing around on the floor before the door bursts open and Sienna stands there screaming. It catches me off-guard and allows Max to plant a fist into my cheek. Before I can regain my control over him, two orderlies have my arms and are pulling me backwards.

'You fucking maniac,' Max is yelling at me hoarsely, rubbing his neck gingerly.

'Uncle Max, it's okay,' I hear Sienna saying as she helps him back to his feet. 'Dad is in shock after what I told him, and—'

'It's too late, Sienna,' I yell at her, as I see the glint of a needle in one of the orderlies' hands. 'I already told Max what I did. You have my confession, don't you, Max? You heard me admit to killing Lucy. I did it.'

Sienna's hands shoot up to her mouth.

'No, Dad, you can't do this. I just got you back after all these years.'

'You did nothing wrong, my darling,' I yell as I feel the needle pierce the skin in my upper arm. 'It was all me.'

This is my last chance to protect her, and these will be my final words to her. Under permanent sedation, I might as well be dead, but I will go to my grave knowing that I saved her. It's a small price to pay to protect her.

The last thing I see is Sienna's distraught face, desperately trying to find a way to stop me, and the realisation of what I'm doing slowly dawning on her.

She mouths the words, 'I love you,' and then everything fades.

ACKNOWLEDGEMENTS

Thank you for choosing and reading *Sleepwalker*. I hope you enjoyed it (and will now tell all your friends to read a copy). Please do get in touch via the usual social channels and let me know what you thought about it.

I have my own history with sleepwalking, although to the best of my knowledge I've never actually killed anyone (that said, my wife is now genuinely terrified of sharing a bed with me). It isn't a subject that is generally talked about a lot, and yet if you ask people about sleepwalking, or strange night-time escapades, everyone seems to have a story they can tell. As far as I'm aware, I stopped sleepwalking after adolescence, but was delighted to call upon my own experiences when writing this book. The incident of Jake placing the wastepaper basket into Max's wardrobe is inspired by something I (apparently) did when I was about seven and my grandmother was down to visit. I haven't yet caught my own children sleepwalking, so I hopefully haven't passed the trait down.

I'm always looking for new ways to explore the psychological thriller genre, and the idea of using sleepwalking as a key theme was inspired by a post I saw on Twitter in 2023 from the brilliant crime writer Noelle Holten (if you haven't read any of her books, please do so). She posted a picture of a large bruise on her knee with a caption that suggested the bruise had arrived during the night but she had no recollection of how. It got me thinking about what else someone might do when they're fast asleep. From this I stumbled upon the loophole in British law that you cannot be prosecuted for any crime committed while sleepwalking. Of course, proving that you were sleepwalking at the time of the offence is fundamental.

And so, I was inspired to write a story from the point of view of someone accused of such a crime who can't determine whether to trust himself or those closest to him. I completed the first draft of the story in July 2023, but at that stage it involved elements that bordered on science fiction (fans of *Quantum Leap* would have loved it), but with the help of my brilliant editor Emily Yau at Boldwood Books, we were able to rebuild the story, more aligned with what my readers have come to love about my books.

At this point, I feel it is only right to clarify that the Lundy Clinic for Sleep Disorders is not real. I wanted my sleep clinic to be based somewhere remote that would isolate Jake from the rest of the world. I love the movie adaption of *Shutter Island* and hopefully those who've seen that movie will be able to draw comparisons between the stories.

I'd like to thank the real Katy Savage, who bid for the chance to have a character named after in a charitable auction. I should state that the patient-turned-nurse bears no resemblance to the real Katy Savage, but I hope she's happy with the role her namesake plays in the story.

As always, I'd like to thank my wonderful agent Emily Glenister at the DHH Literary Agency, who is always only a phone call or email away when I'm struggling and need her to remind me that I'm a far better writer than I ever give myself credit for. It means so much having someone to champion my books and I'm indebted to her honesty and support.

The whole team at Boldwood Books deserve huge credit for the work they do in producing my books in the array of formats available. From line and copy editing, proof-reading, cover design, audiobook creation, and marketing. The fact that you're reading this acknowledgement is testament to the brilliant job they do.

My children are an inspiration to me every day, and as they continue to grow so quickly, I am eternally grateful that I get to play such an important role in their development. They continue to show one another affection, patience and kindness, and make being their dad that bit easier. I'd like to thank my own parents and my parents-in-law for continuing to offer words of encouragement when I'm struggling to engage with my muse.

It goes without saying that I wouldn't be the writer I am today without the loving support of my beautiful wife and soulmate Hannah. She keeps everything else in my life ticking over so that I can give what's left to my writing. She never questions my method or the endless hours daydreaming while I'm working through plot holes, and for that I am eternally grateful.

And thanks must also go to YOU for reading *Sleepwalker*. Please do post a review to wherever you purchased the book from so that other readers can be enticed to give it a try. It takes less than two minutes to share your opinion, and I ask you do me this small kindness.

I am active on Facebook, X (formerly Twitter), Instagram, and now TikTok, so please do stop by with any messages, observations, or questions. Hearing from readers of my books truly brightens my days and encourages me to keep writing, so don't be a stranger. I promise I *will* respond to every message and comment I receive.

Stephen (a.k.a. M. A. Hunter)

ABOUT THE AUTHOR

M.A. Hunter is the pen name of Stephen Edger, the bestselling author of psychological and crime thrillers, including the Kate Matthews series. Born in the north-east of England, he now lives in Southampton where many of his stories are set.

Sign up to M. A. Hunter's mailing list here for news, competitions and updates on future books.

Visit M. A. Hunter's website: stephenedger.com/m-a-hunter

Follow M. A. Hunter on social media

𝕏 x.com/stephenedger

f facebook.com/AuthorMAHunter

📷 instagram.com/stef.edger

BB bookbub.com/authors/stephen-edger

g goodreads.com/stephenedger

ALSO BY M. A. HUNTER

The Boat Party

One Wrong Turn

Every Step You Take

Sleepwalker

THE

Murder

LIST

**THE MURDER LIST IS A NEWSLETTER
DEDICATED TO SPINE-CHILLING FICTION
AND GRIPPING PAGE-TURNERS!**

**SIGN UP TO MAKE SURE YOU'RE ON OUR
HIT LIST FOR EXCLUSIVE DEALS, AUTHOR
CONTENT, AND COMPETITIONS.**

SIGN UP TO OUR NEWSLETTER

BIT.LY/THEMURDERLISTNEWS

Boldwood

Boldwood Books is an award-winning fiction publishing company seeking out the best stories from around the world.

Find out more at www.boldwoodbooks.com

Join our reader community for brilliant books, competitions and offers!

Follow us
@BoldwoodBooks
@TheBoldBookClub

Sign up to our weekly deals newsletter

https://bit.ly/BoldwoodBNewsletter

Printed in Great Britain
by Amazon